PRAI

'No one is l
Beckerman. *Th* deeply drawn characters that move you, grip you and ultimately shock you. The new queen of domestic noir.'

— Alex Michaelides

'*Three Mothers* is smart, suspenseful and beautifully written.'

—Gillian McAllister

'Suspenseful, spellbinding and profoundly moving, *Three Mothers* is a deliciously tangled web that had me ensnared from page one.'

—Louise Candlish

'Proper edge-of-the-seat writing. There were times reading this that I thought my heart rate would go through the roof! The twists and turns in this story are truly gripping - totally unpredictable, I kept gasping in disbelief at the end of each chapter. I love Hannah's writing and once again she has knocked it out of the park. A great moral dilemma tale with big heart and unconditional love at its centre: superb characterization and observation of how we humans tick and how far we'd go to protect those we love. This is Hannah's best novel yet.'

—Ruth Jones

'I stayed awake till the early hours to finish *Three Mothers*. Oh my god, what a great book! I was agog but also invested and moved. This (like all your novels) is so emotionally intelligent. I found it very affecting... I enjoyed it ENORMOUSLY. It's wonderful.'

—Marian Keyes

'Taut as a wire, *Three Mothers* is an emotionally raw page-turner of a book about family secrets, growing up, sibling rivalry and the lengths a mother will go to protect her children. The characterisation is sublime, the writing is wonderful, and I was gripped from the very first page.'

—Rachel Joyce

'An utterly engrossing read, and almost impossible to put down. Compelling, clever, and compassionate. I loved it.'

—Louise O'Neill

'I loved it so much! It's such a huge page turner and the plotting is pin-point perfect. It's just wonderful. I love how the characters develop over the course of the story and it's a true one-more-chapter book. It's brilliantly written, utterly compelling and such a treat of a story.'

—Joanna Cannon

'Domestic noir at its best; tense, twisty and utterly gripping. The characters are portrayed with such emotional insight and the plot so skillfully controlled that it was impossible to put down.'

—Joanna Miller, author of *The Eights*

'If you like Liane Moriarty's novels, I think you'll love this riveting domestic suspense novel. I began it yesterday morning and finished it 24 hours later unable to stop reading. A tragic car accident brings three mothers and their children into conflict as truths about their relationships are laid bare. How well do we really know our children? Never as well as we think! It's unsettling, surprising and super tense.'

—Fanny Blake

PRAISE FOR HANNAH BECKERMAN

'Mysterious, deeply moving, impossible to put down – and its killer twist left me gasping. Brilliant. Hannah Beckerman's best book yet.'

—Alex Michaelides

'A tense, claustrophobic, sinister portrait of a marriage. Skilfully clued and suspenseful – I loved it.'

—Louise Candlish

'I'm SO wowed! I literally gasped when I realised the twist. How clever, how very clever. It's brilliant. So very effective. This is an excellent, important novel.'

—Marian Keyes

'Emotional, smart and with one of the best endings I've read in quite some time.'

—Gillian McAllister

'It had me absolutely gripped from start to finish and has one of the best story twists I have ever read. I love Hannah's writing – clever, insightful, eloquent and empathetic. Utterly compelling, compulsive reading and superb writing. I could not put it down!'

—Ruth Jones

'An emotionally engaging, clever and wonderfully satisfying novel – proper storytelling at its finest.'

—Kate Mosse

'A tense, stylish thriller. Beautifully written and utterly compelling, with an important message at its heart. It's fantastic.'

—Louise O'Neill

'I loved it.'

—Jojo Moyes

'This is Beckerman's best yet! Tense, twisty and really clever.'

—Adam Kay

'This book is amazing! It's deliciously sinister, deeply twisty, and HUGELY addictive. I love the disquietness of it so much, and Hannah writes into the dark corners of the characters' minds so beautifully.'

—Joanna Cannon

'Absolutely compulsive, wonderfully plotted with a story that resonates long after you turn the final page. It's gripping, surprising, interesting, relevant. I was hooked.'

—Rosamund Lupton

'An emotionally devastating novel. So compelling that I read it, cover to cover, in a single day.'

—John Boyne

'A compelling, claustrophobic story . . . I finished it in one huge gulp, excusing myself unilaterally from any family responsibilities I was so desperate to finish it.'

—*Observer*

'Beckerman's tight, tense prose is fast paced and compulsive. You'll tear through the pages until you get to a final killer twist.'

—*Daily Mirror*

'If you're after a classic page-turner, here it is . . . Menacing and unsettling, this is one compelling read.'

—*Woman & Home*

'An unputdownable page-turner that keeps you guessing until the final chapters.'

—*Daily Express*

'[A] terrifically tense thriller . . . so clever.'

—*Good Housekeeping*

'A brilliantly crafted, tense story.'

—*Sun*

'One of those books that grabs your heart, brain and soul and refuses to let go. Do not miss it.'

—*Stylist*

THREE MOTHERS

ALSO BY HANNAH BECKERMAN:

The Forgetting

The Impossible Truths of Love

If Only I Could Tell You

The Dead Wife's Handbook

THREE MOTHERS

HANNAH BECKERMAN

LAKE UNION
PUBLISHING

Text copyright © 2025 by Hannah Beckerman
All rights reserved.

Published by Lake Union Publishing, Seattle

www.apub.com

Amazon, the Amazon logo, and Lake Union Publishing are trademarks of Amazon.com, Inc., or its affiliates.

EU Product Safety contact:
Amazon Publishing, Amazon Media EU S.à r.l.
38, avenue John F. Kennedy, L-1855 Luxembourg
amazonpublishing-gpsr@amazon.com

ISBN-13: 9781662523366
eISBN: 9781662523359

Cover design by Emma Rogers
Cover images: © Jung-Pang Wu / Getty Images; © Xeniia X
© Marijka van Kuik / Shutterstock

Printed in the United States of America

For Aurelia: for whom I would go to the ends
of the earth

Abby

It is ten-fifteen and Isla Richardson is not yet home.

Abby watches the clock above the fireplace, listens to it fill the silence.

It is unlike her daughter to be late.

Picking up the phone beside her, she checks for unread messages, finds nothing, taps out a WhatsApp to her best friend, Nicole.

Any word from Nathaniel this evening? Isla's not back from the party yet and I haven't heard from her. x

She watches her phone, waits for the two ticks to turn blue – Nicole is never very far from her mobile – feels a pinch of concern when they remain stubbornly grey.

There is the metallic slice of a key in the front door lock, and Abby whips her head around, relief expanding her lungs. But when the door to the sitting room opens, it is not Isla who walks through but Clio. She is wearing a pair of grey jogging bottoms and a white crop top that leaves little to the imagination. The outfit exposes far too much flesh for a fifteen-year-old, though Abby never dares mention Clio's clothing choices, is met with a scowl and a lecture on feminist rights if she makes that mistake.

A frown puckers Abby's forehead that Isla still isn't home, but she consciously irons it out, greets her younger daughter with a smile.

'I thought you were staying at Freya's tonight?'

Clio shrugs, does not meet Abby's gaze. 'Changed my mind.'

'You didn't walk home by yourself, did you?'

Clio rolls her eyes, fiddles with the toggle at the waistband of her joggers. 'It's literally a ten-minute walk.'

'Still, I'd rather come and get you when it's late. You know that.'

Clio sighs with teenage forbearance, and Abby studies her daughter's face: watchful blue eyes framed with thick, black kohl; eyelashes caked in mascara; heavily glossed lips pursed in a tight, unyielding line.

'You haven't heard from Isla, have you?'

Clio looks directly at Abby for the first time since arriving home and glowers. 'No. Why would I?'

'I just thought she might have texted you or something. She said she'd be home at ten.'

Clio shakes her head. 'God forbid Little Miss Perfect might be fifteen minutes late.' Contempt smears her voice, and she turns, heads towards the door.

'Are you off to bed?'

'Yep.' The single, clipped syllable hangs in the air as Clio exits the room.

Abby listens to her thump up the stairs, wondering – as she so often does – about the person Clio might be in a parallel world, one in which her father had not died of a stroke a week after her tenth birthday. She had been such a happy child before: brimming with infectious enthusiasm, slightly cheeky, somewhat maverick. A natural charmer, endearing people to her with her impish smile and beautifully naïve, often hilarious observations. The kind of child who managed to attract the affection of a room without ever showing off. But now – five years since Stuart's death – that child has long since disappeared, replaced by a teenager who seems full of disdain for everything Abby says and does, however much she tries to reach out to her.

Glancing down at her phone again, Abby begins typing a message to Isla even as a part of her brain tells her not to. Isla is seventeen. It is not unusual for seventeen-year-olds to stay out late at a party. And ten-fifteen is not late for a Friday night, Abby knows that.

But she also knows that Isla is not like other teenagers. She is responsible, considerate, diligent. She always messages Abby if she will not be home on time. She is the daughter of whom other parents speak in adulating tones, because Isla is always so mindful of Abby's feelings, has been such an emotional rock since Stuart died. And Isla has swimming early tomorrow morning, knows she needs to get a decent night's sleep if she is to have a good session. After a training blip over the summer – a nasty tummy bug followed by a bad shoulder – Isla has been working fiendishly hard at the pool, is determined to qualify for the nationals when trials take place next month. Abby knows Isla is good enough; her coach has made that clear, as have her results at county meets over the past year. All Isla needs to do is train hard. Keep focused. Get enough sleep.

Hey sweetheart. Just checking everything's okay? Let me know if you want a lift home. xxx

Even as she presses her finger down on the send button, she is aware of a sharp flare of guilt. The party at Meera's house is only a short walk away. Isla will be fine getting home. No doubt Jules or Yasmin, who live close by, will walk back with her. Abby is worrying about nothing.

The sound of the doorbell shrieks into the quiet, and Abby jumps up from the sofa, assumes Isla must have forgotten her key. She is usually so meticulous about her possessions, rarely forgets or loses anything.

Opening the front door, Abby is aware of something pushing down hard on her chest.

It is not Isla, smiling apologetically at her.

Instead, two police officers stand on the doorstep. And neither of them are smiling.

'Mrs Richardson? I'm PC Kelly and this is PC Hessell. Do you mind if we come in?'

Nicole

Nicole tiptoes from her son's bedroom, closes the door with a barely audible click.

For a moment, she listens, ear pressed against wood, waiting to see if he will stir.

It is years since she has done this. At fifteen, Jack does not need her – want her – tucking him into bed at night. But this evening was different.

From behind the door, she hears the sound of deep breaths, allows herself a sliver of relief.

Creeping down the stairs, she exhales silently, tries to block images of the evening's events flashing behind her eyes.

Jack is asleep. That is enough for now.

Walking into the kitchen, she startles to find Nathaniel leaning against the butler sink, gulping a glass of water.

'When did you get home?'

Nathaniel drains the glass, wipes his mouth on the sleeve of his jacket, and Nicole resists the urge to tell him not to do that. In ten months' time, Nathaniel will officially become an adult – he already resembles an almost-adult with his tall, gangly frame, his limbs slightly too long as though they have grown unilaterally and failed to alert the rest of his body – and Nicole knows that her licence to chastise him dwindles with each passing day.

'A few minutes ago.'

Nicole walks past the kitchen island, reaches into the cupboard above the wine fridge for a glass. She watches – as if in slow motion – as the glass slips through her fingers and shatters onto the slate-grey tiled floor.

'Are you okay?'

Nicole nods, though the effort feels gargantuan. 'Sorry. Be careful where you tread.'

Reaching past Nathaniel, she opens the cupboard beneath the sink, grabs the dustpan and brush, begins sweeping the floor with wide, jolting movements.

'Are you alright? You're being a bit . . . weird.'

Nicole stops, sucks in a deep breath. She does not know how it is possible to feel both exhausted and adrenalised in the same moment. 'I'm fine. It's Jack. He's been really unwell this evening.'

'In what way?'

Nicole hesitates, unsure how much detail to offer. 'He just couldn't stop vomiting. It was awful. I almost took him to A&E.'

'Shit, I hope I don't get it.'

Nicole hurries to reassure him. 'He seems a bit better now. He's asleep. Hopefully he'll have improved in the morning. But I suspect he'll be a bit off-colour for a few days.'

She stands up, tips the broken glass into the bin before remembering that she should have wrapped it in newspaper, knows Andrew will comment on it later, whenever he finally gets home from work.

Pulling her mobile from the back pocket of her jeans to see if Andrew has messaged, she sees a WhatsApp from Abby sent a few minutes earlier.

Any word from Nathaniel this evening? Isla's not back from the party yet and I haven't heard from her. x

Nicole glances across the kitchen to where Nathaniel's face is buried in his phone.

'How was the party?'

Nathaniel shrugs. 'Fine.'

'Was Isla still there when you left?'

He looks down at the floor, and Nicole thinks she sees an almost imperceptible trace of something – embarrassment? self-consciousness? – flit across his face.

'I dunno. I left early. Went to Elliot's. Why?'

'Abby messaged, asking if I'd heard from you. Isla's not home yet.' She studies her son's face, searches for a flicker of the emotion she saw a moment before but finds a blank canvas. 'What time did you leave?'

Nathaniel shrugs. 'Not sure. Nine, maybe? What's the big deal? It's not exactly late.'

Nicole picks up a cloth, cleans some stray crumbs from the worktop. 'Abby was just a bit worried, that's all.' Rinsing the cloth, she wrings it out, hangs it over the tap. She dries her hands in preparation to respond to Abby's message.

'By the way, where's your car?' Nathaniel barely glances up from his phone as he asks the question.

Nicole feels herself frown. 'What do you mean? It's in the driveway.'

Nathaniel looks up, shakes his head. 'It's not. I thought you must be out when I got home.'

There is a moment's hesitation, the cogs whirring in Nicole's brain: thinking about Jack upstairs, rewinding her memory, recalling the events of the evening. 'It must be. I parked it there earlier when I brought Jack home from football.'

'Well, it's not there now.'

Nicole heads out of the kitchen, into the hallway, across the black-and-white tiled floor. Opening the front door and stepping onto the driveway, she sees the empty space where her car should be. Thoughts scramble in her brain, trying to form a coherent narrative.

'I bet you it's been stolen.' Nathaniel's voice appears over her shoulder, full of prurient interest. 'Dad said there's been loads of car thefts round here lately.'

For a few seconds, Nicole does not reply, her thoughts like a smudged canvas.

'Are you going to call the police?'

Nicole turns, finds Nathaniel staring at her. Something clicks inside her head – a need to act, to deal with the situation – and she nods, opens her phone.

'I think I'll have to.'

Jenna

Jenna stares at the paperwork piled up on the sofa beside her, experiences a sense of oppression just looking at it. She debates the pros and cons of ploughing through more of it now, at almost ten-thirty on a Friday night, or calling it a day and cracking on tomorrow. Not for the first time, she wonders whether her bosses at the council have any conception of how much graft beyond their contracted hours the average social worker devotes to their job each week.

From the flat above begins the repetitive thudding of a bass line. Irritation clenches Jenna's jaw. It is like clockwork, this nightly invasion from the neighbouring flat, music that often persists until the early hours of the morning. Jenna has tried talking to the occupier, asked him to be a little more considerate, but the young man who answered the door – topless, tracksuit bottoms hanging low against his pelvic bones – just curled his top lip at her, told her 'I'll do what I want in my own home, alright Granny?' Jenna is only thirty-nine, her son is seventeen; she hopes not to become a grandmother for many years to come.

'Hey, Mum.'

Turning around, she finds Callum standing behind her, hoodie pulled up high over his head, hands thrust into the pockets of his jeans. There is still, sometimes, a momentary shock when she sees him, her little boy now resembling a grown man: six foot two, broad-shouldered, lean and toned from his athletics training. She realises she is biased but she thinks he is handsome, the kind of capable young person you'd want with you if you were stranded on a desert island: strong, honest, dependable.

'I didn't hear you come in.'

'Course you didn't with that prick's music thumping through the ceiling. Do you want me to go and have a word?'

Jenna raises her eyebrows. 'You know full well I don't. He's a nasty piece of work – just steer clear of him, okay?'

Callum slouches into the armchair, and Jenna resists the urge to tell him to sit up straight.

'Did you have a good evening?'

'S'okay.'

'Only okay?'

Callum shrugs, and Jenna is aware of tension puckering in her chest. 'Was Isla at the party?'

He nods.

'And?'

'And what?'

'Was everything alright?'

Callum shifts awkwardly as though he cannot, all of a sudden, get comfortable.

'Callum?'

His eyes flicker towards her and then away again, like moths too close to a flame. 'We had a bit of a row.'

Jenna forces herself to pause, not to jump in, feet first. 'What about?'

'Doesn't matter.'

'Of course it matters.' She can hear the effort in her voice to remain neutral. 'I thought everything was okay between you now?' She thinks about how crushed Callum was when Isla broke up with him last spring, how it has taken over five months for him to find his feet again. How Jenna's own feelings towards Isla swerved so abruptly from affection to anger when she broke Callum's heart. How difficult she has found it to fix a polite, magnanimous smile on her face when she has seen Isla at school events since.

'It is. We're fine.' He chews at the corner of his mouth. 'I'm going to make some toast. Do you want anything?'

Jenna shakes her head, and Callum launches himself out of the armchair. As he does so, the hood of his sweatshirt slips back, revealing a scarlet weal across his cheek.

'How did you get that scrape on your face?'

Callum's hand shoots up to his cheek. 'I walked into a door. At the party.' He does not wait for a response before heading into the small, square kitchen attached to the sitting room.

Jenna listens as Callum prepares a snack – the clank of the bread bin, the suction of the fridge door, the clatter of cutlery – aware that her pulse is racing. She thinks about the past three years, about her efforts to extract Callum from his previous school, to distance him from influences intent on destabilising him. She thinks about his stellar GCSE results that won him a sixth-form bursary to the private school he now attends, the school at which he has been flourishing, academically at least, over the last year.

She thinks about the trajectory of Callum's adolescence, about his involvement in events that could so easily have set his life on a different path, and about her determination that, in changing schools, he should be allowed to begin afresh. About how she thought he was achieving that when he began dating Isla: clever, popular, level-headed Isla. A nice girl, Jenna had thought. About how worried she has been since Isla dumped Callum that it may, possibly, derail him.

And then she thinks about the bright red streak on Callum's face, about his implausible explanation, about his row with Isla, and there is nothing she can do – nothing she can tell herself – to stop a spiral of anxiety weaving between her ribs.

Abby

Hit-and-run.

Paramedics did everything they could.

Pronounced dead at the scene.

The words reverberate in Abby's ears.

They do not make any sense. Nothing these two young police officers are saying makes any sense.

'I'm so sorry, Mrs Richardson. We know what a terrible shock this must be. There's a family liaison officer on the way, but in the meantime, is there someone we can contact for you, someone who could come and be with you?'

Abby hears the officer's words but cannot connect them to any comprehensible meaning.

'Mrs Richardson? Can I get you anything? A glass of water?'

Sound crackles on the radio attached to the female officer's shoulder, and her hand darts towards it, turns down the volume until silence engulfs the room.

The floor seems to sway beneath Abby's feet.

None of it makes any sense.

'Can I call someone for you – a friend or family member?'

Time seems to have paused, the breath in Abby's chest stilled. Sounds are muffled in her ears, belonging to some distant, parallel world. A world in which her seventeen-year-old daughter cannot possibly be dead.

'Where is she? Where's Isla?' The words burn in Abby's throat, but she needs to know, she has to find out.

A flicker of unease passes between the two officers, and Abby wishes they would wipe their faces clean of that abominable concern, that they would stop staring at her with such appalling sympathy.

'Isla's at the mortuary, Mrs Richardson. At the hospital.'

The mortuary. The words hit Abby as though she has been physically assaulted.

From behind the sofa, she hears the quiet click of the sitting room door, and for a split second, Abby feels a rush of incomparable relief; it is all a terrible mistake. The police officers have got it wrong. It is not Isla who has been hit, not Isla who has been killed. Isla is on the other side of the door, preparing to apologise for being late, to tell Abby that she lost track of time, that her phone battery died, that she wasn't able to call on the way home. Isla is going to tell her she is sorry, that she hopes Abby has not been concerned, that she will relay all the gossip from the party in the morning but, for now, she just wants to get to bed, get some sleep before the four-thirty alarm goes off for tomorrow's swim training. Abby will hug her, tell her not to worry; the only thing that matters is that she is home, safe and sound.

For the briefest fissure of time – a split second that lasts a lifetime – Abby is sure that behind the closed door, Isla is home.

And then the door opens, and there is Clio, slouching in pyjama bottoms and an oversized t-shirt, eyes grazing the room. She clocks the two police officers, turns to Abby, face awash with questions Abby does not have the capacity to answer.

At the sight of Clio and the absence of Isla, the full horror of what is happening overwhelms Abby as if she has been flung from

13

a great height, the ground rushing to meet her, air whistling past her ears, no idea how far she will fall or what will happen when she lands. Grief pummels her from every angle, collecting in her throat, threatening to choke her.

She reaches out, takes hold of Clio's hand, pulls her into her arms. Wrapping herself around her daughter's body, she clasps her fiercely as though to let go would risk them both being suffocated by the horror of what has happened. The shock breaches over her, like storm-battered waves, and Abby does not know how they will survive this, how anyone could survive this; how they will both not be drowned beneath the weight of such a loss.

Nicole

'What did they say?'

Nicole turns to where Nathaniel is sitting at the kitchen table, thoughts scrambling in her brain.

'What did the police say? Do they think your car's been stolen?'

She pours herself a glass of water, drinks it thirstily. 'They gave me a crime number and said I should give it to the insurance company first thing in the morning.'

'Is that it?'

'What do you mean?'

'They're not going to send someone round to investigate or something?'

Pain throbs at Nicole's temples and she rubs her fingers in concentric circles against it. 'Like Dad's been saying, car thefts are two-a-penny these days.'

'But who's going to take me for driving practice if your car's been stolen? My retest is in six weeks, and Dad never has time.'

Nicole allows herself a moment before answering. 'We'll figure something out, don't worry.'

From beyond the kitchen, she hears the front door clicking open and shut, familiar footsteps padding down the hall. Glancing at her watch, she sees it is just gone ten-forty: late by any normal person's standards to arrive home from work on a Friday night, but hedge fund managers, Nicole has come to realise over the past nineteen years of marriage, are not like normal people.

Andrew walks into the room, eyes edged by crows' feet, and yet he could still – on a good day – pass for mid-thirties rather than late forties. Friends of Nicole have often commented on how well Andrew has aged, how lucky Nicole is that he hasn't – like so many men approaching fifty – let himself go. But as Nicole looks at him now, she finds herself wondering whether Andrew's relentless drive towards self-improvement, his dogged acquisition of wealth and status, has been right for their family. Whether it might have been better to lead calmer, quieter, less aspirational lives, so that she might have had him at home when she really needed him.

Andrew kisses her cheek. He smells of garlic overlayed with mint, and she does not know if it is his breath or the aftermath of the evening's events that turns her stomach.

'Are you okay? You look shattered.'

'Mum's car's been stolen.'

Andrew eyes her quizzically, and it is all Nicole can do to nod in response.

'Have you reported it to the police?'

She nods again, her head unwieldy on her shoulders.

'Jesus.' Nathaniel's voice bleeds shock, and Nicole looks over to where he is sitting, sees the distress on his face, feels a knot of pre-emptive fear.

'What is it? What's wrong?'

For a moment, Nathaniel says nothing, just stares silently at the screen of his phone. He looks up at Nicole and Andrew, then down at his phone, then back up again. 'It's Isla.'

For a split second, Nicole assumes it is Isla who has messaged him, wonders if she has already been in contact with Abby, if she is already home. But before the thought has time to settle, Nathaniel is talking again.

'Elliot's just messaged me. He says Isla's been in an accident.'

Nicole feels a tightness in her chest, and it is as though the room is hesitating, waiting for whatever Nathaniel is going to say next.

'He says Isla's *dead*.'

There is a rush of blood to Nicole's head, as though she has been submerged in water, pressure bearing down on her.

'That's got to be a prank, surely?' Andrew's incredulous gaze pivots between Nicole and Nathaniel as if searching for confirmation that it is nothing more than a sick joke.

'Meera's messaged me too, saying the same thing. She says there's loads of police at her house.' Nathaniel swipes at his phone, reads something, swipes again, and all the while, the ground beneath Nicole's feet seems to lurch and sway, and she does not know how she is still standing.

'I've got another four messages about it. They're all saying the same thing.' He looks up, face ashen. 'I don't think it's a joke.'

'Where did it happen?' The words are thick, viscous, in Nicole's mouth.

'Outside Meera's house. At the party. I can't believe it.'

Next to her, Nicole is aware of Andrew grabbing hold of the table's edge, lowering himself into a chair next to Nathaniel, burying his head in his hands. Nathaniel gapes at his phone as though, perhaps, the words will shape themselves into a different meaning.

Nicole stands motionless, watching them both, her brain darting with thoughts she cannot grasp. It is as if she has exited her body, as though she is floating out of reach, beyond this unthinkable reality.

She thinks of Abby's earlier message, to which she never replied, too preoccupied with Jack and with phoning the police about her car.

She thinks of Abby – of where she might be right now, who might be with her – and guilt sweeps over her that Abby is going through this alone, no husband by her side to help bear the grief; she will have to withstand another, unimaginable loss.

She thinks of Isla, a teenager she has known since the day she was born. Such a beautiful baby. Such a beautiful child.

And now Isla is dead.

Nicole's stomach convulses and she rushes to the sink, feels an inexorable heaving as the contents find their way into the porcelain basin. The retching continues, like the roiling waves of an ocean, and she feels a hand on her back, a rhythmic rubbing, senses Andrew standing behind her.

She thinks of Isla – *How can Isla be dead?* – and of Abby and Clio, how they can possibly endure this loss. She cannot begin to imagine how Abby must be feeling. She thinks of Jack upstairs in bed, of Nathaniel white with shock at the kitchen table, and it is all she can do not to wrap her boys in a swathe of cotton wool and vow never to let them out of her sight again.

Jenna

Jenna watches Callum on the sofa next to her, eating the last of his toast. She tries not to stare at the red mark emblazoning his cheek, tries not to imagine what may have caused it. Tries not to think about the argument between her son and Isla this evening.

Consternation prickles the back of her neck as she thinks about Callum's precarious standing at school. The only sixth-form student on a full bursary. The only student who has transferred from the local, failing comprehensive. The only student, almost certainly, who is trying to escape a past that so nearly derailed his life.

His relationship with Isla – straight-A student, county swimmer, universally popular – had been Callum's first teenage romance and also a fast-track into the nucleus of the school's social life. Abby had clearly not approved of her daughter's five-month relationship with Callum, had been unable to conceal her displeasure beneath the superficial social niceties when Jenna bumped into her at school events: the tight smiles, the stock enquiries, the supreme effort to pretend that class, wealth and privilege were of no importance when it came to the young man dating her daughter. Callum always insisted that Abby was unfailingly polite to him during all those evenings and weekends he spent at Isla's house, but politeness and kindness were not the same thing.

Jenna has no illusions of ever being embraced by the parental clique at Collingswood; she does not have time for their coffee mornings nor the money for their endless stream of dinners and drinks. She has never sought that kind of inclusion. She knew, before Callum started at Collingswood, that they would be entering a different economic world: a world of seven-figure salaries, affluent houses, second homes, brand-new 4x4s, exotic trips abroad every school holiday. A level of wealth Jenna could barely envisage, let alone compete with. But since Callum started at Collingswood, Jenna has been clear in her own mind that financial parity and parental friendships are not what's important. She just needs the Collingswood students to accept her son. And she is all too aware that if there is going to be conflict between Callum and Isla, there will be only one social casualty.

From deep in the pocket of Callum's jeans comes the familiar sound of his phone.

She watches as he pulls out his mobile, opens a message, observes the rise and fall of his Adam's apple.

'Is everything okay?'

He turns to face her, and there is something unreadable in his eyes: disquiet, upset, angst, she cannot quite tell.

'It's Isla.'

Jenna does not know whether to feel concern or relief. If Isla is messaging him, perhaps things aren't as bad as she feared. Or perhaps the message is a continuation of their earlier argument, an edict for him to stay away from her, to stop hanging out with her friends.

'What does she say?'

Callum scrunches closed his eyes, shakes his head in small, jolting movements. 'Fuck!' He bangs a fist down hard on the sofa beside him, and anxiety wraps itself around Jenna's throat.

'What is it? What's wrong?'

Callum does not reply, presses his hands against the sides of his head as if trying to squeeze out whatever thoughts are inside.

'Callum, please, you're scaring me. What's going on?'

A lone tear slips over the lower lid of Callum's left eye. Jenna has not seen him cry for years – for over a decade – since the last time his dad promised to visit and failed to materialise. The sight of it now shreds a little piece of her heart.

Consciously, she softens her voice, places a hand on Callum's arm. 'What is it, love? What's happened?'

Callum does not speak, passes her his phone.

Jenna reads the message, senses her world tilting at a different angle.

Shit. Have you heard? Isla got knocked down by some fucked up hit-and-run driver. She's been killed. There's police swarming around Meera's. Where are you?

Jenna reads the message, and then reads it again, her eyes swimming from one word to the next, knowing what they say but unable to grasp their meaning. Unable to comprehend that Isla is dead: the beautiful young woman with whom her son, Jenna knows, is still in love.

'Callum, I'm sorry. I'm so, so sorry.'

Wrapping her arms around him, she rocks him back and forth, holds on to him, wishing she could feel his pain for him. And yet, even as she murmurs to him that it's going to be okay, that they will get through this together, she cannot escape the fear tugging deep inside her that perhaps, this time, she will not be able to protect him.

SEVEN MONTHS BEFORE ISLA'S

DEATH

Isla

'What time will you be home?'

Isla folded the items she would need for training after school and packed them into her bag: swimming costume, goggles, swim hat, towel, deodorant. 'I'm not sure. Ten, maybe?'

'And it'll just be you and Callum at his this evening?'

There was a clear, pointed edge to her mum's voice, and Isla pulled her face into a reassuring smile. 'I'm only going there to study, Mum. Callum's going to help me prep for my chemistry test, and I'm going to help him with his application for summer school. That's all.' She could hear the ellipsis at the end of her sentence: *We're not going to have rampant sex. It's not like that. You can trust me to be sensible.*

'Wouldn't Callum rather come here? We've got more space. It would be better for studying. I can order in food for you – whatever you like. Pizza, Thai?'

'Honestly, we'll be fine. Callum's always coming here.'

Isla watched a pleat of concern fold across her mum's forehead. Three months since she'd started dating Callum and her mum still didn't seem to like him any more than the day Isla first brought him home.

'I'm just worried about you getting . . . distracted. You know what an important year this is for you. Your A levels aren't that far away. And if you're serious about making the national swim squad, it's going to take up a huge amount of time.'

Her mum didn't need to complete the speech for Isla to know what she was thinking. *You haven't got time for a relationship. You're only seventeen. Boyfriends can wait until you're older.* Sometimes Isla wondered whether it was having a boyfriend per se that bothered her mum, or whether it was Callum specifically. Whether, had Isla brought home one of her classmates that her mum had known for years – someone who lived in a house like theirs rather than a rented flat in an ex-council block – her mum might have been more accepting. But her mum hadn't really got to know Callum yet; she hadn't allowed herself to see Callum's kindness, his sense of humour, his incredible drive.

Stymieing her frustration at her mum's disapproval, Isla could only hope that, in time, her mum would look beyond her preconceptions to see that Callum was actually really good for her.

'Honestly, Mum, I'm fine.' Isla checked her school bag for her biology, chemistry and maths textbooks. 'I'm not getting distracted, and I'm not letting anything slide. Callum works even harder than I do.'

'Jesus, is that even possible?'

Isla looked over her shoulder to where Clio had appeared in the doorway, arms folded across her chest.

'What do you mean?'

Clio regarded Isla with an air of derision. 'I can't imagine anyone finding more hours in the day to study than you.'

Their mum sighed. 'There's nothing wrong with wanting to do well, Clio. It wouldn't hurt you to take a leaf out of your sister's book occasionally.'

Isla watched as Clio's face tightened like a fist.

'Yeah, well, we can't all be as perfect as Isla, can we?'

Isla baulked at her sister's barbed tone. 'Clee, don't be like that.'

'Like what?' Clio glared at her.

Isla allowed herself a breath. Sometimes, only by closing her eyes and forcing herself to remember, could she believe that once, not so very long ago, she and Clio had been close.

'Clio, can you please finish getting ready for school? You don't want to be late again.'

There was a moment's hesitation before Clio scowled, turned, and thumped down the stairs. Isla listened to her retreating footsteps, wondering if there was anything she could do to re-ingratiate herself with her sister; to help make Clio less resentful, less awash with a sense that the world was against her. Ever since their dad died, Clio had been like a coiled spring, her feelings tightly wound, as though restraining her grief was an act of self-preservation. It didn't matter how many ways Isla tried to reach out to her, or how endlessly patient their mum was with her outbursts; Clio's anger was now like a fourth member of their family, to be considered, managed and placated at all times.

Glancing at the photo on her bedside table – Isla and her dad standing in front of the Great Geysir in Iceland not long before he died – she was aware of a familiar cramping in her chest; the loss of him, the love for him that she did not know what to do with now he was gone. The disbelief, even after all this time, that she would never see him again. Sometimes, she could not help feeling that if her dad had not suffered a stroke at the age of forty-one, her and Clio's lives would be different beyond all comprehension; his death marked a bifurcation in the road that sent them both on different paths, and they would never know how their experiences may have been different – better – had he lived.

'How will you get home? I'm happy to come and collect you.'

Isla shook her head. 'It's fine. I'll jump in an Uber. Callum will probably come with me and get the bus back.'

'Callum doesn't want to be traipsing back all that way at night. It'll be arctic out there.'

'Honestly, Mum, it's okay. Callum doesn't mind.' Glancing at the clock beside her bed, she saw the time. 'I'd better go. I said I'd meet Meera in the library before school.' Grabbing her swim bag and rucksack, she slung them over her shoulder, leaned forwards, kissed her mum goodbye. 'I'll see you later.'

Running down the stairs, Isla became aware of something fluttering in her chest, like the beating wings of a caged bird, a feeling she'd first noticed soon after her dad died. A sense of responsibility and expectation, and a need to keep paddling furiously beneath the surface so that nobody – not even her mum – knew quite how much effort it took to maintain the perception everyone had of her: the perfect student, the perfect daughter, the perfect athlete. People seemed to think it came effortlessly to her, that she was blessed with the ability to hold all this together without stress, anxiety and inordinate, Herculean effort. Ever since her dad died, she'd felt a pressure to mature overnight, to morph from a twelve-year-old girl into an adult; to be there to look after her mum, keep an eye on her sister, and be the teenager nobody had to worry about because they already had enough worries of their own. For the past five years, she felt as though she'd been trying to become the person other people wanted her to be – the person other people needed her to be – and now, sometimes, she was not quite sure what the true version of herself was any more.

◆ ◆ ◆

'Forty-eight out of fifty. You're totally going to nail that chemistry test.'

Isla turned onto her side, where she was lying on Callum's narrow, single bed, and propped her head on her arm. 'Which ones did I get wrong?'

Callum's eyes skimmed over the pages of the textbook. 'One on hydrocarbons and one on aldehydes.'

Isla frowned. 'Are you sure? We revised aldehydes in class today. I shouldn't have got that wrong.' Taking the book from Callum's hands, she scanned the page, saw that Callum was right. Anxiety flickered inside her like a faulty lightbulb, and she wondered whether she could feasibly cram in any more revision before Tuesday's test. Earlier today, Mr Vyleta told her she'd got one hundred per cent on a mock paper they'd sat in class last week. But now she was only pulling ninety-six per cent on a stupid class test and there wasn't really any excuse for it.

'Stop looking so worried. It's just one practice test. It's not a big deal.' Callum kissed her, reached for his study folder, and Isla tried to convince herself that he was right; she still had time to improve before next week's test.

Looking around Callum's bedroom, Isla noted the slim wardrobe, the melamine bedside cabinet, the thin curtains that failed to block out sufficient light from the single-paned window. No chest of drawers, no chair, no desk to work at. Callum usually did his homework at the fold-out table in the kitchen or in the library at school. Sometimes, when the two of them hung out at her house, Isla felt an urge to apologise, to say she knew it was absurd, her having a bedroom almost as large as Callum's entire flat, complete with double bed and built-in wardrobes, two chests of drawers, a solid oak desk, a sofa beneath the window overlooking the garden. But she couldn't find the right words – the right tone – without running the risk of sounding patronising.

As Isla watched Callum read through his summer school application, she tried to imagine how the next eighteen months might play out: whether they'd both get the grades they needed for Oxford, her to read medicine, Callum to read PPE. Whether he would still, in a year and a half's time, be as keen as he was now for them to study at the same university. The prospect of them having to go their separate ways felt unthinkable. She had never been interested in dating anyone before Callum, but now – three months into their relationship – he already felt such an important part of her life. The possibility of them not being together at university felt too big, too unwieldy, and she pushed it to a corner of her mind before it took up too much space.

From the top of the bedside cabinet, Isla's phone bleeped. Reaching across Callum, she picked it up, found a message from her mum.

> *How was swimming? Just checking you definitely don't want me to collect you from Callum's? It's freezing out there! Xx*

She was about to tap out a reply, tell her mum she'd be home around ten, just as she'd promised, when an image slipped into her head: her mum at home alone, at nine o'clock on a Friday night, no doubt worrying about Clio's whereabouts, an unread novel beside her on the sofa, the house throbbing with silence.

Before she was aware of her thoughts coalescing into words, she turned to Callum. 'Do you mind if we do your application on Sunday? I think I should get home, check my mum's okay.'

Stepping out of an Uber at the end of her street where she'd asked the driver to drop them, Isla slipped a hand beneath Callum's coat, wrapped an arm around his waist.

In the artificial light, her breath snaked in the air before evaporating like a puff of smoke in a magic trick. The darkness was illuminated only by streetlamps and a faint glow that stole around the edges of closed curtains from the large bay windows of detached Victorian houses identical to her own.

An image of her dad appeared suddenly in Isla's mind: him cupping her hands inside his on a cold winter's day, breathing hot air onto them, rubbing them until the numbness subsided.

There were still so many moments when Isla was seized by grief. Moments when it felt physical, tangible, oppressive. Moments when it seemed incomprehensible that the rest of her life lay ahead and her dad would share in none of it. He had not been there to witness her clean sweep of top GCSE grades, had not been sitting by the side of the pool when she'd won a gold medal at the county championships. He would not be there to find out her A-level results, or drive her to her first day at university. He would not watch her graduate, secure her first job, move into her first home, get married, have children, maybe. It seemed surreal to her that all those milestones would occur without her dad being there to witness them.

'You okay? You're shivering.'

Isla tilted her head up towards Callum's face. 'I'm fine.'

As they neared her house, Isla spotted a silhouetted figure leaning against her garden wall, hood pulled up over his head. Instinctively, her arm tightened around Callum's waist. But then the person turned around, and she saw it was just Nathaniel.

'Hi.'

'Hey. What are you doing here?'

'Hey bro.' Callum reached out a hand, fist-bumped Nathaniel.

'I was just passing. Thought I could pick up those maths notes.'

'At nine-thirty on a Friday night?' Isla heard a note of mild mockery in her voice. She saw colour bleed into Nathaniel's cheeks, felt a rush of guilt. Nathaniel had never liked being teased, even when they were little, and she knew he would resent it even more with Callum to witness it. 'Sorry, I haven't finished going through them yet. I can email them over on Sunday morning?'

'Great, thanks.'

For a few moments, none of them spoke. A security light clicked on outside a neighbouring house, and Isla watched as a fox slunk past a garden wall and disappeared through a gate.

'Right, well I'd better get indoors. It's freezing.' Isla shivered.

Nathaniel looked down at the ground, scraped his trainer against the edge of an uneven paving slab. 'Can I talk to you about something?' He paused. 'In private?'

Isla felt herself falter, glanced at Callum.

'No worries. I'll head off. Call me tomorrow, after training?'

'Yep. I should be finished by lunchtime.'

Leaning forward, Callum slipped a hand gently around the back of her neck, kissed her lips. Isla tried to relax but it was difficult when she could sense Nathaniel's eyes boring into the side of her head.

'Don't stay out here too long – you'll freeze.'

Isla watched Callum leave before turning back to Nathaniel. 'What did you want to talk to me about?'

Nathaniel peered into the darkness, where Callum had disappeared. 'I don't get what you see in him. You could do so much better.'

An icy breeze weaved its way around Isla's neck, and she pulled her scarf tighter. 'You've made it clear you don't like him, Nate. But no one's asking you to hang out with him.' Her tone was harsher than she'd intended, but his repeated jibes about Callum were becoming tiresome, and it wasn't any of Nathaniel's business who she dated anyway.

Thrusting his hands deep into his pockets, Nathaniel kept his eyes trained on Isla's face. 'I'm just looking out for you. There's no need to bite my head off.'

Isla averted her gaze from Nathaniel's scrutiny. It was no secret between her and her friends that Nathaniel liked her. It had become obvious in Year 11 with the endless excuses to pop round to her house, the blushing whenever she spoke to him, the stream of extraneous questions in the common room about homework, lesson notes, deadlines. At first, Isla had brushed it off, assumed it was just a phase he was going through, that he'd get over it soon enough. She couldn't think about Nathaniel like that. She'd known him all her life; their families were entwined, their personal histories inextricably linked. The only guise in which she could think about Nathaniel was fraternal. An annoying brother sometimes, but fraternal nonetheless.

But now, over a year since it began, Nathaniel's crush showed no signs of abating, and Isla was beginning to feel that he was making their lifelong friendship almost impossible. Every conversation seemed loaded with a subtext she'd rather not acknowledge, and their former childhood ease had been replaced by an awkward, uncomfortable sense of expectation. Sometimes Isla wished Nathaniel would strike out on his own, make some new friends.

'What did you want to speak to me about anyway?'

'I just wanted to check you were okay. You seemed a bit . . . preoccupied in maths today.'

Isla shook her head, tried not to betray her impatience. 'I'm fine. Just got a lot on.' She paused, saw a light click on in the hallway of her house, wondered what her mum was doing. 'My feet are starting to go numb. I'm going to head in. I'll email those notes to you on Sunday, okay?'

For a few seconds, Nathaniel studied her face, the air between them charged with hope or disappointment, Isla couldn't quite tell. And then he gave a brief nod. 'Sure, thanks.'

Turning and walking along the garden path, Isla retrieved her key from her bag, slotted it into the lock. As she stepped inside the house and closed the door behind her, she caught a glimpse of Nathaniel standing on the pavement, lurking in the shadows, and she could not escape the feeling that should she open the door in an hour's time, he would still be there, watching and waiting in the darkness.

THE PRESENT

Abby

Abby stands outside the cemetery chapel as mourners file past: shaking her hand, offering condolences, saying how sorry they are for her loss. One by one they tell her that Isla was wonderful, that they will miss her so much, that her death is an unspeakable tragedy.

Abby listens and yet she does not really hear. The words are like a phantom hovering in front of her, but she cannot think, cannot respond, does not know what these people want her to say. A part of her seems to have been frozen in time, paused the moment she opened the door to the two police officers just over a fortnight ago. Because she does not understand how it can have come to pass that she is here, again, for the second time in five years, standing outside a chapel, having just cremated one of the people she loves most in the world. It does not seem possible.

Beside her, Clio is mute, motionless, her face impassive. Abby does not know what she is thinking or feeling. She has barely reacted to her sister's death; Abby has not even seen her cry. The night it happened, Clio stood rigid inside Abby's embrace, did not make a sound. She disappeared to her room soon after, left Abby to deal with the police alone. Since then, all Abby's attempts to comfort Clio have been met with stony silence or benign passivity. It is as though Isla's death has cemented an insurmountable wall between them. Abby wants to look after Clio, to share their grief, to eliminate some of her daughter's pain. But it is as though Clio is exuding a force field of self-protection, and she will not let Abby get close.

The October sunlight flares and then darkens as clouds drift across the sky. Abby has a sense of being disconnected from herself, as though her body is present but her mind, her heart, her soul, are somewhere else, somewhere distant she cannot reach. She is aware of a gaping chasm at the centre of her being: an excavation, an infinite abyss. And yet, at the same time, there is a constant churning, a debilitating sensation: a permanent sense of loss.

As mourners continue to exit the chapel, the events of the past fortnight play in her memory like a horror film she does not want to see. The visit to the mortuary to identify Isla's body. The endless phone calls to notify family and friends. The day of the post-mortem, the unbearable thought of a stranger slicing open her daughter's body, examining it, putting it back together as though Isla could be restored anew. The funeral arrangements that Nicole has overseen but about which Abby had to make decisions nonetheless: choosing a coffin and a headstone, finalising music and readings, confirming an order of service for a funeral she never once imagined might take place during her own lifetime. The countless hours she has spent visualising the final moments of her daughter's life: questioning why Isla was outside when she should have been indoors at Meera's party; speculating whether she was on her way home or en route elsewhere; wondering whether she saw the headlights of the car speeding towards her, knew in those final, unimaginable seconds what was about to happen. They are imagined scenes which haunt her day and night.

'How are you doing?'

She feels a hand on her arm, finds Nicole standing beside her.

'You don't have to do this. Nobody expects you to stand here, thanking everyone for coming.'

Thanking everyone for coming. A part of Abby's brain understands that this is what she ought to be doing. But still, as the next mourners traipse past, no words emerge from her lips.

'Come on, you've been standing far too long. Come and sit down. You too, Clio.'

Abby allows Nicole to lead them away, to chaperone them to a quiet bench in the cemetery garden. She senses dozens of eyes on her, wishes they would all go away, wishes everyone would just leave her alone.

'Why don't you sit here for a moment before we go to the hotel.'

The hotel. For a moment, Abby cannot make sense of what Nicole is saying, thoughts blurring in her head.

And then she remembers. The wake – Isla's wake – is being held at a hotel not far away, on the bank of the Thames. The wake that Nicole has organised. The wake that will involve more well-intentioned sympathy from people who cannot possibly understand the depth of Abby's grief.

The thought is unpalatable: having to mingle with family, friends, parents, students, teachers, as though they are attending a wedding or an afternoon tea party rather than her daughter's funeral. It is incomprehensible to her that she is expected to converse with guests when every fibre of her being wants to howl into the wind.

Across the lawn, her eyes land on Callum and Jenna, talking with the Head of Sixth Form, and she experiences a stab of envy that Jenna's seventeen-year-old child is still alive while hers is not. She wishes they had not come, does not want to be reminded of Isla's relationship with Callum.

Jenna catches her eye, nods, offers a cautious smile. Abby turns away, resentment throbbing beneath her skin.

'Why haven't the police found out who did this yet? What's taking them so long?' The words erupt from her mouth in a voice she does not recognise, her tone replete with unrestrained vitriol.

'It's still early days, isn't that what the police said? I'm sure they're doing everything they can.'

There is something unnatural in Nicole's voice, like an automated response, as though she no more believes what she is saying than Abby does hearing it. Abby is sick of platitudes. She does not understand how it can be possible that the person who is responsible for killing her child – for knocking down her daughter in the street and leaving her for dead – is still walking free. 'The police are hopeless. You know they are. They haven't even managed to find your car yet. How do we know that the person who stole your car isn't the same person who killed Isla?'

She sees the look of horror on Nicole's face, knows she has gone too far. She understands that she should feel guilty, but there is no room for guilt when there is already so much rage, so much grief. 'The police are incompetent. Do you know what percentage of hit-and-runs go unsolved?'

'Mum, for god's sake, stop going on about it.'

Abby darts a glance at Clio, turns back to Nicole. 'Ninety per cent. *Ninety per cent.* Do you know what it's like to feel that there's only a *ten per cent* chance that the person who killed your child will get caught?'

Nicole pauses, takes a deep breath. 'I know. They're appalling stats. But getting angry isn't going to help anyone, least of all you or Clio.'

A switch flicks inside Abby: a sense of maternal fury that her daughter's killer is still at large and nobody but her seems to care. 'Do you know what I hope?'

Nicole shakes her head.

'I hope they find the person who did this and that when they go to prison, it destroys their life as much as they've destroyed mine.'

Abby hears the venom in her voice – sharp, caustic – sees the shock on Nicole's face quickly smoothed into something more benign. And in that fleeting moment, Abby is struck by how alone she is in her grief. Stuart is not alive to bear it with her, Clio will not allow her to get close, and not even her best friend can withstand the depth of her loss.

Nicole crouches down, places a hand on Abby's knee. 'I can't begin to imagine how you're feeling today, and I'm so sorry you're having to go through this. It's every mother's worst nightmare, I know.'

Abby hears the fracture in Nicole's voice, does not know whether she wants to rage at the world or if she wants it all to stop; whether she just wants to hide beneath a duvet and stay there forever.

'I know it doesn't feel like it now, but you will get through this. You're strong, Abby, and you have so much love around you. You *will* get through this.'

Abby feels herself drifting, out of her body, away from tropes which can offer no solace. There is nothing anyone can give her – nothing anyone can say or do – to make this better, and she almost resents them trying. It is an affront to Isla to believe that this is something from which she will ever recover. She does not want to recover. To grieve is an act of remembrance, she senses that keenly. The only thing anchoring her to the world – the only reason she has not already drowned beneath the weight of her loss – is Clio.

'I just need to find Nathaniel, see how he's doing, and then I'll be back, okay?'

Abby watches Nicole walk away, sits silently on the bench beside Clio, aware that they have lost a father and a sister, a husband and a daughter. Looking out over the chapel gardens, at the hundreds of people who have come to pay their respects to Isla, Abby experiences a desolating, all-encompassing sense of loneliness, and it is all she can do to close her eyes and wait for it to be over.

Nicole

Nicole looks over her shoulder to where she has left Abby on a bench with Clio. She sees Abby close her eyes as though to shut out the world and all the pain it inflicts, and her own mind is awash with feelings too complicated to articulate, even to herself. She sees Clio turn her head away from Abby, as though proximity to her mother's grief is dangerous and she cannot bear to witness it. Nicole experiences a surge of love for Clio, a wish that she could – somehow – insulate her from all this. She's always had a soft spot for Clio, has seen how difficult it's been for her, growing up in her sister's shadow, has watched Abby's efforts to assure Clio that she is loved every inch as much as Isla. She has observed, over the years, Clio's inability to believe it, and the steely carapace Clio has erected around herself: a failed attempt to shield herself from her own vulnerability.

Looking around the gathering, Nicole's eyes scan the crowd for Andrew and Nathaniel, but she cannot see them anywhere. Nathaniel barely said a word this morning before they left, has been quiet ever since the news of Isla's death, and Nicole does not know how best to help him. For the past couple of years, Nathaniel has tried to keep his feelings for Isla a secret, but Nicole has seen the flush in his cheeks whenever her name is mentioned, heard the longing in his voice when he is talking to her. And she has also seen Isla's tactful attempts to deflect Nathaniel's unwanted attention, understood that Isla never thought of Nathaniel that way, that her feelings towards him were purely platonic. Many times, Nicole has begun to broach the subject with Nathaniel – gently, sensitively – but each time Nathaniel has shut her down, his humiliation so acute that Nicole has felt it unkind to continue. Now, given what has happened, she does not know how to acknowledge the exquisite pain of Nathaniel's grief without embarrassing him, feels paralysed by an overwhelming sense of her own impotence.

'How's Abby doing?'

Nicole feels a hand on her arm, turns to see Sita Rani standing next to her.

'Not great, to be honest. I'm hoping she'll feel a bit better once today's out of the way.'

Sita shakes her head. 'I feel so guilty. If Dev and I hadn't gone away for the night and said Meera could have a party, this would never have happened.' She holds her hands up against Nicole's attempt to interrupt her. 'I know, it's a futile way of thinking, but I can't help myself.'

'You can't torture yourself like that. It's not your fault.' Nicole squeezes Sita's hand, thinks about this group of parents she has known for almost seven years, whose children she has watched grow from prepubescence to near-adulthood.

'I haven't seen Jack today. Did he not want to come?'

Something catches in Nicole's throat, and she swallows before answering. 'No, we decided against it. We felt it was too much for him, at his age. He's gone to a friend's for the day.'

She thinks about Jack, about how withdrawn he has been over the past two weeks, even more so than usual. Nicole has already spent months worrying about him. Since his diagnosis six months ago, she has been aware that Jack has behaved differently, perceived himself differently. However many times she tells him that a diagnosis of Inattentive ADHD does not make him a different person – it does not change the way anyone thinks or feels about him – Jack does not seem able to believe her. It's true that his condition makes him more forgetful, more disorganised, more distractible – these were the reasons she got him tested in the first place – but it does not alter fundamentally who he is: the kind, thoughtful, funny teenage boy she knows him to be. And yet, Jack seems to have become unsure of himself: tentative, less confident, less sociable.

'How's Nathaniel doing? It must be hard on him. I know he and Isla have been friends their whole lives.'

As if in Pavlovian response, Nicole's eyes sweep across the assembled mourners, alight on Nathaniel leaning against a tree trunk, alone. 'He's found it tough. But then, it's been tough for all Isla's friends.'

'It's different for you guys, though. I know how close you all are.'

It is all Nicole can do to nod in response. Memories flit through her mind like grainy footage on an old cine projector. Isla and Nathaniel as toddlers playing in sandpits, in paddling pools, at soft-play centres. Isla and Nathaniel standing side by side, holding hands, grinning impishly on their first day of kindergarten. Isla, Nathaniel, Clio and Jack dressed in costumes to perform plays Isla devised. The four of them jumping off the side of Stuart's boat into the water at Newtown Creek. Isla comforting Jack after he failed to win a prize in the treasure hunt at Clio's seventh birthday party, giving him a bumper bag of Haribo instead. Isla and Nathaniel lounging on the sofa in the den, in fits of laughter, watching *Elf*, *Bill and Ted*, *School of Rock*. So many shared memories. So much shared history.

'It must be especially difficult for Nathaniel, given all the friendship drama over the past few weeks.'

The words jar in Nicole's head. 'What friendship drama?'

There is an almost imperceptible flicker of surprise across Sita's face before she neutralises her expression. 'Sorry, I just assumed you knew.'

'Knew what?'

Sita smiles with exaggerated reassurance. 'I'm sure it's nothing.'

Impatience stipples Nicole's skin. 'It's clearly not nothing or you wouldn't have mentioned it. Seriously, Sita, I don't have space in my head to be worrying about things I don't even know about. What's going on?'

Sita looks over her shoulder as if to check nobody's eavesdropping, lowers her voice. 'It's just that Nathaniel seems to have been . . . slightly frozen out lately. It's probably just a passing spat or something. You know what teens are like – there's always friendship issues going on. But Meera said that's why he wasn't invited to the party.'

For the second time in less than a minute, Nicole is aware of words snagging in her head as if on a rusty nail. 'What do you mean, he wasn't invited to the party?'

'Meera's party, I mean. The night of the accident. Sorry, if I'd known in advance that she wasn't going to invite him, I'd have had a word, told her to be a bit kinder. To be honest, it's probably a blessing he wasn't there. I'm not sure any of our kids will ever recover from finding Isla like that.'

Questions scramble in Nicole's brain, as if she is trying to collate pieces of a jigsaw without knowing what the picture should be. 'Do you know if Elliot was at the party?'

'Elliot Mercer?' Sita nods. 'Yes, he had to give a statement to the police. So did Meera, obviously.'

Sita continues to talk – about friendships and social cliques and how she wouldn't want to be a teen again for anything – but Nicole isn't really listening. Her attention wanders to where her son

45

stands alone, his tall, thin frame like a newly planted sapling that has yet to take root.

Her memory rewinds to the night of the crash: coming downstairs to find Nathaniel in the kitchen, how his presence had startled her after everything she'd been through with Jack. She remembers him telling her that the party had been fine, that he couldn't remember if Isla was still there when he left, that he had gone to Elliot's for most of the evening. But now she learns that he had never been at the party and that he couldn't have gone to Elliot's because Elliot had been at Meera's.

Nathaniel leans against the tree, chews at his thumbnail, looks around surreptitiously as though unnerved by his own presence. Something wrenches inside Nicole at the thought of her son being ostracised by people he's been friends with for years, and she cannot separate her worry for him from her dismay at their behaviour. There is pain that he has not felt able to confide in her, regret that she has not noticed something is wrong. She thinks about the past fortnight, about how preoccupied she has been in the aftermath of Isla's death, and chastises herself that perhaps she has missed some vital clues as to Nathaniel's state of mind.

And yet, while her heart breaks for her son, she cannot silence a voice in her head asking the same question, again and again: if Nathaniel was not at the party on the night of Isla's death, and neither was he at Elliot's, where was he until ten-twenty at night?

Abby

Abby stares straight ahead at the groups of mourners, incapable of focusing on any single, specific thing, as though to pull the world into focus would be to view it in all its current horror. She does not dare lift the lid on the emotions raging inside her, knows how dangerous it would be to open those floodgates. For now, she must anaesthetise herself if she is to survive the minutes, hours, days ahead.

Next to her on the bench, Clio's phone vibrates, and she pulls it from her pocket, clicks on something, reads whatever is on the screen.

'Mum, look at this.'

Clio holds out the phone, and Abby does not have the strength, nor the will, to tell her to put it away, that this is neither the time nor the place to be looking at messages. Instead, she watches as her hand reaches out, takes hold of the mobile, as though her limbs are operating of their own volition.

Looking at the screen, she sees a local newspaper report from a neighbouring borough, experiences a sense of disorientation as her eyes scan the headline.

Teen Joyrider Sentenced while Accomplices Escape Punishment

'Why are you showing me this?' Abby hears the rebuke in her voice, does not want to read about joyriders who have been caught and punished while her daughter's killer remains at large.

'Just read it.'

Clio's voice is impatient, insistent, and Abby turns back to the screen, does as her daughter asks, too beleaguered to resist.

On Thursday morning, eighteen-year-old Ryan Marsh was sentenced to 11 years and 7 months in prison for causing death by dangerous driving. The teen joyrider had been at the wheel of a stolen car at the time of the offence. In her sentencing, Judge Cayburn pronounced Marsh 'a heartless and irresponsible young man who has failed to demonstrate any remorse during the course of the trial'.

In August last year, Marsh and two accomplices were seen running from the scene of a collision after a stolen vehicle crashed into a lamppost on the junction of Heathfield Road and Browning Avenue. A passing police car chased the offenders, arresting two of the culprits. A third was identified later that evening. Shortly before crashing the vehicle, Marsh had knocked down twenty-seven-year-old Hayley Everson – a promising young barrister at St Mark's Chambers – and had fled the scene of the crime. Everson later died from her injuries.

The two accomplices – both aged fourteen at the time of the offence, who cannot be named for legal reasons – were last month tried in court. Both escaped without custodial sentences. One of the teens was issued with a two-year youth rehabilitation order. The second – who was described as

*a promising young student of prior exemplary character,
and who Judge Cayburn concluded had been 'coerced'
into participating in the offence by Marsh's 'aggressive and
intimidating' behaviour – was given a six-month youth
referral order.*

*The family of Ms Everson said in a statement that while
they were pleased about the sentence handed down to
Marsh, they were disappointed that his accomplices did
not face custodial punishments: 'If you knowingly get into
a stolen car with someone, you're aware of the potential threat you're causing to other people. Being fourteen
should not have abnegated them from all responsibility
for their actions.'*

Abby finishes reading, does not understand why Clio is showing this to her, today of all days. 'Clio, I don't want to—'

'For god's sake, Mum, just read Shani's message.'

It takes a moment for Abby to pull Shani's identity from the
recesses of her memory: a friend Clio met on an art course last
summer.

Clio swipes at her phone, hands it back to Abby. Abby reads
the message, the words hammering in her brain until she can no
longer hear her own thoughts.

Looking up and across the cemetery gardens, her eyes find
Jenna placing an arm around Callum's shoulders, pulling him close:
the perfect image of the grieving ex-boyfriend.

Before she knows what she is doing – before she is conscious
of her legs lifting her from the bench, her feet making contact with
the gravel path – she is striding across the garden, grief and fury
pounding through every footstep.

49

Jenna

Jenna shivers in spite of the tentative autumn sunshine. Overhead, thin shreds of cloud like cigarette smoke drift across the sky. She tries to focus on the conversation she and Callum are having with Mr Marlowe, Callum's Head of Sixth Form, but she is distracted by a sense that everyone is watching her, silently questioning why she is there.

Glancing past Mr Marlowe, she sees Nicole talking to one of the other parents. Nicole, as always, is perfectly turned out: calf-length cashmere coat buttoned up to the neck, dove-grey pashmina draped across her shoulders, blow-dried hair, make-up so subtle it looks professionally applied. Jenna does not know Nicole well – nothing more than fleeting social niceties at sports day, school plays, parents' evenings – but sometimes Jenna wonders about Nicole, wonders whether her life – so neat, so perfect on the outside – can be as ordered and well-organised on the inside. She cannot, in truth, imagine what either Abby's or Nicole's life is really like; cannot imagine not having to work for a living, to have financial security from husbands earning seven-figure salaries or generous life insurance policies. To have the freedom for leisurely lunches, exercise classes, meetings of the school parent committee. On the rare occasions she has spoken with Abby or Jenna, they have always complained about being busy, but Jenna has never been able to establish with what, precisely, they fill their days.

Studying Callum's face, she sees the shadows beneath his eyes, the tightness of his jaw as though he is physically clamping down on his grief. Whenever she tries to talk to him about Isla's death, he becomes withdrawn, says he is fine, and for now she just wants him to know she is there for him, whenever he is ready to talk.

Mr Marlowe pats Callum's shoulder before moving on to talk with another family, and Jenna looks down at her watch, wonders whether or not it is a good idea for them to attend the wake. Since Callum's break-up with Isla, she has been aware of his possible social isolation, and she cannot bear to think what he might do – with whom he may choose to associate – if his peers at school decide to exclude him.

'Was it you?'

Jenna turns around, finds Abby standing close beside her, fury in her eyes, the full force of her anger directed at Callum.

'What do you mean?' There is a slight tremor in Callum's voice, like the aftershock of a distant earthquake.

'Was it you driving the car that killed my daughter?'

Callum is shaking his head even before Abby has finished speaking. 'Of course not, of course it wasn't.'

'Abby, I know how hard this must be for you, but—'

Abby pivots her gaze, glares venomously at Jenna. '*You* know how hard this must be for me? How could you possibly have *any idea* what this is like?'

'I don't, obviously, but—'

'I know what your son did. I know what he did to that woman.'

For a moment, Jenna cannot move, cannot speak. But she knows she needs to do something, to stop Abby revealing whatever she has uncovered in front of the families who have halted their conversations to listen to her raised voice. But before Jenna has a chance to speak, Abby is turning back to Callum, announcing the secret Jenna has worked so hard to conceal.

'Were you out joyriding again? Is that what happened? Were you out in another stolen car? Did Isla get in your way? Did you kill her just like you and your friends killed that other poor woman?'

All at once, the world seems to spin at a different speed. Jenna looks at Callum, watches the blood drain from his face, feels the past rushing to catch up with them. Something hardens within her, a determination that Callum's future will not be ruined by past mistakes. She turns back to Abby. 'Callum didn't kill anyone. I know you're grieving, but you can't go throwing around accusations like that.'

Abby glowers at her. 'Are you denying that your son was in a stolen car with . . .' She looks down at the phone in her hand, then back up at Jenna. '. . . with Ryan Marsh and another boy when they killed a woman? Are you denying that he ran away from the scene, and left the woman for dead? Or that he was caught, that he was charged, that he got off scot-free?'

Poison bleeds through Abby's words. Jenna looks at Callum, sees his panic, feels his fear.

'That was *not* his fault. He was just a passenger. He was fourteen years old, for goodness' sake.'

She takes hold of Callum's arm, wants him to know she is there, by his side, just as she had been throughout those eight months of hell.

Memories play out in her mind like a film running at an accelerated speed. The phone call from the police station that night, telling her Callum had been arrested. The sight of him in the interview room when she arrived: so vulnerable, like a little boy. The torturous months until the court case, petrified he would receive a custodial sentence, painfully aware that if he did, the teenager who entered the youth detention centre would not be the same young man who emerged however many months or years later. The day of the court case, Callum in a suit she had borrowed from a friend's husband, the material hanging from his shoulders. Sitting before the three magistrates, his face ashen with dread. Her own heart pounding so fiercely she thought everyone must be able to hear it. The three teachers from his former school who had lined up to be character witnesses for him, who had – she knows only too well – saved him from prison. The magistrates' verdict – when it finally came – like a stay of execution. The relief palpable, visceral. And then the decision – the desperation – to extricate Callum from the possibility of ever getting embroiled in something like that again. The application to the local private school armed with a string of top predicted GCSE grades. The persistent encouragement for him to work hard, the constant hum of awareness that this was his chance – possibly his only chance – to escape a culture that might otherwise destroy his life. And then his acceptance to Collingswood, the offer of a full bursary, the beginning of new opportunities for him. A fresh start which – she had hoped – meant he could leave the past behind. But now, here it is, staring them in the face, witnessed by dozens of families from Callum's school, destined to become common knowledge before the day is out.

'Did you know Callum was seen arguing with Isla less than half an hour before she got killed?'

Thoughts race in Jenna's brain as she scrambles to salvage something from the situation. She steadies her voice – consciously, deliberately – softens her tone. Thinks about how she would handle the situation if this were one of her social work cases. 'I can only imagine how hard this is for you, Abby, but lashing out at Callum isn't the answer.'

Abby shakes her head disbelievingly. 'So you're telling me it's just a coincidence that my daughter got killed in a hit-and-run moments after having a row with your son – her ex-boyfriend – who also happens to be a convicted joyrider? Someone who's already responsible for the death of another young woman? Do you really expect anyone to believe that?'

Jenna is aware of Callum's body tensing beside her, fear emanating from him as though seeping through his pores. 'Callum didn't kill anyone. He was just a passenger in that car. He wasn't even driving.'

'And that makes it okay, does it?' Abby stares at her, daring Jenna to contradict her in front of all these witnesses.

'Of course it doesn't. But that doesn't mean he had anything to do with what happened to Isla. You must be able to see that.' She has kept her voice steady, but her pleading tone is unmistakable nonetheless.

'So where was he? At the time Isla was killed? Where were you, Callum? Because I know you weren't still at the party.'

Jenna senses Callum hesitate, feels the weight of a guilty verdict being borne down upon him from the silent onlookers, hears herself speak before she knows what she intends to say. 'He was with me. At home. He was nowhere near the party when Isla was killed.' The lie burns in her throat. She is sure they must all be able to sense it, must be able to hear that her words are alight with untruths.

Before Abby has a chance to say anything more, Jenna grabs hold of Callum's arm, steers him away, through the spectating crowd, past the cemetery gates and on to the street.

'Are you okay?' She studies Callum's face, tries to contain her rage towards Abby for having excavated his secret, today of all days. She knows she needs to keep calm for Callum's sake. 'Come on, let's go home.'

Callum – six foot two, strong, capable – allows Jenna to lead him home, like a little boy who's lost his way.

All the way back, as the two of them sit on the bus in silence, Jenna tells herself that Callum is not the person Abby thinks he is. What happened before wasn't his fault. It was a moment of stupidity with tragic consequences. Callum has learnt his lesson, would never be so foolish as to joyride again. He would never run Isla down and leave her for dead. She knows it, indisputably, with as much certainty as it is possible to know anything. And yet she cannot silence the fears whispering in her ear, about what Callum and Isla were rowing about the night she was killed. About how he really got that red mark on his face that evening. And about where he was at the time Isla was knocked down if he wasn't at the party and he wasn't at home with her.

Nicole

Nicole scours the cemetery grounds, trying to spot Andrew among the throng of people. She realises she hasn't seen him since the end of the service, knows he is not with Nathaniel, who is still standing alone beneath a sycamore tree, staring at the ground as though fearful of making eye contact with anyone.

If Nathaniel wasn't at the party, where was he that night?

The question repeats in Nicole's head like a record stuck beneath the groove of a needle. But for now, she does not have time to entertain it. She needs to find Andrew, enlist his support in shepherding mourners to the wake.

Walking out through the cemetery arch and towards the road where they parked Andrew's Tesla, Nicole experiences a sudden stab of irritation that perhaps he's sitting in the car reading emails, or making work calls, when he should be at the cemetery, supporting Abby.

Nicole and Andrew have barely talked about Isla's death in the fifteen days since it happened. There has been neither the space nor the time for the two of them to converse; Andrew has been at work – busier than ever – and Nicole has been comforting Abby, or being present for Nathaniel and Jack, trying to hold things together emotionally for them all. She has, in truth, felt too exhausted – too drained – to talk about things with Andrew.

Rounding the corner into the small cul-de-sac where they parked the car, she sees Andrew's outline sitting in the driver's seat, hunched over what is no doubt his mobile phone. Frustration needles her skin, and she strides towards the car, yanks open the passenger door, ready to castigate him for his absence. But as soon as she faces him, words temporarily elude her.

Inside the car, Andrew's shoulders heave, tears streaming down his cheeks.

Nicole is aware of a momentary paralysis, unsure of herself suddenly. Sliding into the passenger seat, she closes the door behind her.

'Are you okay?'

Andrew drags a hand across his eyes, wipes away his tears, forces his lips into an apologetic smile. 'Sorry. I'm just finding today quite overwhelming.' His voice wavers, and there is something out of kilter in it, like a badly tuned instrument trying to bring itself up to pitch.

Nicole hesitates, wishes the clock could be turned back, that they could return to a time before any of this happened. 'I know. I still can't get my head around it.' She thinks of all the nights over the past two weeks that she has lain awake in the early hours of the morning, watching the minutes tick sluggishly by, going over and over the events of that evening, wishing it could have been different. Worrying about Abby and Clio, worrying about Nathaniel and Jack, possessed by an overpowering desire she has not experienced since the boys were little: the need to keep them close, watch over them, shield them from whatever adversity may come their way.

Glancing across at Andrew, expressions of panic and shame chase each other across his face. It is unlike anything she has seen before, in nineteen years of marriage. It is an expression that sends fear hurtling through her mind, dangerous suspicions she dares not entertain. She knows, instinctively, they have the power to unravel the stitching binding her family until there is nothing left beyond strands of loose thread.

For a brief moment – a split second in time – Andrew's eyes dart towards hers and then away again, as though to hold her gaze puts them both in danger.

She studies his face, can read him like a book after all their years together, can feel something coming – an acknowledgement of guilt – but if it is what she fears, she does not want to hear it. If he is going to say what she suspects, she knows there is no way back for their family. She cannot allow him to do this to them.

But then Andrew buries his face in his hands, his shoulders wracked with fresh grief, his voice muffled through closed fingers. 'I'm sorry. I never meant for it to happen. I don't know what I was thinking. It was some kind of temporary madness. I'm so sorry.'

Waves of nausea wash over her, and she understands what he is telling her without him having to articulate it: a confession Nicole would not have believed possible were she not seeing the irrefutable proof on Andrew's face. And she knows, in that moment, that everything has changed irrevocably, that there is nothing either of them can do now to halt the sequence of events he has put in motion.

SIX MONTHS BEFORE ISLA'S DEATH

Isla

Isla waited outside the swimming pool for her Uber to arrive, scrolling through her phone. It never ceased to amaze her how many messages were sent on various WhatsApp groups during the ninety minutes she was at swim squad training; one group from school had managed to clock up seventy-seven comments in that time, most of them about the school ski trip that Isla wasn't even going on because she didn't want to miss a week of swimming.

Zipping up her coat in defence against the brisk March wind, she wished her mum had been able to collect her tonight. But Clio was having some sort of crisis about a maths test she'd failed to revise for, and her mum had texted earlier asking if Isla minded getting a cab this levening so she could stay at home and give Clio some moral support. Isla wondered about offering to help when she got back, but every time she'd made overtures in the past, Clio had rejected her with an air of derision. There were moments when the loss of Isla's childhood friendship with Clio was like a physical ache, but her mum kept assuring her it was just a phase Clio was going through, that she'd come through it eventually. That they would be close again in the future. Isla wanted to believe it but sometimes – when Clio glared at her with that expression of contempt and resentment – she found it hard to trust that it might be true.

Her phone pinged, and she smiled as she opened a message from Callum.

Hey beautiful. How was training? Call me when you're done. Cx

Before she could phone him, a large black SUV pulled into the lay-by beside her. Isla was aware of her body tensing, her hand reaching into her bag for her house keys, her fingers wrapping around them in pre-emptive self-defence.

The window of the car wound down, and Isla felt her body relax as Andrew Forrester smiled at her from the driver's seat.

'Hey. Are you okay?'

Isla nodded. 'Just waiting for an Uber. It was supposed to be here five minutes ago but now it's saying it'll be another six minutes.'

Andrew gestured to the passenger seat. 'Hop in. I'm heading home. I'll drop you off.'

Isla glanced down at her phone, knew Callum would be waiting for her to call. She was on the verge of politely declining Andrew's offer when another gust of wind snaked around her neck. Figuring she'd be home in fifteen minutes and could ring Callum then, she looked back into the car. 'Are you sure you don't mind?'

'Course not. Come on, get in. It's freezing out there.'

Scanning the road for oncoming traffic, Isla ran around to the passenger door, got in the car, cancelled the Uber. Andrew waited for her to fasten her belt before pulling out into the road and heading towards home.

'Have you been swimming tonight?'

'Yep.'

'How many times a week are you training now?'

'Six.'

'God, that's a lot. You must be phenomenally fit. At least you get Sunday off, I guess.'

Isla laughed. 'Actually, I don't. If I'm not competing at the weekend, there's a two-hour training session on Sundays. I usually only get Mondays off.' Isla thought about how much she loved swimming: the feeling of her body streamlined in the water, the adrenaline when she competed. And yet sometimes, her training schedule felt like a treadmill without a stop button, and there were days when she wished she could take a break – just for a week or two – so that it didn't feel quite so relentless. But she knew she couldn't take time off, not if she wanted to make the nationals. None of her competitors ever took a break, and Isla couldn't afford to slip behind.

'That's so impressive. You must be really dedicated.' Tapping a couple of buttons on the car's digital screen, he increased the air temperature. 'That okay? You're still shivering.'

'Great, thanks.'

For a few moments they drove in silence, Isla looking out of the window at parades of shops, blocks of flats, rows of terraced houses lining the main road.

'Did you know I used to be a competitive swimmer, back in the day?' Andrew glanced across at her before turning back to the road.

'Really? Who did you swim for?'

'My local club in Wiltshire. Swam for the county for a couple of years too. Only narrowly missed out on the nationals.'

'I'm hoping to make the nationals later this year, but I don't know if I'll be good enough.'

Andrew smiled. 'I'm sure you will. You clearly train exceptionally hard, and from what I hear, you're an incredible athlete.'

Heat rose into Isla's cheeks. 'I'm not sure about that. But I do love it.'

'Even the five a.m. starts?'

Isla laughed. 'Okay, maybe not those in winter. But I do love training, and I really love competing. Even when I've had a really hard race, I always come out feeling energised.'

'I know what you mean. There's such a rush with competitions. Just knowing you're pushing yourself to the limit is a huge buzz.'

'That's exactly what I always tell people, but I don't think anyone really understands if they haven't experienced it themselves. Callum says he has a similar thing with running.'

'Callum?'

'My boyfriend.'

'Right, of course.' Andrew swung into the outside lane as they crossed the bridge over the Thames. 'How do you manage to stay on top of it all? Your work and swimming? Nathaniel doesn't have half the commitments you have and yet he's always complaining about not having enough free time.'

Isla thought about her weekly schedule: two early mornings and two evenings at the pool, Saturday and Sunday spent training or competing. Most lunchtimes running clubs for younger pupils: the debating club, the dissection club, the Young Medics Society. Staying on top of her homework. Finding time to hang out with Callum and her friends. Making sure she was always there for her mum when she needed her. Having the energy to deal with Clio's strops. Sometimes, if Isla dwelled for too long on the various demands on her, she could feel something pressing down on her chest, had to breathe deeply against it. 'I'm not sure, to be honest. If you want a job done, ask a busy person? Isn't that what people always say?'

Andrew laughed. 'That's definitely true. But it's all very impressive. If only all young women could be like you.'

For the second time, Isla felt herself blush. She looked down, fiddled with the toggle on her swim bag.

Andrew's Tesla pulled into her road and stopped outside her house.

'Thanks for the lift.'

'No worries. Any time. It was really nice to chat.' Andrew smiled, locked eyes with her, and Isla was aware of a change in the atmosphere, a moment of temporary discomfort she could not quite decipher.

Opening the car door, she stepped out onto the pavement. 'Thanks again.'

'My pleasure. I'll see you soon.'

Isla closed the car door, turned, walked along the garden path towards her house, her head suddenly light, vertiginous. Entering the hallway, she told herself it was just hunger, tiredness, that she would feel fine after some food and a good night's sleep.

Isla shut the lid of her laptop, slid it into her bag.

'Are you leaving?' Callum looked up from his economics textbook, his voice a low whisper. On adjacent tables in the school library, fellow sixth formers worked in silence.

'Yep, Paul's focusing on my tumble turns tonight so I want to get some lengths in before he gets there.'

'Cool. And you're still okay to come to mine tomorrow night? Mum's making a lasagne.'

'Course. Right, I'd better get going. Call you later?'

Callum nodded. Isla picked up her bags, headed out of the library and into the quad, where the sky was a smudged grey, like pencil marks badly erased from a sheet of white paper.

'Hey, Isla, wait up.'

Looking behind her, Isla saw Nathaniel running across the quad – awkward, ungainly – his long, skinny legs uncoordinated with the rest of his body. Isla felt herself tensing even as she pulled her lips into a smile. It was the third time today Nathaniel had stopped her en route from one part of the school to another, each reason for delaying her more spurious than the last.

'What's up?'

Nathaniel caught up with her, panted breathlessly. 'I just wanted to ask if you knew when the maths homework was due?'

Isla swallowed her frustration. 'Monday morning. Ms Rawlence said it at the end of the lesson.'

Nathaniel hauled his rucksack onto his back. 'Right, sorry. I must not have been listening.'

There was an uncomfortable silence, and it was Isla who broke it. 'I'd better go. I need to get to swimming.'

'Course, yeah, right, sorry.' Nathaniel's words tripped over each other as though they couldn't agree about the order in which they should emerge. 'Can I tag along? I was only going to head home anyway.'

She allowed herself a beat. 'It's in the opposite direction.'

A deep shade of red coloured Nathaniel's cheeks. 'I just thought you might like some company.' He looked down at the ground, pushed his shoe against the edge of the lawn.

Why don't you just tell him you're not interested?

Ignore him – he'll soon get the message.

I don't know why you put up with him following you around all the time.

He's a weirdo.

Her friends' comments circled on a loop inside her head. But it wasn't as easy as that. She'd known Nathaniel her whole life. Their families had been entwined for as long as she could remember. Until about a year ago, when he'd started behaving creepily around her, they'd been really good friends. She couldn't just tell him to get lost. 'Thanks, but I need to clear my head before training. I'll see you tomorrow, okay?' Without waiting for a reply, she turned, walked across the quad and out of the school's wrought-iron gates.

Heading towards the bus stop – still undecided whether to catch the bus or get an Uber – she thought about Callum, about training, about the mountain of homework she had to get through at the weekend. Sometimes it felt as though she were running to stand still; that however hard she worked, the goalposts were forever shifting, the expected levels of attainment ever increasing. She was aware of a constant thrum inside her – a need to do well, to maintain the perception that she was good at everything: academics, swimming, family, friendships, involvement in school life. She didn't, in truth, know where the feeling came from: whether from her mum, or her teachers, or somewhere deep within herself that she didn't really understand. All she knew was that it was there, like a constant, ambient noise that she couldn't silence. Or perhaps she didn't dare try.

A car horn beeped behind her, and she whipped her head around, expecting to see some of the idiots from the school rugby team who thought blaring car horns at women was entertaining. Her expectations adjusted as Andrew Forrester's black Tesla pulled up beside her, the second time in ten days. For a moment, she thought perhaps Nathaniel was inside, perhaps Andrew had collected him from school and he'd asked if they could give Isla a lift. But looking through the open car window, she could see Andrew was alone.

'Where are you off to? Need a lift?'

Isla shook her head. 'No, I'm fine thanks. I'm going to order a cab to the pool.'

'Don't be silly – I can scoot you up there in fifteen minutes.'

Isla hesitated, thinking about the biology reading she'd intended to do en route. 'Honestly, I'm fine.'

'It's no trouble. And there's something I want to talk to you about anyway. You'll be doing me a favour. Hop in.'

Wavering momentarily, Isla opened the door, slid into the passenger seat, crammed her bags into the footwell.

'How was your day?' Andrew looked into the wing mirror, pulled out into the road.

'Fine thanks. How was yours?'

'Busy. And not over yet. I've still got a mountain to get through when I get home.'

He stopped at a red light, looked across at her for what felt an inordinately long time, and Isla was overcome by an intense, inexplicable feeling of self-consciousness. 'What did you want to talk to me about, anyway?'

The lights changed to green, and Andrew pulled away, faster than the twenty-miles-per-hour speed limit. 'I was just thinking about all the swimming I used to do, and realised I missed being involved in it.'

'You want to start competing again?'

Andrew laughed. 'Definitely not. I was thinking more about training to be a part-time coach. You've really inspired me.'

He turned to her, smiled, and it was there again: the feeling that he was studying her with disproportionate intensity. Disquiet skittered across her skin, and Isla forcibly dismissed the sensation, told herself she was being ridiculous. This was Andrew Forrester: Nathaniel and Jack's dad, one of her mum's best friends. He wouldn't be looking at her in that way. 'To be honest, I don't really know much about that. Both my coaches are full-time instructors. I could ask them, if you like?'

Andrew shook his head. 'No, don't worry. I'll do some research online. Do you think it's a good idea though?'

'I guess so, if you really want to. I think it's quite a big commitment, though, even if you only do it as a volunteer. Would you have time?' Isla thought about the conversations she often overheard between Nicole and her mum, Nicole bemoaning how hard Andrew worked and how little she saw of him during the week.

'Probably not. But I'd like to get involved somehow. Maybe I could come and watch you compete one day, see you in action? From everything I hear, you're pretty amazing.'

Isla felt herself blush. 'I'm not sure about that. My coach says I need to do loads of work on my tumble turns.'

Andrew smiled. 'Ah, I used to practise those for hours. It's worth it in the end, though – even a fraction of a second can make all the difference. But I don't need to tell you that.'

Pulling into the swimming pool car park, Andrew veered into a space at the far end, switched off the engine.

'Thanks for the lift.' Isla leaned forward to collect her bags from the footwell.

'You've got something on you. Here, let me.' Without waiting for a reply, Andrew reached out his hand, ran his fingers across the bare skin at the side of her neck.

Isla was aware of something stilling in the car, as though time were unmoving – as though she were unable to move – as though all noise, all movement, had evaporated. It was as if the tableau they were in had frozen – her in the passenger seat, Andrew's hand skimming the surface of her flesh – a moment that lasted no more than a few seconds and yet felt unending.

'Got it. It was just a little spider.' Andrew rubbed his fingers together, flicked something onto the car floor.

For a moment, Isla said nothing, the imprint of Andrew's fingers still warm on her skin, her feelings too confused to decipher. And then she pulled her bags onto her lap, hugged them tight to her chest. 'I'd better go. I don't want to be late.' Her voice sounded strange in her ears, as though trying and failing to mimic normality.

'Sure. Hope it's a good training session.'

Opening the door, she stepped onto the asphalt. 'Thanks for the lift.'

Andrew presented her with a wide, open smile. 'Any time. I'll see you soon.'

Shutting the car door, Isla swung her bags over her shoulder. As she walked away, towards the leisure centre entrance, she thought about what had just happened, tried to organise her feelings into some logical order. But the sensation of Andrew's hand on her neck was still there, an act that had roused in her a response that felt muddled, confused. Dangerous.

Swiping her membership card against the turnstile, she headed for the changing room, unable to untangle the knot of conflicting feelings: part confusion, part disquiet, and something else to which she dared not give a name.

Isla sat on a stool at the kitchen island, scrolling through her phone, trying to avoid her mum's questions.

'Are you *sure* everything's okay, sweetheart? You've been very quiet since you got home from training. Was everything okay at the pool?'

Isla forced a smile. 'I'm fine. Just tired.'

It had been nearly three hours since the incident in the car with Andrew, and she had thought about little else since: the memory of the way he had looked at her, the recollection of his fingers on her skin. She'd said nothing about it to anyone: not to Callum when she'd spoken to him after training, not to her mum, not to any of her friends. She could not articulate why she was keeping it a secret: only that she knew she felt unable to share what had happened.

'Are you sure you don't want something to eat? There's some sushi in the fridge. Or you could order in if there's something you fancy.'

'That's not fair. I'm never allowed takeout on a weeknight.' Clio appeared in the kitchen doorway, scowled, strode across the kitchen towards the fridge.

Their mum sighed. 'That's not true. You're forever ordering in, even when I've made dinner.'

'So? You made dinner tonight and you're still saying Isla can order in. But why am I surprised? There's always one rule for Isla and another rule for me.' Clio yanked open the fridge door. 'Am I allowed a can of San Pellegrino or are they all reserved for Isla?'

'Clee . . .' Isla glanced at their mum, at the lines pinching the corners of her eyes.

'What?' Clio glowered at her.

'Just calm down, okay?'

'I *am* calm. It would just be nice if *for once* you didn't get all the preferential treatment around here.'

'Clio, *enough*. Just stop it, please.' Their mum's voice bled fatigue.

'Surprise, surprise. All I do is point out how unfair things are and somehow I'm the one in the wrong. As always.' Clio turned and stormed out of the kitchen, slamming the door behind her.

From Isla's phone came a notification. Swiping it open, she found a WhatsApp from Andrew, the first solo message he'd ever sent her. They were both on the joint family thread dominated by her mum and Nicole making plans for various get-togethers, but Andrew had never messaged her alone before.

> *Hey. Great to chat earlier. Any time you need a lift, you know where I am. I want to do everything I can to support a future Olympian.* ☺ *x*

Isla read the message, and then read it again, thoughts jostling for prominence in her head; one part of her brain telling her he was just being kind, that he probably felt sorry for her, that he was just trying to fill the chasm her dad's death had left behind. But another part of her brain would not let her forget the way he had looked at her, the sensation of his hand on her neck.

'Everything okay?'

Isla scrambled to switch off her screen, looked up from her phone. 'Fine. Just Callum.' The lie tripped from her tongue. Isla couldn't remember the last time she'd told even the smallest fib to her mum. A voice in her head told her to undo it immediately, show her mum Andrew's message, tell her what had happened. But something – she didn't know what – stopped her.

She watched the tensing of her mum's jaw, a Pavlovian response at the mention of Callum's name.

'Actually, I think I'll head up to bed. I'm shattered after training and I've got an early start tomorrow.'

Standing up and kissing her mum goodnight, Isla headed out of the kitchen and up the two flights of stairs to her bedroom, trying to ignore the sense that something significant had happened this evening that she just couldn't allow herself to acknowledge.

Light drizzle fell from low clouds. Isla pulled her hood up over her head. Glancing left and right down the small residential cul-de-sac where she was waiting, half a mile's walk from school, there was no sign yet of anyone approaching. Pulling out her phone to check the time, she saw she was still a few minutes early. She'd rushed out of school, made excuses to Callum and Meera about her need for a hasty exit. She'd told herself they were excuses, but deep down she knew what they were really: lies.

Opening her umbrella, she was unsure whether it was the rain or nerves making her shiver. For the past seventy-two hours, since the arrangement had been made, Isla had not been able to stop prevaricating; fretting that she was being foolish, that she was making a mistake, that she may come to regret it. But each time she'd been on the verge of cancelling, another message had arrived, and her fears seemed to evaporate.

An approaching car caused her to turn her head, and her stomach lurched as she saw the familiar black Model X pulling up at the kerb beside her. Isla opened the door and climbed inside.

'You came.' Andrew smiled, his expression calm and relaxed in contrast to Isla's anxiety, and she could only nod in response as she fastened her seat belt. 'I'm so glad. I've been looking forward to seeing you all day. Are you okay?'

It was such an easy question and yet, to Isla, there was no obvious answer: just a chaos of feelings that refused to fit into any singular box. A part of her brain told her to say she'd made a mistake, she was sorry, she was going to head home and get on with her homework. But then she thought about all the messages between them over the past three weeks: how intoxicating it had been receiving them, sending them, how there had been moments when she'd felt that her communication with Andrew was the most thrilling thing that had ever happened to her.

The capacity to form words still eluded her so she merely nodded again, watched as Andrew put the car into gear, began their journey towards a pub half an hour away.

As they drove, Andrew began telling a story about a colleague at work; the kind of story that made her feel both grown-up and, at the same time, as though she were masquerading as an adult, trying it on for size, unsure whether it fitted. Isla's thoughts wandered over the events of the past few weeks, the sequence of communications that had led to her being here, in the car of a man she'd known her whole life, embarking on what she knew – even though a part of her didn't yet want to admit it – was a date.

She thought back to that first message three weeks ago, and to the second one that had arrived the next morning, a swimming meme that had made her laugh before she'd even got out of bed. She thought about the diving meme she had sent back almost immediately, and the succession of gifs they had sent each other during the course of that day.

She thought about how their messages had moved on to more personal questions, Andrew asking her about school, about training, about life more generally – her hopes, ambitions, fears and anxieties. How he had shared frustrations of his own about work, about the state of the world, about the stasis of his life and how he sometimes thought about shaking everything up, disrupting it all, throwing all the pieces into the air and seeing where they landed. It was so different from her interactions with Callum, who had never been keen on lengthy WhatsApp chats. Conversations with Callum tended to focus on school and homework, university applications and gossip about their classmates. It wasn't that there was anything wrong with that; she'd always loved talking with Callum. But those conversations felt small, somehow, compared to her interactions with Andrew. Small and less significant.

Within a few days, Isla had found herself anxiously awaiting Andrew's next communication, willing it to arrive, experiencing a jolt of adrenaline whenever a new message appeared in the locked chats where she'd moved their thread so it was not easily detectable should her phone fall into the wrong hands. A part of her brain told her that this act alone was significant, that it should reveal to her the clandestine nature of their friendship; but another, reckless part of her resolutely ignored it. Nobody had ever communicated with her like this before. No adult had ever treated her like an equal in this way, had ever shared so much, so candidly, about their own life. Since Isla's dad died, her mum had relied on her – emotionally, psychologically – but that didn't make Isla feel equal, it didn't make her feel like an adult. Often it made her feel as though she'd been awarded a responsibility she'd never even wanted.

And then, three nights ago, the message had arrived that changed everything. The message that exposed what she knew, deep down, was happening but which she had, until then, deliberately chosen to ignore.

> *Isla, I'm about to go out on a limb here, and I sincerely hope I don't live to regret it. I can't stop thinking about you. I think about you pretty much all the time. I love our conversations on here. You're funny and smart and wise beyond your years, and you understand me in a way I haven't felt understood for a very long time. Our WhatsApp chats are the highlight of my day. I think – if I'm not mistaken – you may feel the same way. I suspect we both know this has gone beyond whatever it started out as. All I know is that I love talking with you, and I don't want it to end. Would you be up for meeting, for talking face-to-face? I'd love to see you. A xx*

Isla had read the message, heart thumping, had re-read it countless times, trying to decipher if there was any possible interpretation other than the obvious one. There had been almost an hour of procrastination: thinking, worrying, weighing up countless pros and cons.

And then, a second message from Andrew had appeared.

> *I really hope you're studying or at training, and that's the reason you're not replying, not that I've freaked you out. If I've overstepped, I'm sorry – let's draw a line, pretend it*

*never happened, move on. I just really love talking to you
and it would be great to meet up and do it in person. A x*

Without allowing herself time to entertain doubts for a second longer, she had tapped out a reply, read it through only once before hitting the send button.

*You haven't freaked me out. To be honest, I don't know
what I feel right now, but it would definitely be good to
meet up and talk it through. I x*

That exchange had been only three days ago and yet, already, it felt like another lifetime.

'Here we are.' Andrew pulled into a pub car park on a narrow, rural lane. 'All good?'

Isla nodded, her throat dry, conscious that she had been responding to Andrew's questions for the past half an hour with only a fraction of her attention.

'Wait a sec.' Andrew reached into the back of the car, pulled a Tiffany box from his coat pocket and handed it to Isla. 'Just a little something. I hope you like it.'

Isla watched, as if on automatic pilot, as her hand reached out to take the box. Inside was an infinity pendant on a silver chain.

'I hope this isn't going to sound corny, but I saw it and thought of you. You make me feel as though the world is full of infinite possibilities. Here, let me.' Taking the box from her, he picked up the necklace and unclasped the chain with surprising dexterity. 'Do you want to lift your hair up?'

Isla complied, wound her long, blonde hair around her fingers, held it in a temporary bun.

Lifting his arms, Andrew fastened the chain in place.

Isla sat motionless as his fingers grazed the nape of her neck, his breath skimming her clavicle, the heat of him drifting across her skin, aware that this was no 'little something'. This was a gift loaded with meaning.

As he drew back from her, his eyes fixed on her face, and Isla found that she could not look away even if she wanted to.

And then he was leaning forward, his face moving closer until their lips were touching, and they were kissing, and it was both exciting and terrifying in equal measure. Her mind raced, a thousand different thoughts spinning through her brain that this was wrong, it was weird, he was too old, she was too young, she already had a boyfriend, she didn't want to cheat on Callum, her mum would be appalled. She didn't know how she had ended up here, in a car, kissing the husband of her mum's best friend, a man she had known her entire life. And yet . . . even as each thought hurtled through her brain, they were no match for how exciting it felt, how electrifying, how much she wanted Andrew to continue doing what he was doing.

He pulled away, cupped a hand around her cheek. 'Are you okay?'

She nodded. She could still feel the sensation of Andrew's lips against hers, still taste him, a sensation so different to when she kissed Callum. 'I'm fine.' Her voice surprised her, calmer than she felt.

Andrew kissed her again, gently, on the mouth. 'I can't tell you how much I've been wanting to do that. You're so beautiful.'

His fingers stroked the back of her hand, and Isla felt as though her lungs did not have the capacity to hold all the air she needed.

'Shall we go in, get a drink? I can't keep you in a car park all evening.'

As Isla stepped out of the car and closed the door, Andrew walked towards her, took hold of her hand, interlaced his fingers with hers, and she was aware that, in this moment, her life was bisecting into two distinct parts: the safety of school, family, friends, Callum; and then this, something she could not yet define, could not comprehend. Something that felt both exhilarating and dangerous; something she both yearned for and yet feared. Something a part of her brain was telling her to stop, now, before it went any further, while her legs nonetheless continued to put one foot in front of the other, following the husband of her mother's best friend – the father of her childhood playmate – towards the most reckless thing she had ever done.

THE PRESENT

Nicole

Nicole's heart thunders in her chest.

On the far side of the room, Andrew sits on the edge of their bed, staring at her like a forlorn puppy awaiting forgiveness. But Nicole cannot forgive him, can barely tolerate looking at him; he is the person she should trust above all others, and yet he has committed the most egregious betrayal.

'I'm sorry, Nicole. I don't know how many more times I can say it.'

'Stop saying it then.' The words snap from her lips.

Out of the corner of her eye, she senses Andrew glance tentatively towards her – wanting something from her that she cannot give – before sinking his head into his hands.

All night long they have circled the same conversation: the same apologies, the same entreaties for forgiveness, the same pitiful attempts to excuse what he has done. But there is no excuse. No justification. No feasible defence for the way he has behaved.

It is less than twenty-four hours since Nicole looked at Andrew's tear-stained cheeks as he sat hunched over the steering wheel outside the cemetery and suspected what he was about to tell her, as though his grief were a Greek chorus, impelling her to understand this abhorrent twist in the narrative. Less than twenty-four hours, and yet Nicole understands that their lives have pivoted onto a different axis, that there are no means by which to restore any semblance of the status quo. She cannot unlearn what she knows. Cannot be unharmed by what he has done. She cannot pretend that his actions have not lacerated the safety and security of their family.

The Garmin on her wrist vibrates and her eyes graze its screen. There is a moment's disbelief that it is only eight a.m., that the day has barely begun. She had not managed to sleep at all last night, had watched the clock march inexorably from two a.m. to three a.m. and onwards towards dawn. She had lain awake, alone in bed, having exiled Andrew to the spare room, flabbergasted that he imagined for one second she would be willing to sleep under the same duvet as him, breathing the same, intimate air, after what he had told her.

Recalling it now, she does not understand how they managed to endure the rest of yesterday's funeral, how she and Andrew succeeded in convincing everyone that their marriage had not just imploded. How she managed to speak to Abby – to support her, console her, grieve with her – given all she knew, when the same few words were revolving round and round in her head: *I'm sorry, I'm so so sorry for what my family has done to you.*

'How can I make this better? I want to make it better.' Andrew's voice slices into the silence.

'There's no *making this better*.' Derision curdles Nicole's voice. 'What do you think we're going to do? Take a trip to the Maldives, have a second honeymoon, rekindle our romance?'

'So what are you saying? You're going to give up on nineteen years of marriage because of one error of judgement?'

'An *error of judgement*? You sleep with a seventeen-year-old girl who just happens to be the daughter of our best friend, and you call it an error of judgement? Jesus, Andrew, it's not just disgusting, it's immoral. She's barely over the age of consent, for god's sake. This is Isla we're talking about. You've known her since she was a child – since she was a baby. Do you really not understand how deplorable it is, what you've done? It's practically abuse.'

'Keep your voice down. The boys will hear you.'

The boys. Nicole's heart stutters at the thought of them, at the thought of how Andrew's actions have upended their lives in ways he does not even comprehend.

She thinks about Jack, asleep in bed. At fifteen, he is in that strange hinterland between childhood and adulthood, in the throes of adolescence and yet still so young in so many ways: his failed attempts at shaving, his face resembling that of the youngest member of a boy band, the one prepubescent girls flock towards because he poses no sexual threat. She thinks about how much Jack has had to contend with recently even before the events of the past fortnight; about his weekly sessions with a psychologist to manage the diagnosis of ADHD that Jack seems to feel is a label from which he will never escape.

She thinks about Nathaniel, about his crush on Isla, about how completely devastated he will be if he ever finds out that his dad had been sleeping with her. She recalls Sita's words to her yesterday morning in the cemetery garden: *It's just that Nathaniel seems to have been . . . slightly frozen out lately.*

The thought slips into her mind that perhaps Isla had been excluding Nathaniel because she wanted to keep him at arm's length, to protect the secrecy of her relationship with Andrew. Perhaps the reason her son has been socially isolated is entirely due to the selfish, immoral, destructive behaviour of her husband.

'Does Nathaniel know?'

Andrew stares at her, forehead puckered. 'What?'

'About you and Isla. Does Nathaniel know?'

Andrew frowns, shakes his head. 'Of course not. I was really careful.'

Nicole does not know whether to feel relieved or sickened. The thought of Andrew creating an intricate web of deceit – to deceive her, their sons, their best friend – is like stepping into a parallel world where everything is upside down.

She berates herself for her own stupidity. For not knowing, not guessing something was wrong. For not being alive to her husband's dishonesty. All those small, seemingly insignificant moments when she felt Andrew was being distant, which she discounted as nothing more than the ebb and flow of a long marriage. All those times she has wrapped her arms around him only to find his body stiffen, placated with a platonic pat on the shoulder and an explanation of tiredness. All the times she has spoken and known he is not really listening. She realises there must have been weeks – months – when Andrew was sleeping with both her and Isla at the same time. The idea is nauseating.

She recalls Andrew's sudden suggestion, not long before Isla died, that perhaps they should consider moving house, moving neighbourhoods. He'd mooted the possibility of relocating north of the river – Islington, perhaps, or Hampstead – his sudden enthusiasm for a change febrile, intense. He'd even contacted some estate agents, showed her the details of a few houses, despite her having explained that they couldn't possibly move now, at this point in the boys' education. At the time, she'd thought it was just another symptom of Andrew's general restlessness: always looking for something new to buy, something else to acquire, something different to try. Only now does she suspect there was another reason altogether: to get them away from Abby and Isla, to limit the possibility of detection, to remove them from the scene of his deplorable betrayals.

So many fleeting moments she chose to view in their singularity, to treat as isolated incidents. Failing to view them collectively, ignoring their cumulative impact, overlooking their possible meaning.

Wilful blindness. Woeful naïvety. Misplaced trust. They are the only explanations she has. And now, her acute sense of foolishness is almost as painful to her as Andrew's treachery.

'Nicole, please. Try to understand. It was stupid and irrational, I know. It was just a moment of madness.'

Nicole stares at him, dumbfounded. 'A moment of madness? A moment of madness that lasted *four months*. Don't you *dare* try to belittle what you've done.'

She sees the clench of Andrew's jaw, perceives the regret that he confessed the length of his relationship with Isla, told her it began last April, while Nicole was no doubt packing his underwear for their family skiing trip to Zermatt, and that it ended seven weeks ago, just five weeks before Isla was killed.

Even now, Nicole has no way of knowing if he is telling the truth. No way of knowing whether it was still ongoing at the time of Isla's death, or whether it had begun long before he claims.

'I'm not trying to belittle it. But I think you've got an image in your head and it's not how it was. It wasn't premeditated. It just . . . happened.'

Fury seethes in the pit of Nicole's stomach. 'It doesn't *just happen* that you start sleeping with a girl young enough to be your daughter. It doesn't *just happen* that you continue sleeping with her for four months. You *chose* for it to happen. You had a *choice*, Andrew. You had a choice about whether to prey on our best friend's daughter, a child – don't look at me like that, she was a *child* – you've known since she was born. You had a choice about whether to do it a second time, and a third time, god knows how many times.' The thought of it – of how many times her husband may have slept with Isla – is momentarily destabilising. 'This wasn't an accident, Andrew. You didn't *accidentally* have a sexual

85

relationship with Isla. You *chose* to do it. So don't you *dare* try to deny responsibility for it.'

She glares at him, refuses to give way to whatever misplaced self-justification he has afforded himself.

'So what are you saying? You want me to move out?'

Exasperation claws at Nicole's throat. 'Of course you can't move out. Don't be stupid.'

He blinks at her, confused, and she cannot believe she is having to spell it out for him. 'If you move out, people will ask questions. They'll want to know the reason why. I presume you're no keener than I am to tell them the truth.'

Fear passes like a shadow across Andrew's face, and Nicole experiences a moment of satisfaction that – for a few seconds, at least – he seems to understand a small fraction of the damage he has caused.

'So what do you want to do? What do you want to happen?'

Nicole studies the lamentable face of the man she believed, for the past two decades, to be strong, decisive, purposeful. She is aware of her respect for him rushing away from her like meltwater from a glacier. 'Honestly? I don't care what you do. Just move your stuff into the spare room. I don't want you in here.'

There is a moment's hesitation before Andrew stands up, turns to her with a self-pitying expression. 'What will we tell the kids?'

'What about?'

'About why I'm sleeping in the spare room.'

For a few seconds, Nicole does not respond, astounded that he should think her responsible for all the decisions – all the lies – they will have to employ to conceal his duplicity. 'I don't know. But deception seems to be a forte of yours, so I'm sure you'll come up with something.'

He gazes at her for a second before shaking his head – as though he, somehow, is the wronged party – and walks past her towards the bedroom door.

'Where are you going?'

'I need some air.'

His hand is already opening the door when words begin to tumble from Nicole's lips. 'I hope you never have to fully understand the damage you've done to our family. To our children. I hope for your sake – for all our sakes – you never have to truly comprehend that.' She thinks of Jack, of Nathaniel, of all the potential repercussions of Andrew's actions. But the thoughts are too unwieldy, too overpowering, and she has to shut them down, like a metal grille at a shop window.

Andrew doesn't respond before heading out of the bedroom, and she listens to the sound of his feet padding down the stairs, to the quiet click of the front door that tells her he is gone, for now at least.

Exhaling the tension gathered in her lungs, she lowers herself onto the sofa beneath the window, allows the minutes to tick by in silence.

The bedroom door opens again, and Jack stands in the doorway in bare feet, boxer shorts and a t-shirt, as if awaiting permission to enter. His face is pale, two red nicks on his cheek, the result of his latest attempt at shaving.

'Have you just woken up?' Nicole tries to keep her voice calm.

He nods, rubbing his eyes as he enters the room. Sitting down beside her, he allows her to put her arm around him. It is unusual, this early-morning affection, and she waits for him to speak, gives him the space to say whatever is on his mind.

'What were you and Dad arguing about?'

She hesitates, represses a knee-jerk reaction to tell him it's nothing, to brush it under the carpet. 'We're both just pretty tense at the moment, what with everything that's been going on.' The partial explanation hangs in the air between them, and she has no desire to elaborate.

Jack lifts his head from her shoulder, and she sees it in his expression: the understanding that Nicole has not divulged the whole story, and the tacit agreement that Jack will go along with it, for now, to make all their lives easier.

'I'm going to have a shower.'

'Okay. Do you fancy pancakes for breakfast?'

Jack shakes his head. 'I'm fine, thanks.'

She watches him slope out of the room, wishes she had the words – the courage – to say all that needs to be said. Instead, she must content herself with the hope – the belief – that there will come a time when they are both ready.

Blinking against the dehydration in her eyes, scenes play out in her mind from yesterday's funeral. Abby, at the wake, seemingly frozen in shock, as though her body were protecting her from the enormity of what had happened. Nathaniel standing alone, on the periphery of every group, as though an invisible barrier prevented him from getting too close. Jack, when they got home, quiet, watchful. Nicole so preoccupied with Andrew's revelation that she could not fully attend to how the boys might be feeling.

But today is different. Today – and from this day forth – all her energies will be focused on her sons. Whatever happens in the future between her and Andrew, it is only Nathaniel and Jack's wellbeing she cares about now.

Abby

Abby curls herself into a ball, knees tucked tight against her chest, arms wrapped around her shins. Eyes firmly shut, she inhales deeply, tries to absorb the essence of her daughter from the pillow where Isla last laid her head three weeks ago.

The muscles in Abby's throat constrict as though invisible hands are wrapped around her neck. Guttural sobs rise up in her chest, out through her lips. She sinks into her grief, as though being pulled deep into a vortex, water engulfing her, dragging her down. She does not try to fight it.

She has no conception of how long she lies there, on Isla's double bed that has not been slept in now for twenty nights, or how many minutes pass as tears leak from her eyes as though from a limitless reservoir. Grief simmers within her: burning, smouldering, scorching her from the inside out, bewailing the injustice of it all. It is only when her throat aches and her body is depleted of energy that her crying finally stops.

There is a moment of panic as she wipes her tears, feels the dampness of the pillow, fears that perhaps she has diminished Isla's scent from the bedding. Burying her head in the pillow, she breathes it in, smells her daughter, experiences a rush of relief. But the feeling is followed by a sharp stab of realisation that it will not always be so. One day she will come into Isla's bedroom, and Isla will be gone: the smell of her erased from the world. The thought is untenable, and Abby banishes it to a corner of her mind.

Her eyes land on the unfinished novel by Isla's bedside, a bookmark poking out two-thirds of the way through: *Emma* by Jane Austen. It is a book Isla will now never finish. She will never learn that Emma marries Mr Knightley, that Harriet finds happiness with Mr Martin, that Frank Churchill was not the man they believed him to be. Looking around the room, she sees the clothes that will never again be worn, the textbooks that will never be studied, the laptop that will never compose another essay or email.

It seems impossible to Abby that there is an entire adult life of Isla's that will now never be lived. Decades of learning, love, work, travel. A plethora of experiences never to occur because they were part of Isla's future.

Closing her eyes, Abby's thoughts ramble through unanswerable questions. She has never been fatalistic, never subscribed to the idea that your destiny is laid out, pivotal moments predetermined. She has always been a firm believer that you forge your own path. And yet now she finds herself speculating about all the other lives that will unwittingly be affected by her daughter's death. The students at university Isla will never befriend. The professors by whom she will never be taught. The men she will never kiss drunkenly on a nightclub dance floor in the early hours of the morning. The colleagues who will win promotions because Isla is not there to compete for the job. The man she will not marry. Who will he marry instead, Abby wonders, and what life will he lead? Will he be happy? Will he be as happy as if Isla had lived and he had married her instead?

She thinks about Stuart, and for a few short, perverse moments, envies her husband his untimely death. Envies the fact that he had a stroke at the age of forty-one, that he is not alive to endure this grief. That he does not have to abide the acute, inarticulable pain of losing their daughter.

The sudden slamming of a door makes Abby start. Glancing at the alarm clock beside Isla's bed she sees it is almost five in the afternoon. Confused, she checks the watch on her wrist, is greeted by the same, disorienting time. It is not possible that it can be so late. She remembers Clio leaving for school this morning, remembers clearing away her daughter's half-eaten bagel and glass of mango juice. She remembers coming up here, to Isla's room, remembers lying down on the bed. But the intervening hours are a blur. She cannot, surely, have been here all day. Cannot have spent nine hours in Isla's bedroom, in a fog of grief. But there is no other explanation to account for the missing hours.

Footsteps trudge up the stairs, and Abby swings her legs over the side of the bed, wipes the tears from her cheeks. As Clio reaches the landing, Abby pulls her face into something resembling a smile.

'Hi, darling. How was your day?'

Clio eyes her suspiciously from the hallway that separates her bedroom from Isla's. 'What are you doing?'

Abby surveys the room as though she has only just realised where she is. 'Just sorting a few things out.' The forced smile aches across her cheeks.

Clio loiters in the doorway, chews on her thumbnail, seems to be waiting for something more to be said.

'Did you have a good day?' The words scratch at Abby's throat. There is something perverse in these attempts at normality, as though it is a betrayal of Isla to continue with quotidian life.

Clio nods, evading Abby's gaze.

'Are you hungry? I could make you something to eat.' Keeping busy, that's what Abby needs to do. Everyone keeps telling her so. It is advice, she is aware, that she is failing miserably to follow.

Clio shakes her head. Abby waits for her to go to her bedroom, slip her noise-cancelling headphones on, pretend to get on with homework while watching mindless videos online. But Clio doesn't move. She lingers at Isla's bedroom door, and Abby doesn't know if she is awaiting an invitation to come inside or if she wants to talk about Isla. For three weeks now, Clio has resisted all Abby's attempts to share their grief, and Abby doesn't know how best to console her.

'Are you okay?'

Clio shrugs. 'Fine. Just thought you might want to know the outcome of the art competition.'

Something jars in Abby's head and then slips into place. The annual Collingswood Art Prize. Clio spent half the summer holidays preparing her portfolio: a series of self-portraits in oils, charcoal, pen and ink.

'I'm sorry. It just slipped my mind. How did it go?'

Her daughter glares at her with naked fury. 'I literally reminded you this morning.'

'I know, I'm sorry. I've just . . . had a lot on today.' She thinks of the nine hours she has lost to her grief, still cannot comprehend how it happened.

Clio continues to glower at her. 'It's fine. I mean, why should I expect Isla not to be the focus of all your attention just because she's dead.'

The words detonate in the air between them. For a moment, Abby cannot speak, cannot move, cannot breathe. Violence lingers in the air, like vapour from a fire which, now lit, cannot be extinguished. A line has been crossed, a boundary traversed, and they both know there is no going back.

Before Abby can conjure any words in response, Clio emits a deep, frustrated sigh, turns around and storms into her bedroom, slamming the door behind her.

Shock paralyses Abby. Never before has she heard such venom in Clio's voice. Never has she felt such intense heat from Clio's rage, her rivalry, her sense of injustice.

Something opens up inside Abby: a chasm of abject failure. She has failed Isla, failed to fulfil the sole objective of a mother's purpose: to keep her child safe, well, free from harm. Failed to ensure the correct order of things: not to outlive her own child. And she has failed Clio in ways she does not even understand: to help her feel every bit as loved, valued and cherished as Isla ever was.

She has failed both her daughters, and guilt ferments inside her, alongside her unassailable grief.

Jenna

'I'll see you in a fortnight. Any problems in the meantime, just give me a call. But you're doing really well.'

Jenna smiles before turning and heading along the external walkway on the twelfth floor of the council flat block where she has been visiting one of the families in her care.

Walking past the broken lift and down the concrete stairs – walls daubed with graffiti, floor littered with crisp packets, spliff butts, empty lager cans – she scrolls through the calendar on her phone for the rest of the afternoon's appointments: a core group meeting at a local school to discuss a child's protection plan, and her weekly catch-up in the office with a newly qualified social worker. Looking at the time – almost three o'clock – she thinks about the mountain of paperwork she will have to complete before the day's end.

Getting into her battered Vauxhall Corsa – pulling hard on the door that fails to shut without a determined slam – her phone rings, and she registers the number on the screen, feels a flutter of concern. Callum may be almost eighteen but the sight of the school's phone number still induces a moment of quiet apprehension.

'Hello?'

'Ms James?'

'Yes, speaking.'

'It's Mr Marlowe from Collingswood. I wondered if you might have a moment?'

Jenna thinks about all she still has to do today, but she knows the question is rhetorical.

'Of course.'

There is a moment's hesitation before Mr Marlowe begins to speak.

'It's come to our attention that Callum has some . . . complicated personal history that we've only recently been made aware of.'

Jenna allows herself a beat. She has been anticipating this call for almost a week, but now that it is here, she is not sure how best to handle it. She knew, deep down, that Callum's school would find out about his joyriding, that Abby or Nicole or one of the other parents would make Collingswood aware of it. Six days since Isla's funeral and now she is only surprised it has taken this long to circle back to her.

'What do you mean?' If Mr Marlowe wants to condemn her son for his involvement in something when he was fourteen years old, he will have to be explicit.

'We understand that Callum was involved in an incident that required police intervention.'

All these euphemisms. It's one of the things she can't bear about the teachers and parents at Callum's school. Nobody is ever upfront. Nobody ever dares say anything difficult or controversial.

'That was quite a long time ago now.' She can hear the defensiveness in her voice, wishes she were able to curb it; wishes she had learnt – like all those polished, confident Collingswood parents – how to take command of a situation like this, defuse it before it becomes an issue.

Mr Marlowe clears his throat. 'As I understand it, it was just before Callum started Year 10? Not that long – relatively speaking – before he applied to Collingswood?'

It is phrased as a question, but Jenna is aware that this is a game of cat-and-mouse, a game where she will, inevitably, get caught. 'Yes, but that was still over three years ago now.'

There is another uncomfortable pause. 'I'm sure you can appreciate our concern. I've spoken with the Headmaster and we do feel that this information would have been best disclosed during Callum's application process rather than us finding out about it now, from a third party.'

Jenna hears the ellipsis in Mr Marlowe's short speech, understands enough about this rarefied world to read between the lines: *We don't want our students involved in this kind of grubby behaviour. It brings the school into disrepute. We'd never have awarded your son a place – let alone a full bursary – had we known.*

All the moisture evaporates from Jenna's mouth. Callum cannot lose his bursary. He cannot – he simply cannot – be forced to leave Collingswood. It is inconceivable that he should return to his previous school. She will not let it happen.

'I'm so sorry, Mr Marlowe. I can see how it looks. It's just that by the time Callum was applying to Collingswood, we felt he'd put it all behind him. He'd learnt from his mistakes and moved on.' She senses the flimsiness of the excuse, understands Mr Marlowe's frustration. But she knows – as well as he must know – that had she divulged Callum's unlawful behaviour during the application process, he'd have been rejected out of hand.

'Like I say, we just wish you'd told us—'

'I know, and I'm so sorry. I can't apologise enough. But it really was just one moment of stupidity on Callum's part. It was completely out of character for him. He loves Collingswood so much. He's really settled and happy there. It's been so good for him, and we really are grateful for all the opportunities he's being given.' She hears the grovelling tone in her voice, winces at her own servility. But she is painfully aware of the power dynamic at play, knows it is the school who holds all the cards, and that her hand is as good as empty.

'We know Callum's thriving at Collingswood. We never had any doubt he would. But if we'd known about Callum's history, we could have ensured he was properly supported if ever it became common knowledge. As it is, we do now find ourselves on the back foot, somewhat.'

It is there again, the admonition for her failure to reveal Callum's joyriding history sooner.

'Of course, I understand. And I really am very sorry I didn't tell you myself. I just want what's best for Callum, that's all.'

'I'm sure that's what we all want. We do understand this must be a very difficult situation for Callum, and we do want to support him in whatever way we can. But I'm sure you can appreciate that there are particular sensitivities around this issue at the moment. Shall we catch up in a week or so, see how things are? And if you want to speak about anything in the meantime, just drop me an email and we'll arrange a call.'

Jenna is so grateful that Callum isn't being immediately suspended – or, worse still, expelled – that she thanks Mr Marlowe profusely, exhales a sigh of relief as he says goodbye and ends the call. But she knows Callum is skating on thin ice, understands this is possibly only a temporary stay of execution. It is imperative she does whatever she can to keep Callum out of trouble, keep him away from any whiff of controversy.

All she wants is for Callum to have a fair chance in life. The chances she never had. The chances all those other students at Collingswood have because their parents are rich enough to pay the fees.

When she thinks back now to Callum's attitude at his previous school – beleaguered by the disruptions to lessons, the lack of discipline, the open secret that drugs were being sold and taken on school premises – it is unconscionable that Callum may have to return there. The change in her son since he started at Collingswood has been transformational. He is more confident, more articulate, more secure in his thoughts, opinions, feelings. More equipped with a sense of self-belief; a burgeoning awareness that he is bright and capable – as Jenna has always known him to be – and that, if he works hard, he has every chance of success.

Looking at the time, she realises she will now be late for her meeting. Putting the location into Google Maps, she begins to rehearse all the arguments she will employ should her next conversation with Mr Marlowe take a different turn. Arguments, she knows, which amount to little more than begging for Callum not to be excluded from the school he has come to love: a school which, Jenna knows only too well, holds the ticket to his future.

Abby

Abby checks the time on her watch. Three-thirty. About an hour until Clio will be home. Today, Abby promises herself, Clio will not return from school to find her in Isla's bedroom, as she had last Friday. Today, Abby will be in the kitchen, doing whatever normal things parents do when their children arrive home from school. In the three days since Abby forgot about the Collingswood Art Prize – a competition in which Clio came second, despite the top prizes usually going to sixth formers – Clio has been sullen, angry, withdrawn – even more so than usual – and Abby knows she needs to make amends.

An hour. That is all she has left in Isla's bedroom, where she now seems to spend most of her days.

She is overcome by an urge to look at photos Isla has taken over the years. Isla's phone was destroyed in the hit-and-run, but all her pictures will be backed up in the cloud. Sitting down at Isla's desk where her daughter's laptop has remained untouched for over three weeks, she lifts the lid, types in the password that Isla was always happy to share with her, is greeted by the sight of Isla's laughing face: her wallpaper photo, taken at Reading Festival the summer before last, in which Isla is sandwiched between Meera and Yasmin, their arms flung around one another's shoulders, sun flaring above their heads like the illuminating halos of angels.

Grief wrenches in Abby's chest. There will be no more festivals for Isla: no more dancing, no more long summer nights with her friends.

Clicking the Photos icon, she scrolls through the tranche of pictures, slips back through the days, weeks, months as though in possession of a time machine: photos documenting almost every day of the past few years. Isla standing at the poolside before a meet, swim cap curtailing her long, blonde hair, goggles strapped across her forehead. Isla at school, messing around with friends. Isla on her Silver Duke of Edinburgh expedition to Snowdonia two years before she died.

It is overwhelming, suddenly, all these visual reminders of the exuberant life her daughter is no longer leading.

Closing the Photos gallery, Abby experiences a renewed sense of fury that Isla's killer is still at large. Three weeks and three days since Isla was killed, and the police have achieved nothing in their search for the driver: a motorist who left Isla for dead, like a piece of roadkill, did not even take the trouble to call an ambulance. Every time she phones the detective in charge of the case, he tells her they are doing all they can, surveying CCTV footage, making enquiries, but Abby finds this hard to believe. It seems incomprehensible to her that in this day and age – with surveillance cameras on every street corner, in shops, on office buildings – they have been unable to unearth a single clue. And even if the perpetrator is caught, the very worst they might face is a prison sentence; that is negligible compared to the life sentence of grief that awaits Abby.

Turning back to Isla's laptop, Abby's eyes rest on the Gmail icon, and she feels herself hesitate. It is a world to which she has never, rightly, had access. Even now, a part of her feels it would be an invasion of Isla's privacy. But something inside her yearns for a new connection with her daughter, something that will bring her closer to Isla.

For a few seconds, her hand hovers over the trackpad, unsure what to do next. And then she watches as she makes contact with the aluminium base, feels the click beneath her fingers.

Opening Gmail, she finds ninety-eight unread emails. Her eyes scan through them, and she sees they are mostly junk or circulars: clothing sales, concert promotions, newsletters from swimming associations.

Scrolling back in time, familiar names begin to appear: Yasmin, Meera, Kit, Jules. Friends Isla has known since she was eleven, longer in some cases. Abby does not open any of the messages, has no desire to inveigle her way into the private correspondence of seventeen-year-olds.

On the navigation bar, she sees a number of named folders: 'School', 'Swimming', 'Uni Applications'. At the sight of the third folder, Abby is aware of her breath catching in her throat: Isla's unfulfilled future laid out so starkly before her.

Beneath the university folder is another labelled 'WSE', an acronym Abby does not recognise. Curiosity gets the better of her and she clicks on the folder, sees a string of emails from an address without a name, simply a collection of random letters and numbers: FSW23BS@gmail.com. None of the emails have a subject heading, and before Abby has time to consider what she is doing, she opens the email at the top of the list.

As her eyes scan the contents, her heart rate begins to accelerate.

She reads the email twice, closes it, opens the next, reads that one too. Closing and opening, she reads one message after the next – another and another and another – each one a variation on the same theme. Her head spins, the muscles in her throat constricting until it does not seem feasible that sufficient air can pass through.

Because every message is from the same anonymous account. Every message is an iteration of the same appalling accusation.

You're a whore, you know that, don't you?

Is he paying you for it? Is that why you've been fucking him for weeks now? Or do you actually get off on shagging men twice your age?

You know he's only doing it because you offered it to him on a plate. You're literally nothing more than somewhere for him to put his dick. Slut.

How about I tell his wife? Or your mum? Or everyone at your school? What do you think people's reaction would be? Wouldn't be Little Miss Perfect then, would you?

He'll get bored of you, you know that. And then you'll be nothing but a tragic little slag who let an old man fuck her.

Have you got NO SHAME? You go around pretending to be so perfect when all you are is a dirty little whore.

What kind of 17 yr old sucks off a married man old enough to be her dad?

The vile messages go on and on – a dozen or more – and Abby reads them with a vertiginous sense of disgust. She tries to grab hold of her thoughts but it is like clutching at air.

She does not understand why anyone would send messages like this to her daughter: such hideous, revolting messages. She does not understand why anyone would make such outlandish claims. Isla was not that type of teenager.

She reads the messages again, studies the email address for any clue as to the sender's identity, but her head is fuzzy, she cannot think straight, cannot decipher the code if there is one.

She notices that some of the messages have a reply arrow next to them, and she clicks on the sender's email address, copies it, goes into Isla's sent items and pastes the address into the search box.

A stream of responses appears, and Abby starts with the most recent.

> *It's over. I told you already. Now just leave me alone. Please.*

A sinkhole seems to open up beneath Abby, and she feels herself tumbling into it with no idea how deep it is, no clue what might await her at the bottom. She clicks on the next reply and then the next, travelling back in time with each new message, her heart thudding, hands shaking.

> *It's over. Happy? Now STOP MESSAGING ME.*

> *Please don't tell anyone. Please. It's not what you think.*

> *Please just keep it to yourself. We didn't mean for it to happen. I don't want anyone to get hurt.*

> *Stop emailing me. If you carry on, I'll go to the police.*

> *Whatever you think, you've got it all wrong.*

> *Do you get off on sending abusive messages to young women?*

*Who are you? You know only cowards send anonymous
messages?*

Abby hears an involuntary cry emerge from her lips as her
brain scrambles to make sense of what she is reading.

It is not possible. It is just not possible. Isla would never have
done something like this. It was not in her character.

And yet . . . here are responses from her daughter's email
account all but admitting to the charges of which she has been
accused. All but admitting to having an affair with an older man.
A married man. A man old enough to be her father. A man Abby
cannot bear to imagine without hatred filling her lungs.

Thoughts hurtle through her mind, as she tries to imagine who
it might be, where Isla might have met him. Whether it was through
swimming, or school – not a teacher, surely? Abby wracks her brain
trying to think of any Collingswood staff who have ever given her
cause for concern, can think of no one – or someone she has met on
an evening out with friends. Speculations rampage in her head and she
cannot think straight – cannot fix upon a viable face, a likely name, a
realistic suspect – feels as though the conjectures will drive her mad.

Checking the dates of the emails, she sees that the first was
sent less than three months ago, the last one just a few weeks before
Isla died.

According to these emails, three months ago Isla had already been
sleeping with a married man for 'weeks'. Since before the summer
holidays began, when Abby thought Isla was busy with friends, with
school, with swimming: with being a normal seventeen-year-old girl.

Nausea rises into the back of her throat. It is as though she is
being forced to watch a movie she has seen a thousand times before
but this time with a perverse alteration to the narrative. She is being
made to view her daughter through a shifting prism, portraying her
in a different, disorienting light.

And yet, suddenly, it all makes sense: Isla ending her relationship with Callum when she had seemed so besotted with him just weeks before. At the time, Abby had been relieved, had silently thanked the universe for making Isla come to her senses. Now, all too late, she realises she should have been careful what she wished for. It had never occurred to her that perhaps Isla finished with Callum because she'd met someone else. But the dates line up, and it is the only reasonable explanation. Isla must have ended things with Callum because some predatory, married man – a man whose identity Abby will uncover and, when she does, she will not be held responsible for her actions – somehow coerced her daughter – her beautiful, innocent, inexperienced daughter – to involve herself in a relationship with him.

Abby's eyes skim the computer screen, over the anonymous emails and Isla's responses.

And then another thought slips into Abby's head, quietly at first as if unsure it wants to be seen, before it begins to shout, loudly, demanding to be heard.

Someone was sending abusive messages to Isla: anonymous emails, threatening to expose her. If someone was malicious enough, angry enough, sinister enough to send those vile messages – to still be sending them just weeks before Isla was killed – what else might they have been capable of?

Where might they have been – what might they have been doing – the night Isla was killed?

TEN WEEKS BEFORE ISLA'S DEATH

Isla

Isla turned onto her side, the crisp white duvet tucked beneath her bare arm. Sunlight bled through a gap in the curtains, and she lifted her head, looked at the alarm clock by the side of the bed: just gone half past six. She thought about where she'd usually be at this time on a Thursday evening: in the pool for a training session, a session she had missed for ten consecutive Thursdays now. For the past ten weeks, she had instead boarded the train to Waterloo and walked the short distance to a large, corporate hotel. She'd given a false name at the front desk, been issued with a key card, and made her way up in the lift and along the carpeted corridor. Ten weeks of walking into an empty hotel room feeling both unfeasibly grown-up and yet out of her depth at the same time. Ten weeks of putting her redundant swimming bag by the wardrobe, sitting in the armchair by the floor-to-ceiling windows overlooking the main road, and waiting for Andrew to arrive.

Next to her in bed, Andrew snuffled quietly. In a few minutes, he'd awake with a start, look down at his Garmin, seem surprised by the time. He'd lift his arm so she could lay her head on his chest, run his fingers through her hair before heading into the bathroom for a shower. It seemed both strange and wondrous to Isla that she already knew what he would do, that they already knew so much about each other's habits. Sometimes, looking at Andrew's face while he slept, Isla felt as though she were finding the answer to a question she hadn't known she'd been asking.

We understand each other, you and I. There's a connection that goes beyond words, beyond the age gap, beyond rational explanation. I knew it the first time I gave you a lift. It just felt so easy. Everything with you is easy. It just feels right.

Isla recalled Andrew's short speech to her just over two months ago, when they'd been sitting in the pub that had, by then, become their regular Thursday evening haunt. They'd been nestled in their usual quiet corner – Andrew with a glass of red wine, Isla with a lime and soda – when he had taken hold of her hand, delivered that speech. Four weeks after their initial kiss, it had been the first time he told her he loved her. That night, she had known, unequivocally, that Andrew would be the first man she would sleep with. It was the evening she'd agreed to meet him in a hotel room in Waterloo the following Thursday, knowing full well what would happen.

Only now did she realise the real reason she'd never slept with Callum: not because she'd wanted to hold on to her precious virginity, but simply because he hadn't been the right person.

Andrew emitted a small, light snore and turned onto his back. Scrolling back through the years she'd known him – all her life, in fact – she thought about all the weekends and holidays she had spent in his company: Christmas Eve at Andrew and Nicole's, New Year's Eve attending the same parties, summer barbecues in each other's gardens. The bank holiday weekends spent on her dad's boat, the half-term holidays they'd all decamped to coastal cottages, the joint family skiing trips in the Alps. Looking at Andrew now, she couldn't understand how it had taken her until a few months ago to realise how handsome he was.

Through the seventh-storey window came the purr of traffic from the street below.

Isla thought back to the afternoon in Andrew's car when he'd brushed his fingers along her bare neck. How flustered she'd been, how confused. How uncertain she had felt when his first texts arrived, convincing herself he was simply taking a paternalistic interest in her given the absence of her dad. A part of her feeling foolish for imagining a flirtatious undertone. And yet, within days, she had become aware that she was anticipating messages from him, that she was excited when one arrived and disappointed when she did not hear from him for a few hours.

Now, when she looked back on those early days of their relationship, she felt embarrassed that she'd been so anxious: so unsure of herself and of her response to Andrew's attentions. So unsettled by the idea that he might be attracted to her. Just months since their first kiss, and already it felt like a different version of herself: a childish, unsophisticated version she was pleased to have left behind, like discarded clothes she had once loved but now found gawkish.

Outside, a police siren wailed, and Isla waited for Andrew to stir. But his breathing did not alter, his body deep in slumber.

This relationship was so different to her one with Callum. She thought back to the evening she'd broken up with him, the day after her first kiss with Andrew, too much confusion and guilt for her to continue as if everything were normal. Callum had begged her to change her mind, asked her again and again what he'd done wrong. He'd thought they were happy, that she loved him. There had been moments during that conversation when Isla had felt she was making a terrible mistake, that she would come to regret it. That she was being rash, ending a five-month relationship because of one evening – one kiss – with another man. Her guilt at hurting Callum had been overwhelming. But as she'd looked at him, she'd known something had shifted between them, something profound and irrevocable. She could not turn back the clock, could not pretend she didn't know what it felt like to be desired by an older man. She could not change what had happened between her and Andrew, or how she was beginning to feel about him.

With Callum, she had felt like a teenager. Their relationship had been firmly rooted in the hermetically sealed world of school. But with Andrew she felt more adult; cleverer, wiser, more knowledgeable. He listened to what she said, encouraged her in her opinions, made her feel as though maturity was not a distant place she'd reach after university but somewhere she was already inhabiting. She felt safe with him and yet, at the same time, exhilarated. He had already taught her so much.

It was strange, how much she'd changed in the months she'd been with Andrew: as though she were no longer the person she used to be but was not yet sure who it was she was becoming.

Her eyes caught the small, square purple box by the side of the bed. Andrew had given it to her as soon as he'd arrived, half an hour later than planned having been delayed on a work call. Isla had got used to him being late, had become accustomed to opening a textbook, fitting in some study before he arrived. Today when he'd walked in – smiling apologetically, cupping her face in his hands, kissing her tenderly on the lips and asking whether she could forgive him for being so monstrously late – he'd pulled the small purple box from his pocket and handed it to her. A pair of delicately crafted silver earrings to join the three pairs he'd already bought her, the two necklaces, the Montblanc fountain pen, the Mulberry crossbody bag. The trunk at the end of her bed at home was now layered with well-concealed objects that she couldn't wear or use without arousing suspicion. But she knew that at some point in the not-too-distant future, once she was at university – at Oxford, hopefully – she would be able to wear the jewellery when Andrew came to visit.

By the side of the bed, the screen on Andrew's silenced phone lit up, and Isla lifted her head to look at it.

A WhatsApp from Nicole, the short message visible on the home screen.

Hi darling. Just checking if you know what time you'll be back. x

Guilt snagged in Isla's throat at the thought of all the different versions of Nicole she had known over the past seventeen years. Nicole who had wiped Isla's childhood tears, bathed her grazed knee or held her hand as they crossed the road on the way to school. Nicole who had cooked so many of Isla's favourite childhood dinners during playdates with Nathaniel – lasagne, spaghetti bolognese, meatballs – always looking after her as if she were part of their family. Nicole who had supported them all with unwavering care and compassion since Isla's dad died. Nicole who had, so often, sat at the kitchen table, sharing a glass of wine with Isla's mum, making her laugh on days when Isla thought it was an impossibility in the face of her grief. So many years during which Nicole had shown Isla unfaltering love and kindness: the most trusted adult in her life, after her mum. And yet, here Isla was, committing the most terrible betrayal.

Squeezing shut her eyes, Isla tried to stem the rising tide of panic. Consciously silencing her guilt, she replayed everything Andrew had told her about his marriage: the complacent companionship he and Nicole had slipped into over the past few years, the lack of passion, the separate emotional lives. The enormous amount of respect and love he had for Nicole alongside the deep-seated awareness that they were together mainly for the sake of Nathaniel and Jack. The tacit agreement that they would go their separate ways once Jack went to university, if not before.

'You're not asleep, are you?'

Isla opened her eyes, found Andrew awake, looking at her. She shook her head. 'Just thinking.' Pushing thoughts of Nicole out of her mind, Isla slipped under Andrew's arm, rested her head on his chest.

She watched Andrew reach across for his phone, sensed him reading Nicole's message, waited to see what he would do.

'Do you need to go?' She tried to keep her voice neutral.

Andrew ran the tips of his fingers through her hair. 'Not yet. I want to make the most of every second we have together.' He paused. 'What do you think about us going away together for a few days?'

Isla shifted from beneath Andrew's arm, leaned up on her elbow. 'Really? Do you think we could?'

'Why not? As long as you can come up with a viable excuse. I can say I'll be away for work.' He nuzzled his face against her neck, his stubble rough against her skin. 'Wouldn't it be great, a couple of days away, just the two of us, not having to watch the clock? There's a hotel just outside Oxford I think you'd love.' He smiled at her. 'What do you think? Are there any friends you could say you were staying with? Or some swim thing you could say you were going to?'

Isla breathed deeply, told herself to stop feeling nervous, that this was what adults in grown-up relationships did. 'Definitely. I'll think of something.'

Stroking her face with his fingers, he gazed at her intently. 'Our time together is the highlight of my week, you know that, don't you?' Leaning forward, he kissed her gently on the mouth. Reciprocating, Isla instructed herself not to think about Nicole or Nathaniel, about her mum or Clio, about Callum or school or the weeks of missed swimming sessions that she knew, at some point in the autumn season, she may come to regret.

◆ ◆ ◆

'You sure you'll be okay from here?'

Isla nodded. 'I'll be fine.' The quiet residential street where Andrew sometimes dropped her was only a ten-minute walk from home.

Andrew glanced down at his watch. 'Sorry, I should get going. There are some documents I need to review this evening.'

He kissed her, and Isla tried not to think about the message from Nicole she'd seen on his phone; tried not to speculate that he was, in fact, going home to spend time with his wife.

'I'll message you later. And you're okay for next Thursday?'

Isla nodded, grabbing her bags from the footwell. Kissing Andrew one last time – wishing she didn't have to leave him, wishing they could spend the whole night together – she got out of the car, gave a small wave and watched him drive away.

'What are you doing?'

Isla spun around, felt as though her heart had dropped into the pit of her stomach.

'What's going on?'

Isla stared at Callum, panic disorienting her for a few seconds. 'What are you doing here?'

'*That's* your response? I see you getting out of Andrew Forrester's car after he's been mauling you for the past five minutes and all you can ask is what *I'm* doing here?'

'It's not what you think—'

'I'm not an *idiot*. I know what I saw.' Callum shook his head, incredulous. 'Seriously, Isla. *Andrew Forrester?* He's Nathaniel's *dad*, for fuck's sake. It's . . . it's weird, you know that, right?'

Isla winced, her fist tightening around the strap of her bag.

'How long's it been going on?'

She looked down at the ground, could not find the words she needed to defend herself.

'Shit. Is that why you broke up with me? Because of *him*?'

Colour rushed to fill Isla's cheeks, and she couldn't look up, did not want Callum to see the guilt written on her face.

'It is, isn't it? Jesus, Isla, this is fucked up. He's taking advantage of you, you know that, don't you? He's a fucking creep.'

Isla forced herself to look directly at Callum. 'It's not like that—'

'Not like *what*? He's practically fifty, Isla. You're seventeen. What part of that is not fucked up?'

'You don't understand—'

'Oh, don't give me that. What did he tell you? That his marriage was shit and he's only staying with his wife for the sake of the kids?'

A fresh rush of blood bloomed on Isla's neck.

'For fuck's sake. It's such a cliché. You're smart. How did you fall for that bullshit?'

Something snapped inside Isla: a need to exonerate herself, to validate her relationship, to counter the false narrative Callum was constructing. 'It's not bullshit. He loves me.'

Callum groaned, but Isla pressed on.

'I'm sorry. I know you're still upset about what happened with us. I never meant to hurt you, you must know that.'

Callum watched her through narrowed eyes. 'I presume you're sleeping with him?'

'That's none of your business.'

'It's obvious. Jesus. How can you be so gullible?'

'I'm not—'

'What do you think's going to happen? You think he's going to leave Nathaniel's mum? That you're going to move in together? Ditch university to play Happy Families with a bloke old enough to be your dad? A bloke who used to be *friends* with your dad, for fuck's sake. How can you not see how screwed up it is? He's using you, Isla. How can you not see that?'

Tears pricked Isla's eyes, and she blinked them away. 'You have no idea what you're talking about. I don't have to listen to this.' She turned around, began to walk away, felt a hand on her arm.

'Stop, please. I'm worried about you. I'm worried what you've got yourself into.'

Isla pulled her arm free. 'You don't need to worry about me. I'm fine.'

Callum looked at her, a frown pinching the bridge of his nose. 'Seriously. Just think about what you're doing. And if you ever need to talk . . .'

His softened voice trailed off, and suddenly fresh anxiety plucked at Isla's fears. 'You won't tell anyone, will you?'

For a few seconds, Callum stared at her, a flurry of emotions crossing his face, too fast for Isla to read. 'You need to end it. You know you do. Just stop it now, before anyone else gets hurt.'

Without waiting for a response, Callum turned and walked away.

Hugging her bag to her chest, Isla watched him go, cursing herself for having been so foolish, for having forgotten that the place Andrew sometimes dropped her was close to Callum's athletics club.

But mostly, she thought about Callum's expression: the shock, the disgust, the disappointment writ large. And as much as she tried to reassure herself that Callum wasn't vindictive, that he'd keep it to himself in spite of the pain she had caused him, dread churned in her stomach. Because now Callum knew. And Isla had no way of predicting what he might do with the information.

◆　◆　◆

As soon as Isla stepped through the front door, she heard voices coming from the kitchen, felt a lurch of apprehension.

Slipping quietly out of her trainers, she began to creep up the stairs, hoping to avoid a conversation. But her rucksack knocked against a picture on the wall, sent it rattling in its frame.

'Isla, is that you?' Her mum's voice called through the closed kitchen door.

Silently cursing her clumsiness, Isla tried to inject some brightness into her voice. 'Yep. Just going to take a shower.'

'Come in and say hello first.'

Heading back down the stairs, Isla walked along the chequerboard floor of the hallway, stretched her lips into a pronounced smile before pushing open the kitchen door.

Sitting at the table with a bottle of Pouilly-Fuissé between them were her mother and Nicole.

'How was swimming?'

'Good thanks.' Isla swallowed the lie, her attention darting round the room, trying not to lock eyes with Nicole.

'School okay?'

'Yep, fine.'

'Did Nathaniel seem alright? He was a bit off-colour this morning and I haven't seen him since.'

Nicole's question was directed at Isla, and she couldn't avoid her any longer. Turning to look at her, she implored her guilt to keep itself hidden. 'He seemed fine in maths this morning.'

'Good. It's a relief school's broken up today. You all need a holiday.' Nicole's smile was wide, trusting, affectionate.

'Nicole just popped over for a glass of wine.' Her mum's cheeks were flushed, and Isla suspected they'd had more than a glass.

'Andrew's still at work, so I thought I'd come over and keep your mum company.' Nicole clocked the time on her watch. 'Actually, I ought to make a move. His text said he'd be home by half eight and I promised we'd eat together.'

Isla's cheeks ached with the effort of smiling. A voice in one ear told her not to worry, that of course Andrew would need to have dinner with his wife sometimes, that it was no indication of his true feelings. But another voice whispered that he had not been entirely honest with her, that he'd told her he was going home to work when all along he was planning to have dinner with Nicole.

Drinking the last of her wine, Nicole stood up from the table. 'See you at Pilates in the morning?'

Abby nodded. 'Absolutely. I'll see you out.'

As her mum and Nicole walked into the hallway, chatting about school PTA events they were planning for the next academic year, Isla's phone pinged, and she pulled it from her pocket, opened the message.

> *Hi beautiful. Thanks for this afternoon. I wish you could know how much I love our time together. Connections like ours don't come along very often. I miss you so much when we're not together. I can't wait for us to have a couple of days alone. I'll look at my diary and let you know dates. I love you. x*

Isla read the message, butterflies dancing in her stomach, and tapped out a reply.

> *I'm so excited about going away together. It'll be perfect. I love you too. X*

As she heard the click of the front door, she exited WhatsApp, slipped her phone into her pocket, and willed the guilt to erase itself from her face.

◆ ◆ ◆

It had been a week since Callum spotted Isla getting out of Andrew's car. Seven days during which Isla had waited – breath bated – to see if he would do anything, tell anyone. Seven days of Isla trying to prepare herself for the worst. But nothing had happened. School had broken up and she had not seen Callum since: he was away for a few days at a summer school. He'd sent her some messages, asking if she was okay, and she'd replied with anodyne emojis; she didn't want to ignore him for fear of provoking him, but equally had no desire to continue their last conversation.

The evening sun veined the sky as she stepped through the train doors and onto the station platform. She thought about Andrew, back in his office by now after their truncated evening together. He'd been full of apologies that he couldn't stay, had told her the US stock market was behaving erratically and that he needed to get back to work, however much he wished he could stay longer. But he'd shown her the hotel he'd booked for their mini-break later in the summer: a Cotswold country house with beautifully land-scaped gardens and a Michelin-starred restaurant. All Isla had to do was concoct an alibi for her mum, the one part of the plan she wasn't looking forward to; she'd never lied to her mum before her relationship with Andrew – never had cause to – and the current layers of subterfuge in her life were beginning to weigh on her like strata of rock.

'Hey Isla.'

Isla whipped her head around, startled by the sight of Nathaniel standing on the platform inches behind her – too close for comfort – his unfeasibly long arms dangling at his sides, his spindly legs and bony knees protruding ridiculously from a pair of shorts miles too large for him.

Isla tried to gather her thoughts, but her mind was replete with anxiety.

Nathaniel had just got off the same train as her. The train from Waterloo that Isla had travelled on having spent two hours in a hotel room with Nathaniel's dad.

'Hey. How are you?' Her voice was unexpectedly steady, but she looked away as Nathaniel fell into step beside her, through the automatic ticket barrier and out onto the street.

'Good thanks. What have you been up to?'

It was an innocuous enough question but to Isla it felt loaded, accusatory.

'Just in Wimbledon seeing a friend.'

'Anyone I know?'

Isla tried to breathe slowly, steadily. 'No, just someone I used to train with.' Above the sound of commuters hurrying past and traffic on the main road, Isla was sure Nathaniel must be able to hear the false note in her voice.

'Aren't you supposed to be at training tonight?'

Thoughts stumbled in Isla's head. The lies she was telling. The spontaneous excuses she was having to conjure, like a magician pulling a rabbit from a hat. 'Honestly? I just needed an evening off.'

She could feel Nathaniel's eyes drilling into the side of her face, tried to avoid the intensity of it, focused instead on the collection of acne spots dotting his forehead.

'That's weird. I got on at Wimbledon and I didn't see you on the platform.'

For a moment, Isla was blindsided. She felt under interrogation, as though anything she said risked incriminating her further. 'I almost missed it. Had to jump on at the last minute.' The lie blazed in her cheeks: hot, unsettling. 'Don't say anything to anyone about seeing me here, will you? My mum'll be annoyed I didn't go to training. But I just really needed a night off.'

Nathaniel nodded. 'Course.' A smile curled at one corner of his lips as though they were now bound together by the secret she had asked him to keep.

A bus trundled past, diesel fumes acrid in the back of Isla's throat. As they turned off the main road and towards both their homes, Nathaniel stopped suddenly, put a hand on Isla's arm, his fingers clammy against her skin.

'Listen, I don't know whether I should tell you this or not.' He paused, like a judge on a television talent show. 'I don't want to stir things up, but I think there might be something going on between Callum and Yasmin.'

Isla felt herself frown. 'Why?'

'I saw them in the park together at the weekend. Callum's arm was round Yasmin's shoulders. They looked . . . close, you know?'

Jealousy contorted beneath Isla's ribs. It was hypocritical, she knew. She was the one who had ended the relationship. She was the one who had betrayed Callum: who had kissed another man while they were still dating. And yet the thought of him in a relationship with someone else – with one of her friends – was too painful to contemplate. 'They're mates. Why wouldn't they hang out?' She could hear the defensiveness in her voice.

'They weren't just hanging out, though. It was obvious from the way they were together that something's going on.'

The muscles tightened in Isla's throat. 'When was this?'

'Sunday.'

The timeline mocked her. Three days after Callum had seen her with Andrew.

Nathaniel squeezed Isla's arm, and she felt herself flinch from his touch. For years, she and Nathaniel had hugged without a second thought. Now, every instance of physical contact between them was charged with one-sided desire that made her flesh crawl.

'Sorry, I shouldn't have said anything. I just thought you'd want to know. You're way prettier than Yasmin anyway.'

Nathaniel tried to hold her gaze, but it was fervent, uncomfortable, and Isla looked away.

'No worries.' She pulled her lips into a determined smile, swerved the conversation onto a different subject. 'What were you doing in Wimbledon, anyway?'

Nathaniel paused, and Isla sensed his disappointment that she wouldn't gossip about Callum and Yasmin. 'I had to take my bike to the repair shop. Brakes kept squeaking. Was driving me nuts.'

Finally, they reached the interchange that bisected their routes home, and Isla said goodbye, felt relieved to be free of Nathaniel's cloying presence.

And yet, his words echoed in her ears: *It was obvious from the way they were together that something's going on.* She tried to tell herself that Callum wasn't malicious, that he wouldn't go out with one of her close friends just to wreak revenge. But the timing was indisputable, too suspicious to be a coincidence: just days after he found out about her relationship with Andrew.

However much Isla tried to view Callum's actions through a generous prism, they kept refracting in the same distorted way: with the fear that if Callum was resentful enough to start dating one of her best friends, perhaps it was foolish of her to trust that he would keep her relationship with Andrew a secret.

THE PRESENT

Nicole

It is only just gone seven when the doorbell rings. Nicole hopes it is not Andrew back early from his morning run. The longer he is out, the better. Ten days since Andrew confessed to his affair with Isla – ten days since Nicole began fabricating excuses to Nathaniel and Jack about the sudden onset of insomnia necessitating Andrew's move into the spare room – and she is beginning to feel she is existing in two parallel worlds: the world of heinous lies and secrets that must be kept at all costs; and a world in which she must feign normality in order safeguard her family. The duality is exhausting and there are moments she fears her ability to maintain the pretence.

Closing her laptop – where she has been filling out yet more insurance forms about her missing car – she walks along the wide, tiled hallway, towards the front door. Opening it, she finds Abby standing on the other side.

Nicole has seen Abby almost every day since Isla was killed: days when Abby has raged with grief, days when she has been withdrawn and silent. Days when she has been apoplectic at the police's ineptitude, and Nicole has tried to placate her, reassure her, steer her onto a calmer path. There have been moments when Abby's rage has felt almost engulfing, when Nicole has felt overwhelmed by the sheer power of it. But today Abby seems different: adrenalised, febrile almost.

'Can I come in?'

'Of course.' Nicole steps back, allows Abby to pass by, follows her into the kitchen. Glancing up the stairs, she silently wills Jack and Nathaniel to stay in their bedrooms, does not want them faced with Abby's grief at seven o'clock on a Tuesday morning. She hopes Andrew does not return from his run, that she is not forced into yet another marital charade, not least in front of Abby, the person to whom Andrew has wrought so much damage.

'I found something in Isla's emails.'

A knot tightens in Nicole's throat. She thinks of Andrew's revelation, and a thousand possibilities hurtle through her mind that she cannot – in this brief splinter of time – believe she has not contemplated before. The possibility of a digital footprint between Andrew and Isla, a trail of virtual breadcrumbs just waiting to be followed.

'What did you find?' Nicole's voice shrieks with guilt but Abby does not seem to notice, pulls a ream of paper from her bag.

Please let it not be what I think it is. Please let it not betray what my family has done to you.

'A whole tranche of messages on Isla's computer. Anonymous messages. I printed them off.'

Nicole breathes against the thundering in her chest. As she opens her lips, her tongue peels from the roof of her mouth. 'What kind of messages?'

'Vile messages. Just vile.' Abby pauses as if steeling herself to reveal whatever she has uncovered. The sheaf of paper crumples beneath the tightness of Abby's grip, and Nicole has a sense of watching someone unravel before her eyes.

'Read for yourself.' Abby thrusts the bundle towards Nicole. She reaches out, takes it, forces her eyes to focus on the printed words.

*What kind of 17 yr old sucks off a married man old
enough to be her dad?*

You're a whore, you know that, don't you?

*Is he paying you for it? Is that why you've been fucking
him for weeks now? Or do you actually get off on shagging
men twice your age?*

Acid pools in the back of Nicole's throat, and she dares not
look up, dares not face whatever is coming next.

'I don't know what to do. I feel sick . . .' Abby's voice trails off,
and Nicole instructs herself to read the rest of the messages, hunting for any mention of Andrew's name. But there is nothing. Just
one abusive message after another.

Something clicks inside Nicole, some instinctive drive for self-
preservation; a primeval need to protect her family. If Andrew's
affair with Isla is revealed, there is no telling what the ramifications
might be. It is not a risk Nicole can afford to take. Not a risk she
dares take. 'These are probably from some bored kid at school with
nothing better to do than troll seventeen-year-old girls. You can't
possibly believe it's true. It'll be nothing more than a stupid, sick
prank.'

Abby shakes her head. 'It's not a prank. There are replies from
Isla, asking them to stop. It's clear from what she wrote that it's true.
I don't understand. How can I not have known? How could something like this have happened and I didn't even know? I mean, she
must have been manipulated or coerced or something, mustn't she?
Isla wouldn't do something like that. It's just not like her. Maybe
this man had some kind of hold over her?' Abby is gabbling, her
thoughts outrunning her tongue.

Nicole thinks – as she has done, so many times – about how the relationship between her husband and Abby's daughter may have begun, about Andrew's explanation that he gave Isla a lift a couple of times and it 'just developed' from there. She cannot stop herself wondering – fearing – that it was more deliberate, more targeted on Andrew's part, but it is a thought she cannot allow herself to consider right now. She takes a moment to collect herself. 'I'm so sorry. This is the last thing you need. You must be reeling.' A question flashes in neon lights at the forefront of Nicole's mind. 'Is there any mention of who it might have been? Who Isla was . . . seeing?'

There is a moment of silence into which Nicole feels she is tumbling like Alice down the rabbit hole.

Abby shakes her head. 'No. I've scoured every email searching for clues but there's nothing. I mean, it could be anyone, couldn't it? Someone she met at swimming or through friends or at a party. Literally anyone. How am I going to find out? I have to know who it was. I want them to look me in the eye and tell me why they thought it was okay to sleep with a seventeen-year-old girl. She wasn't even an adult, for god's sake.' Abby buries her face in her hands as though the speculations are taking up too much space in her head.

Coherent thought abandons Nicole, and she desperately tries to imagine what she might say next if she were not harbouring such secrets. 'Have you any idea who the emails might be from?' The thought of someone else knowing about Andrew's relationship with Isla is nauseating, but she cannot indulge that fear now, not while Abby is here.

Abby shakes her head. 'They're all anonymous. But it must be Callum, mustn't it? Who else would be hateful enough to send her messages like that? Nobody else would have any reason, any motive. You know how distraught he was when Isla broke up with him.'

Nicole thinks about Callum, terrified as to what he might do with the information, if it is he who has been sending the emails. She is struck, suddenly, by a bitter sense of regret that she hasn't been nicer to Callum since he arrived at Collingswood, that she hasn't been more welcoming – more effusive – with both Callum and Jenna. She has never been unfriendly, but neither has she gone out of her way to embrace them into the school community. Now, the regret is a stick with which she will beat herself long into the night.

'What do I do? I don't know what I'm supposed to do with this?' Abby wrings her hands as though trying to squeeze some explanation out of them. 'I feel like I'm going out of my mind. I feel like . . . I don't know . . . that I didn't really know Isla at all.'

Nicole rubs a hand across Abby's back. 'You can't think like that. You and Isla had an incredible relationship. You know you did. Whatever this . . . thing was, it was just a teenage blip. Don't let it redefine your relationship with her.'

The kitchen door clicks open and there is Jack, standing in the doorway, bleary-eyed with sleep, his blonde hair dishevelled, looking like the kind of teen who might present a TV show on the Disney channel, and yet, at the same time, still the little boy who used to curl up in Nicole's lap while she read him *Where the Wild Things Are*.

Time seems to warp, to accelerate and slow down in the same moment. Nicole watches Jack clock Abby at the kitchen table, fears what he may have overheard before he opened the kitchen door, berates herself for not having been more careful. She senses the fragility of her grip on her family's welfare, knows she must keep papering over the cracks as best she can.

'Have you just woken up?' She tries to keep her voice bright, optimistic.

Jack's eyes dart towards her: questioning, uncertain. 'Sorry, I didn't know you were . . . I'll just . . .' He pivots around and scuttles into the hall.

Nicole turns to Abby, rearranges her expression. 'I'm sorry. He's just at that awkward age. He didn't mean to be rude.'

Abby does not seem to have heard, stands up abruptly from the kitchen table. 'I'm going to the police. They need to find out who these messages are from. What if there's a link between all this . . .' She waves the sheaf of paper in the air. '. . . and what happened to Isla?'

Nicole feels a bolt of alarm, like a rush of blood to the head. If Abby shows those messages to the police, the trail will lead – eventually, inevitably – back to Andrew, and Nicole cannot allow that to happen. 'But the police have already said they think it was just a random accident. I know those messages are horrible – it must have been dreadful to find them – but they're probably just from someone who was jealous of Isla.'

'But we don't know that for sure, do we? If someone was threatening her online, what's to say they didn't hurt her in real life too?' Abby slings her bag over her shoulder, strides towards the kitchen door like an avenging angel, intent on justice.

Following Abby along the hallway, Nicole tries to think of something – anything – to stem the tide of Abby's fury. 'Let me come with you. I'll just grab a quick shower, and then we can go together. You don't want to go to the police station by yourself.' At least, she thinks, if she is there, then she will know what has been said. At least she will be forewarned, forearmed.

Abby shakes her head. 'Thanks, but I just want to get on with it. I need to get things moving.'

'That's fine. I don't need a shower. I'll get dressed—'

'No, really, I'd rather go on my own.' Abby reaches out, places a hand on Nicole's arm. 'It's not that I don't appreciate the offer. I do. I just need to get this done.'

Nicole nods mutely, unable to find any suggestion that might change Abby's mind. She watches as her best friend opens the front door, walks towards her BMW parked by the side of the road, steps inside.

Panic distorts her thoughts as Abby pulls away, drives towards the police station, where she will show officers the anonymous messages that will, surely, lead back to Nicole's family.

Closing the door, a sense of foreboding overwhelms her. Somebody knows about Andrew's affair with Isla. And if they were angry enough to send Isla those vicious messages, she dares not imagine what they might do next.

Jenna

Jenna slips her coat from her shoulders, hangs it up on one of the pegs by the front door, eases her feet from her shoes.

Walking into the lounge, she calls Callum's name, is met by silence. Glancing down at her watch, she sees it is almost a quarter past seven. Awakening the screen of her phone, she types out a message, asks him where he is, whether he will be home for dinner.

In less than a minute, her phone pings with a reply.

> *Stayed in the library til 7. Heading home now, but just missed a bus and there's not another one for 12 minutes. See you in a bit. X*

She allows herself a moment of relief that he is at the library, being diligent. Since her phone call with Mr Marlowe four days ago, she has been hyper-vigilant about Callum's behaviour, his attitude, any references he makes to school. All he needs to do is keep his head down, work hard, and hopefully the stigma surrounding him at Collingswood will eventually subside.

Heading into the kitchen and opening the freezer to find something for dinner from her stack of batch-cooked meals, she chooses a chilli con carne – one of Callum's favourites – and is about to defrost it in the microwave when the doorbell rings.

As she answers the door, time seems to reverse and comes to a halt in a place Jenna had hoped never to revisit.

'Alright, Mrs J. Callum around?'

Jenna stares at the young man standing on her doorstep, heart hammering in her chest. 'What are you doing here?'

The young man grins. 'That's not a very nice greeting. Just wanna see Callum. He in?'

For a moment, Jenna is speechless. She has not seen Liam Walsh since the day he and Callum appeared together before the youth magistrates' court, charged with aiding and abetting. She has not seen Liam since he was issued with a two-year youth rehabilitation order for being a passenger – alongside Callum – in the stolen car that Ryan Marsh had been driving when he killed a woman. She had hoped never to see him again.

'You gonna ask me in? I could murder a cuppa.' A corner of Liam's mouth curls into a goading smile.

'Callum doesn't want you here and neither do I.' Pulse racing, she moves to close the door, but Liam jams his foot against the frame, pushes against it.

'That's a bit rude. I just wanna see Callum. Can you get him for me?'

Jenna shakes her head. 'Callum doesn't want anything to do with you.'

Liam smirks, his open palm pushing at the door. 'Really? That's not the impression I got when I saw him a few weeks ago.'

For a moment, Jenna is speechless. 'What are you talking about?'

He raises his eyebrows with faux-innocence. 'Didn't he tell you? Maybe he's not such a mummy's boy after all.'

Liam cocks his head provocatively, and it takes all Jenna's self-control not to shove him hard, get him away from her flat. But he is tall, strong, his heavily tattooed biceps well defined beneath the sleeves of his t-shirt.

'Just leave Callum alone. I mean it. I don't want you anywhere near him.' She had hoped her voice would sound threatening but she can hear the tremor in it.

Liam eyes her for a moment, unblinking. And then he laughs, shrugs. 'No worries. I'll catch up with him another time. I know that posh school he goes to.'

Jenna breathes deeply against the pounding beneath her rib-cage. 'Don't you go near him. Do you hear me? I don't want you anywhere near Callum's school.' Images spool through her mind in accelerated time: Liam turning up at Collingswood, causing trouble; Mr Marlowe intervening; the school being handed the excuse they need to expel Callum once and for all. Given the knife edge on which Callum's standing at school already balances, she cannot allow it to happen. 'I mean it. Stay away from my son.'

Liam's eyes narrow at the edges, his smile flattening into a tight, menacing line. Fear prickles Jenna's skin and for a few seconds she is scared – genuinely scared – about what he might do next.

But then he removes his hand suddenly from her front door and begins to swagger away, calling over his shoulder. 'You look after yourself, Mrs J. And tell Callum I'll catch up with him soon, yeah?'

Jenna slams the door closed, pulls the chain across, takes a step back as though, perhaps, Liam is about to burst through. Her hands are clammy and she wipes them on her trousers, tries to steady her breathing.

That's not the impression I got when I saw him a few weeks ago. Liam's taunt echoes in her ears and Jenna tries to tell herself that he was lying, that it cannot be true. Callum is too sensible – too aware of the opportunity he has been given at Collingswood – to jeopardise his future.

But even as she repeats the self-assurances, she cannot silence the other voice in her head, the one reminding her how withdrawn Callum has been of late, not just since Isla's death but before that too. The break-up had knocked his confidence in ways Jenna hadn't anticipated; reigniting his insecurities about Collingswood, about whether he really belonged, about whether he deserved to be there.

The question niggles at Jenna like a pestering child; if Callum was feeling vulnerable about his place at Collingswood, perhaps the obvious place he would seek refuge – the place to which he would retreat for familiarity and security, however perverse it may seem, given the trouble they got him into before – would be with his former school friends. With Liam Walsh.

She recalls Callum returning home the night of Isla's death, the lie he told about the mark across his face – clearly not the result of walking into a door – and wonders what other untruths he may be telling. She recollects the self-satisfied smirk on Liam's face, and the question appears as if by the flick of a switch: how does Liam know where they live if Callum hasn't told him? They moved after Callum got the place at Collingswood. There is no reason Liam should know.

Leaning against the wall, Jenna closes her eyes, tries to regain some semblance of composure before Callum gets home. She will not tell him of Liam's visit, of that much she is sure. If Liam is lying – if his appearance this evening was nothing more than false bravura – she would be playing into his hands by telling Callum.

But doubts continue to circle like vultures over a carcass: perhaps Liam is telling the truth. Perhaps Callum has been spending time with him again.

Jenna's fists curl into tight balls. Because she knows there is only one place that a friendship with Liam might lead for Callum, and it is not a place she has any intention of allowing him to go.

Abby

Abby sits in her car outside the police station, contemplating whether to go inside, whether to reiterate everything she said ten hours ago, at eight o'clock this morning, when she showed the police the cache of anonymous emails sent to Isla.

Detective Webb had read the emails, thanked her for bringing them in, sympathised with how upsetting it must have been to read them. When Abby questioned him outright – wasn't it possible that there was a link between Isla's killer and whoever wrote those emails? – Detective Webb had looked at her almost sadly, the pity unambiguous in his expression, and repeated what he had already told her countless times: that he believed Isla's accident to have been a tragic, random hit-and-run, that there were no grounds to suspect anything more sinister. Abby had waved the ream of paper in the air, asked whether this wasn't evidence enough that there might be another explanation, that perhaps it wasn't random at all, perhaps it was completely intentional. The forbearance on Detective Webb's face had been infuriating as he reassured her that his officers would investigate the emails if she would allow them access to Isla's account, reassured her that they were doing everything they could to uncover the circumstances surrounding her daughter's death. He had concluded far too swiftly, just like Nicole, that the emails were probably the work of a bored teenager, no doubt someone from

Isla's school, perhaps someone she'd fallen out with who was trying to get under her skin. It had taken all Abby's patience to explain that Isla didn't have enemies – she'd been the most popular girl in her year – and her school wasn't like that; it wasn't replete with people who'd do something like this.

Detective Webb had been more interested in the man with whom Isla had been having an affair; did Abby have any idea who he might be? Had Isla given any indication that she was romantically involved? Did Abby think Isla might have confided in any of her friends? Was it usual for Isla to keep secrets? Every question to which Abby had no meaningful response felt like a reproach about her inadequacy as a parent, an open acknowledgement that she hadn't really known her daughter at all: hadn't known what went on in her head, in her heart. Since finding the emails, Abby had been forced to recalibrate everything she thought she knew about Isla: her previously unswerving belief in Isla's truthfulness, her integrity. Now, Abby had to accept that her daughter had been secretive, duplicitous, dishonest. That she must have lied – how many times, Abby would never know – about where she was going, what she was doing, with whom she had been. That she had kept a secret of this magnitude: about an affair with a married man, with someone else's husband, with a man old enough to be her father.

Abby didn't expect a male detective to understand how it made her feel; how she had lain awake last night unable to escape the hideous images of her beautiful seventeen-year-old daughter seduced by a disgusting, middle-aged man: a man old enough to know better. Imagining this man's hands writhing over her daughter's innocent skin. Imagining him touching her, kissing her, inveigling his way into her heart, her body, into places he had no right to be. She didn't expect this detective to understand the pain – the wracking, tormenting pain – that Isla had not felt able to confide in her, that she had kept this part of her life hidden. Or the sheer agonising fact that Abby would now never be able to ask her about it.

When Abby finally left the station this morning – when Detective Webb made it clear he had other things to do, other cases to deal with – she had walked away with exactly the same feelings she'd experienced during every encounter with the police over the past twenty-five days: resentment for allowing herself to be fobbed off, fury with the police for failing to demonstrate any sense of urgency, rage with them for failing to catch her daughter's killer.

On the seat beside her, Abby's phone pings, and she picks it up, sees a message from Nicole.

> *Just checking in to see how you're doing. Any news from the police? X*

Abby drops the phone back onto the seat, feels the temperature of her frustration rise.

She turns back to look at the police station, contemplating whether to go inside, to insist that her visit this morning should have been taken more seriously, that more needs to be done.

And then, suddenly, it hits her. And the moment it does, she cannot understand how it has not occurred to her before. She can only imagine that her anger, her upset, her confusion have mired her thoughts, clouded her judgement. It is so obvious – so transparently, blindingly obvious – that there is a moment's humiliation she has not seen it before, that she was so defensive about the detective's questions earlier. It is clear he reached a conclusion in minutes that it has taken her twenty-four hours to grasp.

He is a suspect. Perhaps the prime suspect.

The man who seduced Isla is the lead suspect in her death. That is why Detective Webb is so interested in uncovering his identity. It is not the person who wrote the anonymous emails that the police think may be culpable of killing her daughter. It is the man who took advantage of Isla so despicably.

The realisation wraps around her throat, presses down on her windpipe.

Thoughts stumble through her mind as if drunk. Perhaps this man – this monster who preyed on her daughter – was angry with her. Perhaps he was desperate to preserve his reputation, his marriage, his family. Perhaps it was over, and Isla was about to expose him.

Perhaps he needed to silence her.

Abby starts the engine, pulls away from the kerb, heads for home, knowing what it is she needs to do. She must scour every inch of Isla's bedroom. She must uncover the identity of the man who coerced her daughter into a relationship. Because if she can do that, she will – she is convinced – find the person responsible for Isla's death.

SEVEN WEEKS BEFORE ISLA'S DEATH

Isla

Isla sat on the closed toilet seat, her hand shaking, holding the thin plastic stick between finger and thumb. The first dawn light glowed feebly through the window, her eyes trained on the test in her hand which would, within the next few minutes, determine her fate.

Sitting, waiting, she could not believe she had been so remiss. The possibility hadn't even occurred to her for days. It had been Sonia – her training partner at swimming – who had expressed relief that she wouldn't have her period for the upcoming county meet. It was only then that Isla realised she couldn't remember when her last one had been. Scrolling through the calendar on her phone and trawling her memory, it dawned on her that she'd missed her period by a fortnight without even realising. Almost two weeks since it was due, and she hadn't even registered it was late. There had been so much else preoccupying her. The upcoming night away with Andrew for which Isla still hadn't fashioned an excuse for her mum. The university application forms to consider, and the increasing awareness that when she returned to school in September, she was only two terms away from sitting her A levels. The swimming sessions five or six times a week and her determination to qualify for the British nationals. And, beyond that, the daily deceptions that made her feel sick to the stomach: the lies, the deceits, the distortions of the truth she concocted every day for her mum, her sister, her friends.

Isla looked out of the bathroom window, across the garden. She was reminded of a weekend in early spring when she and Callum sat out there, books strewn around them, laptops open, studying together. It was only a few months ago, but already it felt like another lifetime.

Isla had barely seen Callum in the two and a half weeks since he spotted her getting out of Andrew's car; she was grateful the summer holidays had begun the same day, and that Callum had gone straight to summer school for a few days. But last Friday, she'd bumped into him outside the local library and had not been able to escape a conversation.

Isla, come on, you must be able to see that it's just . . . really off? He's Nathaniel's dad. He's literally old enough to be your dad. I know you think I'm just pissed off because you dumped me for him. But it's not that. It's just . . . this whole thing is screwed up. Surely you can see that?

Isla had let him rant, knowing she had wronged him, that the least she owed him was the space to vent his grievances. And then, thankfully, her phone had rung – her mum asking if she'd be home for lunch – and she'd had a viable reason to escape.

That evening, unable to placate the gnawing anxiety that Callum might tell someone about her and Andrew, she'd messaged him, implored him again to keep it a secret. His response suggested that all she'd managed to do was offend him even more: *Jesus, Isla, what do you take me for?*

And then, last night, she'd received an anonymous email from an account she didn't recognise.

What kind of 17 yr old sucks off a married man old enough to be her dad?

146

Isla had read the message, sick with apprehension.

The only person who knew about her and Andrew was Callum.

Without hesitation, she had pulled out her phone, opened WhatsApp.

> *So now you're sending me anonymous emails? Just stop it, Callum. I'm sorry for the way I treated you – I really am – but we both just need to move on.*

It had taken only a few seconds for a reply to come through.

> *What are you talking about? What anonymous emails?*

Isla had stared at the screen, trying to order her chaotic thoughts. A part of her brain told her that Callum wouldn't write something like that, it wasn't his style to be cowardly, abusive. But then she remembered his anger the day he'd seen her get out of Andrew's car: *He's Nathaniel's dad, for fuck's sake. It's . . . it's weird, you know that, right?* And now she didn't know what to think.

Isla forced her eyes back down to the pregnancy test in her hand, felt her world begin to disintegrate.

The unmistakable second blue line. The irrefutable confirmation of her worst fears. Her life veering onto a different, untenable path.

◆ ◆ ◆

Isla studied Andrew's face, wishing she could know what he was thinking. It was a bombshell, she understood that, but his silence was unnerving.

Around them, in a pub in Barnes where they'd hastily arranged to meet, men in suits and women in maxi dresses drank overpriced cocktails and bottled beers. Isla sipped a glass of sparkling water, tight with anxiety, waiting for Andrew to respond.

Finally, he looked at her, ironing out the furrow in his brow. 'How are you feeling? Are you okay?'

Isla nodded, words like fishbones stuck in her throat.

'Do you know . . . have you any idea how many weeks you are?'

'About six, I think.'

'Okay. That's good.' There was a twitch in Andrew's right cheek. 'And you haven't told anyone else?'

Isla shook her head.

Reaching across the table, Andrew took hold of her hand. 'It's best we keep this just between us, okay? And don't worry. We'll get this sorted. I'll take care of everything.'

Isla found herself nodding even though she wasn't quite sure why.

'I'll book you into a private clinic. And I'll pay, obviously. I promise I'll find the very best place.'

Isla continued to nod, the meaning of Andrew's words slippery in her ears.

'You'll be in and out on the same day. It's a very quick, simple procedure, and completely safe. I know it's a lot to take in, but you'll be fine. It's just lucky you realised so early.'

As Andrew squeezed her hand, Isla was aware that a decision had been made, one in which she wasn't aware of having had any involvement. A part of her wanted to protest, to insist they discuss it further, explore all the options. That she be allowed an opinion on the matter, at least. But when she tried to think about what she might say – what alternative conclusion might be reached – she realised there was no other viable choice. Andrew was being so matter-of-fact because it was the only feasible outcome.

While Andrew continued talking – suggesting that a surgical abortion was preferable because a medical abortion at home would arouse suspicion, telling her he'd send the appointment details first thing tomorrow as soon as it was booked – Isla could feel shame seeping into her cheeks. It wasn't that she expected Andrew to announce he'd leave Nicole and set up house with her. That wasn't even what she wanted. It was the cavalier attitude with which Andrew was speaking, as though the prospect of her keeping the baby was not even a remote possibility. As though her feelings – her thoughts, her views – didn't matter.

'Stop looking so worried. It's going to be okay.' Running a finger inside the crook of her elbow, Andrew smiled. 'I love you. We'll get through this together, I promise.'

Isla tried to return his smile, tried to imbibe some reassurance from his words. But somewhere deep within her was a sense that this was a defining moment in her life. A moment in which her future was swerving onto a different path, and there was no way of returning to where she had come from – the person she had been – before the events of the past few months.

◆ ◆ ◆

'Hey, Isla, wait up.'

Isla glanced behind her, felt a tug of dismay as she saw Nathaniel pedalling towards her on his bike. He had an irritating habit of popping up when she least wanted to see him – which, these days, was pretty much any time.

'Where are you going?'

Isla looked at the quiet residential street, realised she didn't know. She had left home over an hour ago, been walking ever since, but with no sense of direction, no sense of purpose. There had just been a visceral need to get outside, clear her head, to figure out how she felt about her conversation with Andrew last night.

It had been just after nine-thirty this morning when her phone had pinged with a message from him.

Here are the details of the appointment. I've booked it in your name, but I've paid for it, obviously. It's a very well-regarded clinic and they'll take exceptional care of you. I know how hard this is, and I'm so sorry you're having to go through it. But I think we both know that a termination really is the only option. You'll be okay, I promise. I love you. xx

She had read the message, taken a screenshot so she could access the details of the appointment without scrolling through WhatsApp. She'd tried to unpack how she felt about it – tried to envisage what it would be like, arriving at a Marylebone clinic, going through that procedure, recovering afterwards, all without telling her mum – but her imagination fell short.

What she really wanted was to escape her own thoughts, but they seemed determined to follow her wherever she went.

'Just going for a walk along the river. I needed some fresh air.'

'Mind if I tag along?'

Every instinct in Isla's head screamed that she wanted to be alone, she needed space, that the last person she wanted for company was Nathaniel. But she couldn't improvise a viable reason to refuse him, didn't dare do anything to arouse his suspicions. 'Sure.'

For a few moments they walked in silence, over the bridge as the husk of late-afternoon sunshine clung to the surface of the water. Turning onto the path that led along the Thames, they hugged the river, Nathaniel wheeling his bike beside him.

'You got it fixed then?'

'What?'

'Your bike.'

Nathaniel studied the handlebars for a few seconds. 'Yeah, all sorted.'

On the river, a pair of rowers glided past, and Isla's thoughts turned to swimming and the abortion and how soon she would be able to train after she'd had the procedure. She thought about all the excuses – all the lies – she would have to invent if she had to take time off. But she couldn't allow herself to dwell on that, not now. 'I heard about your driving test. I'm sorry. That sucks.'

Nathaniel shrugged. 'The examiner was an idiot. I could tell she didn't like me straight away. Anyway, I've applied for another one. There's no way I'll fail next time.' He picked at a spot on his cheek, and then stopped abruptly, self-consciously. 'Can I talk to you about something?' He glanced quickly at her and then away again.

Isla was aware of the muscles tightening in her throat, lest she betray the secrets she was keeping. 'Of course.' In accelerated time, she imagined Nathaniel finally declaring his feelings for her and the impossibility of dealing with that, right now, on top of everything else.

'It's just that stuff's a bit weird at home at the moment and I don't really have anyone to talk to about it.'

Isla tried to look attentive, tried not to let the consternation show on her face. The last thing she wanted to discuss with Nathaniel was the status of his home life.

'You know my dad's always been a bit of a workaholic? That's nothing new. But lately he seems different. Even when he's at home, it's like his head is somewhere else. Do you know what I mean?'

Isla nodded. Her palms were beaded with sweat, and she wiped them on the cotton of her shorts.

'It's like he's always thinking about something else, as though he's never really *with* us.'

Isla's skin crawled with an acute awareness that she didn't want to be having this conversation.

'I know he can get totally obsessed with work when he's got some big investment going on, but he's been like this for months now. I can't help thinking . . . I don't know . . . maybe there's something else going on with him.'

Panic quickened Isla's breathing. 'Like what?'

Nathaniel shrugged. 'I don't know. Maybe he's ill or something, and he doesn't want to tell us.'

She tried not to display her relief. 'I'm sure he's not. He's probably just got a lot on. Your dad's always seemed super-healthy to me.'

'Yeah, but so was yours.'

There was a moment's silence.

'Sorry, that was shit of me—'

'It's fine—'

'No, it was a stupid thing to say. I'm sorry. I didn't mean to upset you.'

'You haven't. It's okay.' Grief tangled in Isla's chest, and she forcibly ignored it, would unravel it later when she was alone.

Nathaniel stopped walking, turned to face her, leaned his bike against his hip. 'There's something else that's weird. Even though he's hardly ever at home, when he is, he's all over my mum. It's gross.'

Heat wrapped itself around Isla's neck like an unwanted scarf. 'Really?' The word sounded thin, reedy, as though there was not enough space in her throat to let it free.

Nathaniel nodded. 'He'll barely be at home for a few days and then suddenly he'll be telling Mum how beautiful she is, how amazing he thinks she is, acting like he can't be separated from her.'

Isla tried to repress the stab of jealousy, told herself to stop being stupid, that Nicole was Andrew's wife, that of course he had to be affectionate with her sometimes. Of course he had to go through the pantomime that their marriage was happy, especially in front of Nathaniel and Jack. It would be ridiculous to imagine otherwise. And yet she recalled all the times Andrew had told her his marriage had slipped into the realms of the platonic, that he loved Nicole as the mother of their children but that any romance, any desire, had long since evaporated.

Nathaniel squinted at his watch against the glare of the sun. 'Shit, I'd better go. I said I'd be at Elliot's at six.' Swinging one leg over the crossbar of his bike, he perched on the saddle. 'Thanks for listening. I really appreciate it. Sometimes I think you're the only person who really understands me and my family.'

He turned to leave, and Isla felt nothing but relief that he was going.

As she watched Nathaniel cycle away, his words echoed in her ears: *He'll barely be at home for a few days and then suddenly he'll be telling Mum how beautiful she is, how amazing he thinks she is, acting like he can't be separated from her.*

As Isla continued walking along the river, she told herself that it wasn't important. It was irrelevant how Andrew felt obligated to behave at home for the sake of appearances. He loved her – he had told her so, again and again – and that was all that mattered.

THE PRESENT

Jenna

Jenna sits in the darkened auditorium, watching the sixth-form production of *Macbeth*. On stage, students she knows by sight but not by name stride across the floor, brimming with confidence, enunciating every syllable as though they're reading the ten o'clock news.

Next to her, Callum fidgets in his seat, and Jenna wonders whether she was right to insist they came. Even though Callum helped build the scenery, he'd been resistant to attending the performance; he'd said he wanted to keep a low profile, that it was bad enough half the year were still recycling the same old news about his previous joyriding offence. He didn't want to spend his free time surrounded by jackals skirting the carcass of school gossip, awaiting their turn to feed. But Jenna thought it important they show their faces, that their absence didn't fuel further speculation. She wanted to prove they had nothing to hide, that they deserve to be part of the school community, however Sisyphean a task it may seem.

An actor on stage begins one of the few soliloquies Jenna recognises – *Tomorrow, and tomorrow, and tomorrow* – and Jenna finds her attention wandering, her eyes flitting about the auditorium.

Three rows in front of her sit Abby and Nicole, side by side as they invariably are at school events. Jenna is surprised to see

Abby. It is less than five weeks since Isla was killed, and Jenna had assumed Abby would avoid sixth-form events for the remainder of the year. But Abby has always taken her role as head of the parents' association seriously, treats the voluntary position with all the gravitas of a full-time executive job. If Jenna had known Abby would be there, she might have been as keen as Callum to give the play a wide berth. Instead, she had faced an awkward moment in the ladies' bathroom before the performance, emerging from a cubicle just as Abby entered the room. There had been a moment's hesitation, Jenna unsure whether to say anything, uncertain if Abby would be receptive to her sympathy. And then Abby had walked into one of the stalls, closed the door, and the decision had been made for her.

Callum pulls his phone from his pocket, the screen illuminating in the darkness. Jenna nudges him sharply, raises her eyebrows in silent remonstration. As Callum turns his focus back to the stage, Jenna studies his face, as she has so many times over the past seven days since Liam Walsh's unwelcome appearance: trying to detect any trace of deceit, any hint that Callum is hiding something from her. In her line of work, she knows only too well how duplicitous teenagers can be, understands that she would not necessarily recognise the signs even if Callum were lying to her.

The audience begins to clap, and Jenna realises with a start that the play is over, joins in with the applause even though, in truth, she has barely registered the production. The main thing is that they came, they bought tickets, they are seen to be supporting the school. Surely – *surely* – at some point, parents will move on to new gossip, and Callum's classmates will find something else to obsess over. Surely the teachers will remember what a diligent, high-performing student Callum is and forgive the misdemeanours he committed long before he arrived at the school.

Shuffling out of the brand-new, state-of-the-art auditorium and into the quad, Jenna is about to suggest that perhaps they should head home rather than joining everyone for a drink in the school hall. But then she sees a police car pull into the car park, watches two male officers step out. They look around as if finding their bearings before their eyes land on the group milling outside the theatre.

Anxiety coils in Jenna's stomach. She instructs herself to stop worrying, there is no justifiable reason why the police would want to speak to Callum. And yet she feels Callum tense beside her, senses the fear radiating out of him as they watch Mr Marlowe walk across the immaculately cut lawn to speak to the officers.

And then Mr Marlowe's eyes meet Jenna's, his expression unreadable: apologetic or angry, she cannot tell. Before she has a chance to decipher it, Mr Marlowe and the officers are walking across the grass towards them, and Jenna senses two hundred pairs of eyes pivoting in Callum's direction.

'Callum James? Do you mind if we have a word?'

Callum darts a look at Jenna – frightened, vulnerable, a little boy trapped in a grown man's body – and her sense of maternal protection kicks in.

'What's this about?' Jenna tries to make her voice strong, authoritative, has adopted her poshest accent, but she knows it pales in comparison alongside the genuine confidence of the parents who are now all watching them, waiting.

'Mrs James?'

Jenna nods, decides this is neither the time nor the place to correct the police officer; to tell him it's Ms, not Mrs, that Callum's father left them years ago, that the only reason she hasn't reverted to her maiden name is to maintain a sense of shared identity with her son.

'We'd just like Callum to come down to the station, answer a few questions.'

'What about?'

The officers trade a beleaguered look as though Jenna is being obstreperous, asking to know why they want to interview her son. Behind them, Mr Marlowe observes the scene, and Jenna understands this is yet another blot on Callum's school record, that surely there is going to be a time – perhaps in the not-too-distant future – when Mr Marlowe's patience with him runs out. Around them, all is silent, as parents and students pretend to look at mobile phones, feign a sudden interest in the flowers bordering the lawn, delaying their short walk to drinks in the hall, determined not to miss the drama taking place outside the auditorium.

'It really would be better if we could discuss this in private.' The police officer hooks his thumbs into the waistband of his black trousers, hoists them up over his protruding stomach.

'Perhaps you'd like to use my office?' There is a note of authority in Mr Marlowe's voice: the clear desire to remove this spectacle from public view.

One of the officers nods. 'That would be helpful, thank you.'

Without waiting for a response from Jenna, Mr Marlowe strides towards the sixth-form block, next to the auditorium. An officer raises an eyebrow at Callum, tilts his head to the side, an instruction for Callum to follow. Humiliation throbs in Jenna's cheeks as she and Callum trail Mr Marlowe into the Victorian, red-brick building, the officers close on their heels, into his office on the ground floor.

'Right, I'll leave you to it.' Mr Marlowe looks around the room with an air of resignation, as though he has done all he can to minimise the disruption – the scandal – for tonight at least.

'I'd rather you stayed, if you don't mind.' Jenna turns to the officers. 'Assuming you've no objection?' Jenna wants – needs – Mr Marlowe to know she doesn't have anything to hide; that she is being open, transparent, honest with Collingswood about her belief in Callum's integrity.

The two officers share an eye-rolling exchange before indicating their assent.

Mr Marlowe perches on the edge of an armchair near the door. Jenna and Callum stand in the centre of the room, opposite the officers. Through the window, Jenna can see parents and students talking, gossiping, and she experiences a wave of indignation at the scurry of speculations the officers have instigated.

'It's not standard practice to come to a minor's school to question them, is it? How did you even know we were here?'

One of the officers looks temporarily abashed, glances towards the older officer, who raises a defensive eyebrow. 'We did go to your flat, Mrs James, but there was nobody home. We assumed you'd be here as we knew there was an event at school this evening.' He hesitates, as if assessing how much to reveal. 'We were here, earlier today, speaking to some of Isla Richardson's teachers, trying to get a fuller picture of her life, her friendships. Her relationships.' There is a pointedness to his voice, and Jenna feels Callum flinch beside her.

'What was so urgent that it couldn't wait until later, when we got home, or even tomorrow?' Jenna hears the social worker in her voice, knows she has to assert some authority.

The younger officer takes a deep breath as if preparing a rehearsed speech. 'We've obtained some CCTV footage from the night Isla Richardson was killed. It shows Callum running down a street not far from where the incident occurred, around the time it took place.' He turns to Callum. 'We'd just like to know what you were doing there?'

Jenna looks across at Callum, wills him to speak, to counteract the officers' suspicions. But he just stares at the floor, does not seem willing, or able, to exonerate himself from the officer's implication.

Jenna feels herself square up to the officers, will not allow herself to be cowed by them. She has faced situations like this many times before in her job, with the young people in her care. She tries to inhabit her professional persona, tries to imagine what she would say if Callum were one of her cases rather than her son. 'Running down the street isn't a crime, is it?'

The younger officer turns to look at her, seems surprised by the note of challenge – of defiance – in her voice.

'Of course it's not a crime, Mrs James. But there is some confusion that perhaps you can help clarify. On one of the occasions officers spoke to Callum about Isla Richardson's death – in your presence, I believe – both you and Callum claimed he was at home with you at the time Isla Richardson was killed. We're wondering how it's possible that we have footage of Callum on CCTV near the scene of the crime when he was supposedly at home with you, some thirty minutes' walk away. As we understand it, you made the same claim at Isla Richardson's funeral, in front of multiple witnesses.'

The officer surveys her face, eyebrows raised, as though he has just laid down a winning hand in a game of poker.

Jenna feels the collective gaze descend upon her – the two police officers and Mr Marlowe – can feel the guilty verdict being concluded as the seconds tick by. She thinks of the lie she told at Isla's funeral: a lie concocted in the heat of the moment to deflect from the revelation about Callum's joyriding history, to protect her son from accusations she is sure are unfounded.

She steadies her voice, tries to wrestle back control of the situation. 'I must have got my timings mixed up. There was quite a lot going on that evening, after all.' She swallows hard against her own falsification. 'But more to the point, surely if Callum had been in any way involved in the accident that killed Isla – as you're obviously implying – he couldn't have been running down the street at the same time? That stands to reason, doesn't it?' Jenna hears a note of victory in her voice even as disquiet pulses in her cheeks.

'That's precisely what we want to ascertain.' The older officer sighs. 'Mrs James, I really think this conversation would be better conducted at the station. I'm sure you're no keener than we are to prolong any disruption to the school's event this evening.'

Jenna glances out of the window again, sees parents and students still gathered in the quad, senses their morbid curiosity. At the edge of the lawn, near the window, she sees Abby gesticulating wildly to Nicole, and it is as if Jenna can feel Abby's fury emanating from her like solar flares from the sun. She knows she cannot put Callum through this debacle any longer. 'Fine. But I've got my car. We'll follow you to the station.' There is no way she is having Callum carted away in a police car in front of the entire sixth form, knows that the officers have a duty to minimise conflict, that they cannot insist Callum travels to the station with them if he is not being arrested.

The senior officer nods. 'That's fine, Mrs James. It's the station on Broad Street. Do you know it?'

She nods. She's been there with young people under her supervision more times than she cares to remember.

As the officers head out of Mr Marlowe's office, across the lawn, Jenna takes hold of Callum's arm, steers him towards her car. Behind them, she senses dozens of eyes boring into the back of her neck, as though she and her son are figures in a circus freak show, existing purely for the ghoulish entertainment of others.

Resentment simmers inside her; it does not matter how hard Callum works, how clever he is, what he might achieve, he will always be an outsider here, will always be the one at whom people point an accusatory finger. He will forever be the student of whom everyone automatically thinks the worst purely because of his background.

Stepping into her car, Jenna recalls the night Callum was arrested for joyriding: a night during which she discovered just how much fear a person could feel without actually suffocating from it. After Callum's trial and his acceptance at Collingswood, she had allowed herself to believe that perhaps the trouble was behind them. Perhaps there really were such things as second chances and clean slates. But as the police car heads out of the imposing black gates with Jenna following behind, she sees the sea of faces watching them from the school quad, and the thought solidifies in her mind that they will never be free of Callum's past.

All the way to the station, she promises Callum that she's got his back, she will stand by him, whatever happens. She assures him that she believes in him, believes he has done nothing wrong, whatever the CCTV footage may imply. And yet, throughout the fifteen-minute car journey, she cannot silence the voice in her head asking if she is sure, asking whether there is not a sliver of doubt in her mind. Questioning what she will do if it turns out she is wrong.

Abby

Abby listens to the recorded message for the umpteenth time. Swallowing her frustration, she ends the call, puts her phone face down on the kitchen table. It is almost twenty-four hours since Callum was questioned by the police, during which she has left half a dozen messages for the detective supposedly investigating Isla's case, and he has not even done her the courtesy of returning her call. All the information she has gleaned thus far is from third-party sources: the friend who saw Callum and Jenna emerging from the police station on Broad Street at nine forty-five last night; the gossip circulating at school, relayed to her by another parent, that there is CCTV footage showing Callum near the scene of her daughter's death; the knowledge, received earlier from Nicole, whom she had badgered to ask Nathaniel, that Callum has been at school today, tight-lipped and defensive.

The thought of it – the thought of Callum waltzing around school as though he has nothing whatsoever to feel guilty about – causes a knot of fury to pull taut around Abby's heart. She picks up her phone, taps out another email to Detective Webb – her fourth today – asking him to contact her as soon as possible. The detective's lack of urgency is infuriating and incomprehensible in equal measure.

Over the past week, Abby has felt she is going out of her mind, hunting for clues as to the identity of the married man who coerced her daughter into a relationship. She has searched Isla's bedroom, looking for diaries, letters, notes, emails – anything that might shed light on who he was – but has uncovered nothing of use. In the trunk at the bottom of Isla's bed, beneath fleece blankets and some scatter cushions, Abby found a hoard of items she has never seen before: two necklaces, three pairs of earrings, a Mulberry crossbody bag, a Montblanc fountain pen – all extravagant items Isla would never have been able to afford herself: would never have wanted, as far as Abby knows. Items Abby assumes were gifts from the man she was seeing. Abby has examined each item, hoping to find a note, a gift card, anything that might reveal the man's name. But there is nothing beyond the implication that the man in question is affluent, ostentatious.

The thought of Isla hiding all those gifts in her bedroom – hiding them where Abby was unlikely to find them – reignites her fury towards the monster who no doubt gave them to her. But she will not give up looking, however painful it may be. She has to discover the identity of the man who thought it permissible to take advantage of her daughter in such a repugnant way. She has even considered asking some of Isla's friends – Meera, Jules or Yasmin – to see if Isla confided in them, but she cannot bear the prospect of telling them if they don't already know, does not want to tarnish Isla's reputation if she had chosen not to tell them herself.

The front door slams, and Abby looks at the time, realises that Clio must be home. She hears her footsteps clumping through the hall, wonders what version of her daughter she will be greeted by today – quiet and withdrawn or angry and defiant.

As soon as Clio walks into the kitchen, Abby sees the scowl across her forehead and understands immediately that this is a day to tread carefully around her daughter's emotions.

'Hi sweetheart. How was your day?'

Clio walks past Abby, heads straight for the fridge. 'Fine.' Grabbing a can of San Pellegrino, she pulls open the ring, drinks thirstily.

Abby studies her daughter's face. Dark rings hang like crescent moons beneath her eyes, and Abby wonders whether Clio is having trouble sleeping or if she is staying up late, watching TikTok videos or messaging with her friends. 'I thought maybe we could order in sushi tonight and watch a film. What do you think?'

Clio shakes her head, avoids Abby's gaze. 'I'm going out.'

'Where? It's a school night.'

Clio takes another glug of drink before replying. 'Just to Freya's for a bit.'

Abby forcibly instructs herself not to object, to recognise that Clio needs to manage her grief in her own way, even if that means always being with her friends. 'Will you have something to eat first?'

'No, I told her I'd go over as soon as I'd had a shower and got changed.'

'I can give you a lift.'

Clio throws her can in the recycling bin, heads towards the door. 'It's fine, I'll walk.'

Abby hears her trudging up the stairs towards her bedroom on the top floor.

The house feels preternaturally quiet, the lonely hours until bedtime stretching before Abby like a weary yawn. A sudden, over-powering sense of loss grabs hold of her as she imagines a parallel world, one in which Isla is still alive, in which she walks through the door and sees immediately – as she always did – that Abby is feeling fragile, vulnerable. A scenario in which Isla pretends she has no plans this evening, suggests takeout and a movie. Abby will know it is untrue, that Isla would have planned to see Meera or Kit or Jules, will feel equal parts guilt and gratitude that her daughter is sacrificing an evening with friends in order to keep her company.

Grief skewers like a knife in Abby's chest. The enormity of Isla's loss fills the room, her daughter's absence a deafening silence.

Closing her eyes, she tries to manage the pain of her loss. She had believed that nothing could ever hurt as much as the death of her husband. Now she knows there is worse – far worse – than losing your partner at the age of forty-one. To lose a child is to be robbed of your trust in the natural order of things: to experience equal parts rage and despair, resentment and disbelief. It is unnatural, outliving your offspring, wrong in every possible way. Abby feels it – feels that perversity – in every fibre of her being. To lose your child when they are seventeen, on the cusp of adulthood, just when you can see their future stretching out before them, just when you sense that perhaps you have done a passable job at raising them: to lose a child then is the cruellest trick of all. It is insufferable. Sometimes she cannot help feeling that if it weren't for Clio, she would have little reason to continue.

Snapping open her eyes, Abby wipes that thought from her mind. She knows that allowing such ideas to fester is dangerous. She contemplates calling Nicole, seeing if she is free to come over for dinner, as a distraction from her all-consuming grief, but decides against it. She has relied far too heavily on Nicole already over the past few weeks, has relied on her endlessly over the past five years since Stuart died. She does not, in truth, know how she would have got through her grief without Nicole's support.

From somewhere in the hallway comes the trilling of a phone. Abby heads out of the kitchen, spies Clio's mobile – usually permanently attached to her daughter's hand – lying on the wooden radiator cover amidst a mountain of letters that Abby cannot find the energy to open. As she reaches it, the ringing halts.

Picking it up, she notices a message from Freya on the home screen.

> *Don't forget your ID. Tonight is going to be SICK. Sam's got whippets. See you at the station at 6.*

Abby reads the message, disquiet cantering in her chest.

Opening her own phone, she googles 'whippets', discovers they are the silver canisters of laughing gas she sometimes sees strewn across the pavement or collected beneath benches in the park.

Alarm bells ring in Abby's ears. Clio is only fifteen. Abby is aware that teenagers push boundaries, but this is new territory for her: Clio outright lying about where she is going, what she is doing. Clio meeting up with people – *Sam* – whom Abby has never heard of. Clio taking drugs. Except perhaps this isn't new territory at all. Perhaps Clio lies to her all the time and Abby simply hasn't known until now.

Glancing up the stairs, she hears the hum of the shower, turns back to Clio's phone. She has seen her daughter tap in her passcode so many times it is as familiar to her as her own. A part of her knows she is invading her daughter's privacy, but on this occasion it feels necessary, imperative even; she has a duty of care to find out what Clio is up to.

Scrolling through her daughter's messages, she encounters long threads filled with emojis, gifs, slang she does not understand. But nothing obviously concerning; nothing as egregious as the outright lie Clio has told her this evening. Opening Clio's camera roll, Abby scrolls through endless selfies of Clio and her friends in mundane settings, countless screenshots of various TikTok accounts.

And then her eyes alight on a series of photographs from Friday night, two weeks ago. Clio vaping, smoke curling from her lips, her arms draped around the shoulders of boys – young men in their twenties – who look too old to be keeping company with fifteen-year-old girls. Clio drinking from a bottle of beer in what looks to be a bar or club. Clio sitting in the driving seat of a car, hands on the steering wheel, laughing into the camera. Abby clicks on the photo to ascertain the details of when it was taken: 1.04 a.m. And yet, on Friday nights, if Clio stays out, she always says she is at Freya's. Until now, Abby had no reason to disbelieve her. No reason to verify the truth of the claim with Freya's mother.

Looking back down at the photo, thoughts spiral in Abby's mind: where the photo was taken, and by whom. What on earth Clio was doing behind the wheel of a car at one o'clock in the morning. Whether Clio is regularly drinking and taking drugs with older boys and, if she is, what else she might be doing.

Anxiety constricts her throat as she continues to scroll through the photos.

And then she sees something that makes her breath hold still in her lungs.

It is a series of photographs taken the night Isla died. Grainy photos, on maximum zoom. And yet there are two figures, clearly visible.

Isla and Callum, standing on the street close to Meera's house.

Abby sifts through the photographs – so many of them, thirty or more – knowing she has peeked through a door she was never meant to open, unable to close it now that she knows what's behind.

It is a sequence of pictures that tell an undeniable story: arms gesticulating in the air, a palm held out in front of a face, a back turned away. An argument.

Grief and angst entwine in Abby's throat. Seeing photos of Isla the night she died is like being swept out to sea by an engulfing wave. She tries to zoom in on the photos, tries to decipher the expression on her daughter's face, but the images blur and haze, leaving her with nothing but a series of meaningless pixels.

Clicking on the information button, she checks the time one photo was taken, then another and another. Anger swells inside her. The last was taken at nine o'clock, just minutes – literally twenty-five minutes – before people from the party went outside and found Isla's body in the road. Here is proof – incontrovertible proof – of what she has long suspected: that Callum is one of the prime suspects in her daughter's death.

And then another thought dawns on Abby.

Clio has all these photos on her phone, proving that Isla and Callum were arguing outside the party just minutes before Isla's death, and yet she has not shared them with Abby or the police.

A realisation creeps into Abby's mind, unsure it wants to be seen.

If Clio took all these photos of her sister the night she was killed, then Clio had been watching Isla. Spying on her. Photographing her from afar.

Clio was present just before Isla was killed.

Abby spools back through her memory to recall where Clio was supposed to be that night. Freya's, she is sure. She is always at Freya's. And yet, according to the evidence in her hand, Clio was not at Freya's. Clio was standing on Windermere Road, spying on her sister.

Scrolling back further through Clio's photo roll, her eyes catch on a series of pictures that send fear snaking across her skin.

They are photos of Isla, downloaded from the school newsletter, the swim club website, the online albums Abby keeps in the cloud for them all to share.

Except these are not normal photos. Every single picture – a dozen or more – has been doctored. Each one has been altered in the most vile way imaginable.

In one image, blood has been digitally drawn dripping from Isla's eyes. In the next, a crude, animated, thrusting penis has been placed next to Isla's mouth. In another, an arrow pierces Isla's chest.

It is the final photograph, however, that makes Abby's blood run cold.

It is a photograph of Isla on their most recent holiday, on a beach in the Maldives. She is laughing into the camera, having just emerged from the sea, her long hair draped across her shoulders. It is one of Abby's favourite photographs; Isla looks so happy, so ebullient, so full of vitality. It is a photo Abby has framed in her bedroom.

Except this version is nothing like the original. This version is an abomination. In this iteration, someone has drawn a noose around Isla's neck and written, in thick red font, across Isla's body, two words: *Die Bitch*.

Abby stares at the photograph, overcome by a sense of vertigo, unsure of her footing, as though, if she takes a step forward, she may fall into an unknown abyss.

The click of the bathroom door two floors above causes Abby to fumble with Clio's phone. Hands shaking, she exits the photo app, returns to the home screen, places the mobile back where she found it just as Clio arrives at the top of the stairs, wrapped in an oversized bath towel.

'I can't find my phone.'

Abby allows a beat, determined not to give herself away. 'It's just there, by the front door.' She points, as though she has only just seen it herself.

Clio does not answer, does not thank Abby for helping her locate it. Instead, she thumps down the stairs, grabs the phone and tramps back up, one hand scrolling, the other holding the towel tight around her chest.

Watching her go, Abby thinks about all the years since Stuart's death that Clio has been overtly rivalrous with Isla. All the times Isla tried to reach out to her – tried to reconnect with her, to rediscover the closeness they'd enjoyed when they were younger – only to be rebuffed. She thinks about how jealous Clio has been in recent years: jealous of Isla's swimming, her academic achievements, her popularity. She thinks about how emotionally volatile Clio has been since Isla's death – antagonistic, truculent, argumentative – volatility Abby has put down to Clio's grief, but now a niggling suspicion worms its way into her head and will not leave.

She recalls the night Isla was killed: how Clio had said she was sleeping at Freya's and then returned, unexpectedly, without good reason, not long before the police arrived.

Her brain replays the images she has just seen on Clio's phone: photos stalking Isla the night she was killed. She recalls the horrific doctored photos she knows will haunt her in the darkness of night: *Die Bitch*. A voice whispers into the silence, dripping poison in her ear, filling her head with suspicions she dares not entertain. Because she knows that if she allows herself even a splinter of belief that they may be true, there is a risk her whole world will implode.

Nicole

'What's for dinner?'

Nicole looks up from her laptop, pauses writing the email she is drafting to Jack's Head of Year about the management of his ADHD at school.

'I'm doing a Thai curry.' She waits for the inevitable eye roll, which Nathaniel duly delivers. Thai curry is Jack's favourite, and cooking it always seems to provoke some latent sibling rivalry in Nathaniel.

Looking at Nathaniel now – at his tall, angular frame that may never fill out – she wishes there was a way to get inside his head, read his thoughts. Not the thoughts he chooses to share with her – so often full of bravado and bluster that seventeen-year-old boys seem to think is a sign of their masculinity – but his real thoughts, real feelings. His real fears.

'How was your driving lesson?' It is over twelve weeks since Nathaniel failed his first driving test. The backlog is so great that he has had to wait over three months for the re-test he is taking next week.

'Fine.'

'Are you feeling okay about it?'

Nathaniel shrugs, and Nicole does not push him any further, knows how desperate he is to pass, how humiliated he was when he failed the first time around.

The kitchen door opens and Jack walks in – shoulders hunched, head down – the lack of childhood inhibitions long since replaced by adolescent awkwardness; he is not yet fully grown, still four inches shorter than his brother, chest not yet expanded. He is not, she has always thought, like other boys: more sensitive, less full of bravura. He spends his weekends go-karting with his friend, Luke, and Nicole has always been pleased that he is doing something outdoors, not glued to computer games like so many boys his age. But lately Jack has been spending more time at home alone, and Nicole does not know how to draw him out of his shell.

Jack slouches towards the bread bin, breaks off a chunk of French stick, while Nathaniel scrolls through his phone. She suspects neither of her sons believe the story she has concocted about the sudden onset of insomnia that has driven Andrew to sleep in the spare room. She is aware that the friction between her and Andrew is palpable; she can no longer look her husband in the eye, bristles the moment he walks into a room. Not that she and Andrew inhabit the same room very often these days; Andrew prefers to work late every night, goes to the office at weekends as a means of avoiding her, a tactic Nicole is more than happy to encourage. Just a few weeks ago, she believed her family was happy. Now it seems like a tired, worn blanket: one loose thread and the whole thing has unravelled.

'You'll never guess what happened with Callum this afternoon?'

Nicole feels the muscles tighten across her shoulders. 'What?'

'Zach said he didn't want to be diversity and inclusion officer any more so Callum offered to do it instead. Can you believe it? He was practically arrested yesterday and today he wants to be part of the Head of School team. Everyone knows he probably had something to do with Isla's death.'

'Nathaniel, that's enough.' Nicole's voice is sharper than she intended.

'What? It's true—'

'I mean it, Nathaniel. You can't go around spreading baseless rumours about people. You know better than that.'

Nathaniel rolls his eyes. 'Whatever.' Turning around, he walks out of the kitchen, traipses up the stairs.

'You okay?' She looks at Jack – eyes rimmed with tiredness – and wishes she could fast-forward the next few years, catapult him to a time and place where he is more sure of himself, when things have settled down.

Jack nods. 'Fine. Going to my room.'

Nicole watches him slope out of the kitchen. All she wants is for her boys to be happy. For them to be safe and contented and at peace with themselves. It is the most difficult aspect of parenting, she has found: the powerlessness to fashion the world as you would like it to be for your children. Her inability to shield her boys from adversity feels like one of the most inevitable failures of motherhood.

Ever since Abby showed her the anonymous messages eight days ago, Nicole has been waiting for the truth to come to light. She feels as though she is living in a feverish state of anticipation, for the thin thread on which her family's security hangs to finally snap. For the person who sent all those anonymous emails to reveal the name of the man who was sleeping with Isla. Or for the police to tell Abby they have uncovered the identity of both the anonymous emailer and the man who preyed on her daughter. Every time Abby phones or messages her, Nicole is convinced this is the moment her family's lives will implode.

The chiming of the doorbell interrupts the silence. Nicole glances at the time – a quarter to six – suspects it will be one of the Amazon delivery drivers who visit daily with items Andrew has ordered.

Instead, when she opens the door, Nicole is greeted by a pair of male police officers. Fear thrums beneath her ribs, and she is certain this will be the scene she has been dreading.

'Mrs Forrester? Have you got five minutes? We've got an update on your stolen vehicle.'

Nicole does not know whether to feel relieved or anxious. Standing back, she gestures for the two officers to come in, directs them towards the kitchen. Glancing up the stairs, she hopes neither Nathaniel nor Jack emerge from their bedrooms until the officers have left.

Following them into the kitchen, she waits patiently while they introduce themselves. They sit down at the kitchen table, decline her offer of tea or coffee.

'We wanted to let you know that we've found your car.'

'Really? Where?' Nicole cannot hide her surprise. A part of her had wondered if she might never see it again.

'On the Springfield Industrial Estate. Do you know it? It's only about a mile and a half away.'

Nicole shakes her head. 'I don't think so. Is the car okay? Will I be able to have it back?'

The two officers share a loaded glance. 'Actually, it appears to have been involved in a collision. There's a sizeable dent to the front of the vehicle. Some tests are being carried out, but in the meantime, we'll need you and anyone else who regularly uses the car to come down to the station as soon as possible for fingerprinting.'

'Why?'

'We just need to eliminate anyone who regularly uses the car so we can check for unknown fingerprints – prints belonging to whoever stole it. It's routine procedure, nothing to worry about.'

Nicole nods as the police officers give her details about where to go, whom to speak to, impress on her the necessity of getting everyone in the family to be fingerprinted as soon as possible to allow the investigation to proceed. The officers apologise that they do not know when her vehicle will be returned, inform her that she should update her insurance company in the meantime.

Nicole listens, half an ear on the hallway in case the boys should appear. She would rather they hear this news from her than from two anonymous policemen. Because the officers may not be saying it – perhaps they have not even made the link yet – but the circumstantial evidence seems obvious to her. Nicole's car went missing the night Isla Richardson was killed. And now her car has been found on an industrial estate, sporting a dent commensurate with a collision. She would love for it to be nothing more than a coincidence, but the possibility of a connection is undeniable.

She lets the police officers out, bids them goodbye, closes the door behind them. Her mind races and she cannot imagine how she is going to impart this latest update to Nathaniel, to Jack, to Andrew. And, worst of all, to Abby.

SIX WEEKS BEFORE ISLA'S DEATH

Isla

Isla walked out of the clinic, raised a hand to her eyes to shield them from the flare of the sun. Her legs felt unstable, as though the muscles in her thighs had become slack, like the limbs of a newborn foal. She told herself it was all in her mind, that there was no physiological reason for her to feel so unsteady, that the doctor said the procedure had gone well: *'You may feel a bit sore and tender for a few days, and you can expect some bleeding for a couple of weeks. If you're worried at any time, just give the reception team a call. But I'm not expecting any complications.'*

Logically, Isla knew it was a routine procedure, that thousands of women had it every day, that it was unlikely there'd be any medical repercussions. Rationally she knew she was privileged to have access to it, that millions of women around the world weren't so lucky. She knew she was fortunate Andrew had paid for her to go to a private clinic where her room had resembled an upmarket hotel. And yet, she felt overwhelmed by a feeling of vulnerability, of precariousness, as though her sense of equilibrium were balanced on a knife edge, threatening to tip over.

Pulling out her phone, she opened WhatsApp, tapped out a message to Andrew.

I'm all done. x

Watching the two grey ticks turn blue, she experienced a stab of guilt for the lie she had told her mum this morning; that she was heading to the Hunterian Museum, somewhere she'd been meaning to go for ages but never had an opportunity to visit during term time. There had been no hint of disbelief from her mum because Isla never usually lied. She'd never had cause to before her relationship with Andrew, but now her deceptions flooded her with guilt. More than anything, she wished her mum could be with her right now: to comfort her, console her, reassure her she was going to be okay. But Isla knew it was impossible. To open that can of worms was unimaginable.

Her phone pinged with a reply from Andrew.

Hope you're okay. Just on a work call. I'll get a car ordered for you and send you the details. I'll call as soon as I'm done. x

Isla read the message, overcome by a sense of abandonment: the need for someone to be there, to look after her. Tears pricked her eyes and she blinked them away, experienced a sense of preemptive humiliation should she begin to weep on a Marylebone street at half past four in the afternoon.

On the road in front of her, a car sped through the traffic lights, sounding its horn furiously. Isla tensed, her whole body on high alert: taut, anxious, agitated. Looking down at her phone, she willed the booking to arrive, felt inexplicably self-conscious as though every person walking past her – every man in a suit talking loudly through Bluetooth headphones, every woman in a flowery dress, every mother pushing a buggy – knew exactly where she had been and what she had done.

A message came through on her phone and she swiped it open, found a screenshot of a booking from the executive car hire company Andrew always used, along with a message.

*Car should be with you in about 5 mins – I've had it
on standby for the past hour. Booking details above. I'm
really sorry I can't get out of work – just one of those
weeks. But I'll call later, just as soon as I wrap up here. x*

Closing WhatsApp, Isla glanced up and down the street, hoping the black Mercedes – they were always black Mercedes – would arrive soon. The sun glared at her, swathing her in heat, sweat trickling down her spine into the small of her back. Glancing around, she stepped into the respite of a shaded doorway.

Even now, she couldn't decide whether she wished Andrew had accompanied her to the clinic. At least, if he had, she would be on her way home now. But he had apologised profusely, said work was frantic, explained that he couldn't possibly get away for an entire afternoon. *'It's probably too much of a risk anyway, don't you think? If anyone happened to see me going in there with you, that would be disastrous.'*

A black sedan pulled up at the kerb and Isla checked the licence plate against the booking on her phone, walked towards it, tapped on the window. Stepping into the back of the air-conditioned car, she sank into its leather seats, was grateful that these drivers never expected conversation.

A sudden, grinding pain clawed at her and she placed a hand reflexively across her stomach. Looking at the time on the dashboard, she realised it was another forty-five minutes until she could take the next dose of painkillers. She wished she were at home already, under the duvet, curtains drawn. She'd already planned the excuse she would use with her mum: that she must have picked up a tummy bug, that she hoped it was nothing a day or two's rest wouldn't remedy. Her swim coach would be unhappy she'd be missing training but there was nothing Isla could do about that.

Opening her Gmail, she felt a stab of apprehension as she saw the now familiar anonymous address at the top of her inbox, the subject line empty, as always. A part of her brain told her to delete it without opening it, to block the sender, to prevent any more hateful messages reaching her. But she couldn't. She didn't dare. Because she feared the repercussions if she ignored them, feared she might provoke them even more with her silence.

She held her breath as she read the few short lines.

> *You know he's only doing it because you offered it to him on a plate. You're literally nothing more than somewhere for him to put his dick. Slut.*

Isla glanced up at the driver as though perhaps he knew what she was being accused of. But his face was impassive, eyes forward, and she looked back down at her phone, tapped out a reply, acid rising up through her chest and into her throat.

> *Please just keep it to yourself. We didn't mean for it to happen. I don't want anyone to get hurt.*

Her finger hovered over the send button, remembering all the internet safety talks they'd had at school over the years.

Don't engage with trolls.

Never respond to abusive messages.

Always report any unwanted, malicious or harmful communications.

Ignoring the advice in her head, she sent the message, imagined it landing in her stalker's inbox, couldn't help but speculate how they might react, what they might do next. The single most important thing for Isla right now was ensuring that, whoever the sender was, they weren't incited to make her secret public.

Filing the email into her 'WSE' folder – Weird Stalker Emails – she hoped it was labelled blandly enough that should anyone ever get hold of her phone they would be unlikely to find it. She wasn't sure why she was keeping the messages; only that she could not bring herself to delete them.

Slipping off her trainers, Isla brought her knees to her chest, tried to thwart the pain grinding deep in her pelvis. The satnav on the dashboard indicated it was almost an hour's journey home, and Isla silently cursed herself for having forgotten her headphones, for not being able to shut out the world for the next sixty minutes. In truth, she'd hoped Andrew might surprise her, might have been waiting outside the clinic when she emerged. It was a hope she had not allowed herself to acknowledge until now.

A fierce, grating pain made her hug her knees tighter to her body as though she could squeeze the discomfort out of her. She became aware suddenly of a yearning for her dad, for him to be beside her in the back of the car, for her to be able to rest her head against his shoulder. To feel the safety of his embrace and know that whatever mess she was in, he would help get her out of it.

Except she knew that if he were alive, he would not be in the car with her. Because she would have been mortified to tell him she had got herself into this situation. Ashamed of the way she had let him and her mum down. Ashamed that she was not the person they believed her to be.

Leaning her head against the window and closing her eyes, she willed the minutes to pass quickly by until she would be at home, in bed, alone.

◆ ◆ ◆

'How are you feeling?'

Isla looked at Andrew, sitting opposite her in an Italian restaurant, far enough from home that their chances of being spotted were negligible. 'Okay, I think.'

'You sure? I know what a difficult thing it must be to go through and I'm sorry I couldn't be there with you on Tuesday. You definitely feel well enough to be here? We can rearrange for another evening if you'd rather, and I can drop you near home.'

Isla shook her head. 'Honestly, I'm okay.' She wasn't sure why she didn't want to tell Andrew about the stomach cramps she'd experienced for the past two nights, or the heavy bleeding that had required a change of sanitary towel every two hours. She didn't want to tell him about the uncontrollable fits of crying or the debilitating sense of fatigue. She didn't want him to know about the guilt she felt when she'd lied to her mum about a phantom tummy bug, lied again as she left the house to meet Andrew, reassuring her that she was feeling better, that she was going to Kit's for the evening, that she wouldn't be home too late, the lies tripping shamefully from her tongue.

'So the clinic was okay? They looked after you well?' Andrew took a sip of negroni.

'It was fine. They were nice.' The response emerged as if on autopilot and she wished she didn't feel so awkward, so ill at ease in Andrew's company. It was as though they were both on their best behaviour, like strangers on a first date.

'That's good. I know it must have been awful, but at least you were well looked after. That's the main thing.'

There was a strange note in Andrew's voice, and it dawned on Isla that perhaps he wanted to be thanked for finding a good clinic, booking her in, paying whatever the exorbitant fee might have been. For ensuring she would be well looked after by a group of strangers when he wouldn't be there to look after her himself.

Isla pretended to study the menu, told herself to stop being ridiculous. It was sleep deprivation and hormones making her think such stupid thoughts. When she considered it logically, rationally, she understood it just wasn't feasible – just wasn't practicable – for Andrew to have accompanied her on Tuesday. The risks would have been too great.

'What do you fancy to eat?'

Isla continued to study the menu. 'I'm not sure. I'm not that hungry.'

'You usually love scallops. Or sea bass? There are some specials on the board, if you fancy something different. The tuna carpaccio sounds good.' Andrew was waffling as though he, too, was unsure about this new sphere within which they were operating.

The waiter arrived at their table, asked if they were ready to order. Eyes scanning the menu, Isla chose a salad, listened as Andrew ordered a rump steak – medium rare – with a side order of broccoli and a glass of Barolo.

As the waiter left, an uncomfortable silence descended. Isla tried to think of something to say, found that her mind was blank.

'I really am sorry that you had to go through that on Tuesday. It must have been awful. I feel dreadful about it.'

Isla shook her head. 'It wasn't your fault—'

'But it was, in a way. If I hadn't fallen for you, if we hadn't begun this relationship, you'd never have been in that situation.'

Thoughts felt fuzzy in Isla's head, and she could not fashion a response.

'It's made me realise how selfish I've been. How selfish I'm being. You're young, you're beautiful, you've got your whole life ahead of you. You should be spending time with your friends, having fun, going to parties. Not in a relationship with an old man like me.' Andrew forced a laugh that sounded like the low growl of a car engine.

His words felt blurry to Isla, like landmarks viewed through the window of a high-speed train. 'But I want to be in a relationship with you. It's not selfish if it's what I want too.'

Andrew ran his fingers through his hair. 'I just think you deserve to be a normal young woman, doing all the things normal seventeen-year-old girls do.'

'What does that mean?' Isla's breath felt shallow suddenly. Andrew never usually referred to her age. It was a tacit agreement between them not to, to ignore the fact of their sizeable age difference. As he'd said at the outset of their relationship, age was irrelevant when two people felt about each other the way they did.

Andrew studied her face, sighing deeply as though the weight of the world were on his shoulders. 'I think the events of the past couple of weeks have made me realise how unfair our relationship has been on you—'

'Unfair in what way?'

He took hold of her hand. 'Isla, you know how much I care about you. The last four months have been incredible. I've loved our time together. But what's happened . . . It's been a real wake-up call for me that it's just not fair on you. You should be dating boys your own age. You should be out having fun.'

Isla pulled her hand free, wiped her palm on the thick cotton napkin. Andrew's words swam in her head. A part of her needed him to say it out loud, to have the courage to articulate it. Not to hide behind euphemisms and platitudes and cowardly attempts to pretend he was doing this for her. 'Are you breaking up with me?'

The muscles in Andrew's throat rose and fell as he swallowed, as if he were weighing up his words until he had the right measure. 'It pains me to say it, but I honestly think it's for the best. You've got your whole life ahead of you.'

Incredulity made Isla falter for a moment. 'For the best? How is it best for me if you break up with me?'

Andrew glanced sideways to where another couple at a neighbouring table were glancing surreptitiously in their direction. She watched as he smiled apologetically, as though perhaps Isla were a stroppy teen, he the personification of paternal forbearance.

Pushing back her chair – hearing it scrape defiantly across the wooden floor – Isla grabbed her bag, ran out of the restaurant, into the street. She couldn't believe he was doing this. Not now. Not *today*. She'd thought he'd brought her to a restaurant because he wouldn't be so crass as to take her to a hotel room two days after she'd aborted their baby. But now she realised he had a different motivation entirely: to ensure they were in a public place when he dumped her. Somewhere she was less likely to cause a scene.

'Isla! Come back.'

She ignored Andrew's voice behind her, delayed no doubt by him thrusting cash at the waiter to pay for dinner and drinks that would now not be consumed. She continued along the busy London street, where office workers spilled out of pubs enjoying the warm August evening. Turning into a quiet side road that was a shortcut to the station, pain clenched her stomach, a cruel reminder of all that had happened over the past forty-eight hours.

A hand grabbed her arm, and she spun around, shook it off. 'Don't touch me!'

Frustration furrowed Andrew's forehead. 'Isla, please. It doesn't need to be like this. I'm only doing what I think is best for you.'

'Don't give me that. You can't do this. You can't dump me two days after I've had an abortion. Who does that?' Isla was aware of her voice beginning to crack and she swallowed hard against it.

'There'd never be a good time for a conversation like this, you know that. I just think we have to be sensible. You've already been through a horrible experience because of our relationship. There are just too many people who are going to get hurt if we carry on—'

'People are going to get hurt? That didn't seem to bother you when you were taking me to hotel rooms every Thursday. You didn't seem too concerned about hurting people when you were messaging me every five minutes telling me you loved me and that you couldn't wait to see me. Where was your conscience then?'

Andrew pinched the bridge of his nose between fingers and thumb, a pained expression on his face as though he were the one in emotional distress. 'I know this is a horrible conversation to have and I'm truly sorry we're having it. But we both need to take responsibility for what's gone on between us. It's not like either of us planned for this to happen—'

'Really? So all those times you just happened to be driving near my school or my swimming club ready to give me a lift – those were just coincidences, were they? All that rubbish about wanting to train as a swimming coach – that was all true, was it? Don't lie, Andrew. You *pursued* me.'

Andrew frowned, shook his head. 'That's not how it was, and you know it. I understand you're upset but let's not rewrite history. I didn't pursue you. We had a connection, there was something special between us. That's the truth, so please don't start twisting things now.' He took a deep breath. 'You must have known, deep down, that it couldn't go on forever.'

Humiliation blazed in Isla's cheeks. 'You told me you weren't in love with Nicole any more. You said your relationship had been over for a long time, that you were only together for the sake of Nathaniel and Jack. So don't *you* rewrite history. You're the one twisting the truth.' Isla glared at him, willing the tears to be kept at bay.

For a moment, neither of them spoke, thoughts reeling in Isla's head, confirming to herself the narrative of the past few months, determined not to let Andrew convince her of an alternative reality.

'Isla, you're seventeen. You've got your whole life ahead of you. Trust me – in a few months, our relationship will seem like a distant memory. I really don't want us to part on bad terms.'

Isla stared at him, unable to believe this was the same man with whom she had fallen in love. 'Don't patronise me. You break up with me forty-eight hours after I've aborted our baby and you don't want to part on bad terms? What did you think was going to happen? I'd just trot back nicely like the good little girl I'm supposed to be and pretend nothing ever happened?'

'Of course not, I didn't mean that—'

'What if I tell Nicole?' The words blurted from Isla's lips before she knew she was going to say them.

'What?'

'What if I tell Nicole what's been going on? Why should you be allowed to walk away without any consequences?'

Isla watched the colour drain from Andrew's face. Emboldened by the switch in the dynamics of power, she continued. 'If you're so wracked with guilt about what you've done, maybe I should tell Nicole, get it all out in the open.'

Andrew focused his eyes on her, unblinking. 'I don't think you want to do that.'

'Why not?'

He held her gaze, eyes narrowing at the edges. 'What will your mum think? What's her reaction going to be if she finds out you've been sleeping with me? Or that you've had an abortion without even telling her you were pregnant? How do you think she'll feel about that?'

Isla couldn't speak, bewildered as to how her feelings could switch from love to resentment in the space of a single conversation.

Andrew sighed, softened his voice. 'Come on, we both know it's in neither of our interests that this ever gets out. And I don't think either of us really wants this to end on such a bad note.' He reached out, placed a hand on her arm. 'Let's try to be grown-up about this.'

His condescending tone made her seethe. 'I can't believe this. I can't believe you'd do this to me.'

Andrew's grip tightened on her arm. 'Isla, promise me you're not going to talk to Nicole.'

Isla pulled her arm free from his grasp, felt the imprint of his fingers stinging her flesh. 'I don't have to promise you anything. I owe you *nothing*.' Turning around, she ran towards the busy street, heard him call behind her.

'I mean it, Isla. Do *not* say anything. You'll regret it if you do.'

THE PRESENT

Jenna

Jenna sorts through the pile of clean laundry heaped on her bed. It is mostly Callum's: jeans, t-shirts, underwear, athletics kit. She does not know how he gets through so much in a week.

Glancing at her watch, worry needles her like a jabbing finger. It is almost six o'clock. Callum is usually home early on a Friday, has no lessons after lunchtime. He tends to work in the school library for a few hours and is invariably back by five.

Her thoughts spool back through the past seventy-two hours. The sudden appearance of police officers at the school play, the trip to the station, the forty-five minutes of questioning about what Callum was doing the night Isla was killed: what he and Isla argued about, what time he left her, where he went. The officers showed them CCTV footage of Callum running along a street not far from where Isla was knocked down, not long after the accident occurred.

But despite the gravity of the situation, Callum was unable – or unwilling – to provide any insight into his movements for the half-hour window during which Isla was killed. Friends at the party reported Callum and Isla having a row in the hallway and leaving together at about eight forty-five. Callum had not been seen thereafter. And yet, when the police asked – again and again – where he'd gone, what he'd done, Callum's only response was that he 'just wandered around'. Even when the police warned him he was not helping himself by failing to give a more detailed account of his whereabouts, still he refused to provide any more information. And when asked why he had been running along the street, he insisted he'd been racing to catch a bus. It was, in one sense, entirely plausible. But the interviewing officers clearly didn't believe a word of it.

Later, when they were finally allowed to leave, Jenna grilled Callum about his movements that night, about what he'd done for the ninety minutes between leaving the party and arriving home. She reiterated again and again that she wouldn't be angry with him, that she would always support him, no matter what. All she wanted from him was the truth. But Callum kept insisting there was nothing to tell; he'd just been walking around, there was nothing more sinister to it than that. When they got home from the station, Callum went straight to his room and had already left the house when Jenna got up the next morning. He'd been avoiding her ever since, and when they'd been in the house together, told her point blank he didn't want to talk about it.

Jenna's phone rings, and she sees the number of Collingswood School displayed, feels a prickle of anxiety.

'Hello?'

'Ms James? It's Mr Marlowe from Collingswood.'

'Hello. How are you?' Apprehension bristles her skin. For the past three days she has been waiting for this call, waiting for the inevitable remonstration about Tuesday night's events.

'Good, thanks, yes.' There is a momentary pause. 'I'm sorry to call you on a Friday evening. I just wanted to catch up before the end of the week, see how things are.'

The euphemism does not fool Jenna. She knows this is no friendly catch-up. She understands why Mr Marlowe is calling. But she will not pre-empt it. If she is going to face yet another telling-off, he will need to take the lead. 'Yes, all fine thanks.'

There is another brief hiatus. 'I thought we should probably touch base about what happened on Tuesday. I had a chat with Callum on Wednesday, so he's brought me up to speed. Hopefully that will be an end to it, as far as the police are concerned.'

Jenna finds herself on the back foot. If only Callum had told her he'd met with Mr Marlowe, relayed what had been discussed, she would not be entering this conversation in complete ignorance.

Mr Marlowe continues. 'I think what's important now is to focus on next steps – on where we go from here.'

An imagined conversation plays out in Jenna's head: the school expelling Callum, him having to finish his A-level studies by himself, the absence of any reference to accompany his university applications. The fear prompts contrition to tumble from her lips. 'I'm so sorry about what happened on Tuesday night, and I know Callum is too. He loves the school so much and he's working so hard. All he wants is to be able to focus on his schoolwork and prepare for his A levels.' There is an undertone of pleading in her voice and she blanches at the sound of it.

'Actually, that's what I wanted to talk to you about.' Mr Marlowe pauses; just a few agonising seconds into which all of Jenna's worst anxieties seem to coalesce. 'Callum hasn't been quite as . . . focused lately as we've come to expect of him. We understand he's been through a lot these past few weeks. It's been a difficult time for him – for the whole school community. We want to support him, especially after all that's happened.' Mr Marlowe inhales audibly. 'Has Callum mentioned to you that we've suggested he see our in-house counsellor?'

For the second time in as many minutes, Jenna feels as though she is playing poker with a blind hand. 'He hasn't, no.' Just three short words and yet they seem to advertise all her maternal failings.

'Okay, well, we think it's something Callum might benefit from. Help him to . . . reconnect.'

The words hum in Jenna's ears. 'What do you mean?'

There is another loaded pause. 'He's just a bit . . . withdrawn at the moment. His teachers say he's somewhat defensive in class: quick to take offence, easily provoked. It's entirely understandable, of course. But I do think some sessions with our school counsellor might be beneficial, and I wondered if you could maybe speak to him, see if you can persuade him. We all want the same thing, after all: for Callum to be happy and fulfilling his potential.'

Jenna nods before remembering Mr Marlowe cannot see her. 'Yes, of course.'

'Great, thanks. And we do think it would be better for Callum to spend his study periods at school – better for him, and for his focus throughout the day.'

The words jar in Jenna's head like jammed pieces in a tile puzzle. 'I'm not sure I follow.'

'Sixth formers don't have to stay on site all day, of course – that's one of their privileges. But most do; they make use of the library, socialise in the common room, get on with independent study. I think it would help Callum feel more connected with school if he were present more.'

Jenna feels as though she is on a roller coaster, information flashing by so quickly she is unable to take it in.

'I wondered if you knew where he was going during his free periods? Is he coming home? We'd just like to know he's getting on with work at those times.'

Jenna understands this is a question to which she should know the answer, but in truth she doesn't have a clue. She is not at home all day like half the Collingswood mums, who complain about being tired and stressed and are always perennially late for everything even though they seem to have very few tangible responsibilities.

But she does not want to alert Mr Marlowe to her oblivious-ness. Does not want to reveal she had no idea her son was not present at school all day, does not know where he is going instead, what he might be doing. With whom he might be spending his time.

'No, he hasn't been coming home – it's a bit too far on the bus. He's been going to the public library, to the quiet reading room on the first floor. He says he can concentrate better there, without the distraction of his friends around.' The elaborate lie flows seamlessly from her lips, and she does not know where it has come from.

'Ah good. As long as he's still focused on his studies. He has so much potential, we'd hate to see him flounder at this stage.'

Jenna thinks she hears something unspoken in Mr Marlowe's words, her imagination running wild as to what he might be imply-ing. 'I really do appreciate your concern, Mr Marlowe. As you say, Callum has had an awful lot to contend with over the past few weeks. Isla's death hit him very hard – probably more than he's let-ting on. But I'll talk to him, suggest he stays in school for his free periods, and encourage him to go to counselling. I agree it would be good for him.' She hears the conciliatory tone in her voice, hopes it is enough.

'Great. That's much appreciated. And maybe we can catch up in a few weeks to see how things are going?'

It is another of Mr Marlowe's rhetorical questions, and Jenna chooses each of her words carefully: thanks him for calling, says she looks forward to speaking with him again soon.

The phone call ends but the conversation replays in her head like an earworm she cannot shake free.

She thinks about how defensive Callum was both during and after the police interview. She thinks about the CCTV footage of him running down the street, and his alibi about racing to catch a bus. She thinks about the visit from Liam Walsh ten days ago, about his claim of having spent time with Callum recently, and about Liam's threat to visit Collingswood.

Jenna pulls a shutter down on her thoughts. She cannot allow herself to speculate, cannot indulge her fears. She cannot let herself believe that Callum has re-established his friendship with Liam Walsh, or hypothesise about what he was running away from the night Isla was killed. She cannot assume the worst about what Callum is doing during the study periods he should be at school. She has to believe in Callum's innocence, his honesty, his integrity. Because, if she doesn't, she is all too aware that there is no one else who will.

Abby

Abby sits at the kitchen table, drinking a third glass of wine even though it is only five o'clock on a Saturday afternoon. Her eyelids feel as though they are lined with sandpaper, the lack of sleep pressing down on her like a weight she cannot shift.

For the past three nights, she has lain awake in bed, recalling the messages and photos she saw on Clio's phone. Every time she closes her eyes, there they are: the hideous, doctored pictures Clio created. The lens through which Abby views her family has shifted, a different filter put in place: instead of conventional sibling rivalry, there is now something darker, more sinister. Something dangerous. An intensity of hatred that has, in one fell swoop, shattered any illusion of a normal sisterly relationship.

Gulping her wine, she thinks about all the photos she has seen of Clio in inappropriate settings: keeping company with young men in the early hours of the morning when she should be asleep; in bars she is not yet legally old enough to frequent; drinking, vaping, sitting behind the wheel of a car. She cannot – even after three days' procrastination – decide whether to confront Clio about it. It is not possible, she knows, without betraying the fact that she has snooped through her daughter's phone. Part of her wonders whether she is being oversensitive, whether Clio's behaviour is normal; just because Isla never acted like this doesn't mean it's not on the spectrum of typical teenage exploits. Part of her fears that if she asks Clio – however gently – she will only succeed in pushing her further away. Their relationship is already on such tentative ground, she does not dare risk alienating her even more.

Last night, Clio said she was staying at Freya's again, and it took all Abby's self-control not to lock the doors, demand she stay at home, wrap her in cotton wool and never let her out of her sight. But she suspected it would be counterproductive, feared it would drive an even deeper wedge between them. And, if she is being honest with herself, she couldn't face the conflict that would ensue. Clio has become so forthright, so headstrong, so strident in every interaction that Abby doesn't have the emotional fortitude to go into battle with her. Later, or tomorrow, or the next day, she will find an opportunity to check Clio's phone again – even if she has to wait until Clio is asleep – and scour the latest photos and messages. She can only hope she will find no new evidence of misdemeanours. Hope that what she has seen is nothing more than an anomaly, a temporary blip: Clio acting out against her grief.

And yet, even as she rationalises it to herself, she cannot ignore the fact that the real reason she has failed to confront Clio thus far is because she is scared of what the truth may be.

Mostly, she wishes that Stuart were alive, that they could decide together what to do for the best. That she wasn't wading through the quagmire of solo parenting and feeling wrong-footed at every turn.

Draining her wine glass, she recalls the grainy photos on Clio's phone of Isla and Callum arguing the night Isla was killed. Abby has not passed the information on to the police. They already know Isla and Callum were rowing that night. They need no further evidence, seem to have little inclination to pursue Callum as a suspect despite his criminal history, despite the CCTV footage they purportedly have of him running near the scene of the crime. Equally, they have failed to identify the married man by whom Isla had been manipulated, seem to have no leads in that direction either. She knows she cannot rely on the police to find her daughter's killer.

The front door clicks, and Abby calls out instinctively. 'Clio, is that you?'

'Yep.'

'I'm in the kitchen.'

There is a moment's hesitation, and Abby can sense it, like a change in atmospheric pressure before a storm: Clio's reticence to speak to her, her desire to go straight to her room, to avoid her mother altogether.

Rising out of her chair, Abby does not leave it to chance. By the time she has exited the kitchen and made it into the hallway, Clio is already halfway up the stairs.

'Did you have a good time last night?'

'Yeah, it was fine.'

'Were you just at Freya's?'

Clio picks at a knot in the wood on the banister, and Abby resists the urge to tell her to stop. 'We went over to Alice's for a bit.'

'And Freya's mum didn't mind you staying over again?'

Clio glowers at her. 'What is this? The Spanish Inquisition?' She turns around and begins trudging up the stairs. 'I'm going to my room.'

Abby watches her go, knowing she could have handled the conversation better. She reassures herself that later – when Clio is asleep – she can check her phone and find out if her daughter is telling the truth.

The thought of Clio's phone makes Abby think of Isla's mobile, demolished in the crash the night she was killed. All that information – all that potential evidence – wiped out in a single moment. The possible discovery of the man who seduced her daughter destroyed forever.

Over the past twelve days, Abby has continued to hunt through Isla's bedroom, trying to uncover the name of the man who exploited her daughter, but she has failed to unearth anything. Every night, she lies awake, imagining that man's unsavoury hands groping her daughter's innocent body, and there are times when she thinks she will drive herself mad, not being able to put a face to the monstrous image in her head. Not being able to confront him, accuse him, insist the police investigate him.

Heading upstairs to Isla's bedroom, she sits down at her desk, opens her daughter's laptop, clicks on the icon that will take her into Isla's photo roll in the cloud for the umpteenth time.

Scrolling through the pictures, her heart cramps at the sight of her daughter, and she no longer knows whether what she is doing is an act of remembrance, a means of detective work, or simply self-harm.

Her eyes skim over photos she has looked at countless times in the five weeks since her daughter's death. Scrolling down the side-bar, she notices that one of the folders, 'Albums', has an expansion arrow at the bottom that she hasn't registered before. Clicking on it, a whole new collection of folders appears. Abby is aware of a flicker of hope that perhaps, finally, she may find what she is looking for. But just as quickly, she tells herself not to get excited, that she has been here many times already, with the belief that she is on the cusp of a discovery, only to be disappointed yet again.

Most of the albums have self-explanatory labels and thumbnails to match – 'Swimming', 'School', 'DofE', 'Reading Festival'. But one has an intriguing name – 'Mine' – and a thumbnail photograph Abby has never seen before: Isla holding a martini glass up to the camera in a bar that does not look the kind of place she frequented; most of Isla's socialising was done at friends' houses, not in bars or pubs or clubs. She was not that kind of teen.

Clicking open the album, a flurry of images line up on the screen like auditioning chorus girls. As they do, Abby has the sense of having taken a wrong turn, lost her bearings.

She studies the sequence of photographs, unable to make sense of them. Neurons in her brain fire in multiple directions, trying to create a sensible narrative from what she is seeing. Trying to reach a logical conclusion. But she cannot collate the images into a comprehensible story.

In front of her are dozens of selfies of Isla with Andrew. Isla with her arm around Andrew's neck, grinning into the camera. Isla poking her tongue out at Andrew. Isla, head turned, smiling beatifically at him.

Dates, times, events cycle back through Abby's memory as she tries to recall what family events the photos might have been taken at. There have been countless get-togethers between the two families over the years: birthdays, anniversaries, barbecues, lunches. And yet, looking at these photos, Abby cannot determine their locations, cannot decipher when and where they might have been taken.

Scrolling further, a thought sidles into Abby's head, a thought so grotesque, so abominable, she tries to swat it away. But as she skims through photographs of her seventeen-year-old daughter with the husband of her best friend, she is aware of an encroaching sense of disquiet: an awareness that she holds Pandora's jar in her hands and is slowly turning the lid.

And then, there it is, the picture she has spent the past few seconds dreading. A photo that causes every fibre of her being to burn with fury. An image she knows she will spend the rest of her life wishing she had never seen.

Isla in bed – a bed Abby does not recognise – the duvet tucked beneath her bare arms, hair dishevelled, smiling into the camera. Next to her, bare-chested, one arm outstretched where he is holding the camera aloft, the other draped proprietorially around the naked shoulder of Abby's teenage daughter, is a forty-eight-year-old man with whom Abby has been friends for almost two decades.

A voice in her head screams with disbelief, with fury, with unbridled revulsion, telling her she has to do something, confront someone, pummel Andrew with her fists until she has hammered the truth out of him. But the scream strangles in her throat and she cannot seem to make a sound. Her fingers, as if of their own volition, scroll back up the page, back to the beginning, to photos she glossed over because there appeared to be no image of her daughter in them.

Expanding the first, it is a booking from an executive car company, to collect Isla from a street in Marylebone in mid-August. Wracking her brain, Abby combs through her memory, tries to recall why Isla might have been in town that day, but her mind is awash with debris and she cannot swim past it.

She opens another image – a screenshot of a WhatsApp message – reads the words, her head suddenly light, vertiginous, as though her brain is being starved of oxygen.

She reads it again, hoping she has got it wrong, that she is putting two and two together and making five. But it is there, in glaring, unapologetic text, and Abby knows, in that instant, it is knowledge that will plague her for as long as she lives.

It is a screenshot of a WhatsApp thread between Isla and Andrew, with an appointment for a clinic in Marylebone, an appointment dated mid-August, just weeks before Isla died. But it is the message Andrew has sent to accompany the booking that sends Abby's world spinning out of control.

Here are the details of the appointment. I've booked it in your name, but I've paid for it, obviously. It's a very well-regarded clinic and they'll take exceptional care of you. I know how hard this is, and I'm so sorry you're having to go through it. But I think we both know that a termination really is the only option. You'll be okay, I promise. I love you. xx

Abby's stomach lurches and she rushes to the bathroom, retches into the toilet bowl, expels the half-bottle of white wine she has drunk, her throat burning with acid, and with pure, unadulterated fury. All this time she has been desperate to know the identity of the married man who seduced her daughter, but now that she does, she wishes with all her heart that she could unknow it, that she could unlearn every last, sordid scrap of information. Her heart pulses with grief that her seventeen-year-old daughter underwent an abortion by herself, that she did not feel able to confide in Abby, that she endured that experience without Abby by her side. Her body shakes with rage that Andrew put Isla in such a terrible, invidious position, that he so flagrantly abused the trust Abby has placed in him all these years. She thinks about the fortnight in August when Isla suddenly took a break from swimming, when she went to bed for a couple of days complaining of a tummy bug and then shoulder pain, Abby bringing her hot-water bottles and cups of chamomile tea, ignorant of the fact that her daughter had just terminated a pregnancy. Unaware that Isla had gone through that experience alone, all to protect the identity of a man whom Abby should have been able to trust with her children's lives.

All those lies. All that subterfuge. All the emotional pain her daughter suffered because of the actions of that grotesque human being she has spent the past eighteen years believing to be one of her closest friends.

Again and again Abby's stomach heaves, and each time the same thought surges through her mind: he will not get away with this. She will not let him get away with it.

Nicole

Nicole dices an avocado onto a bowl of green salad for an early dinner. Through the kitchen window she watches Andrew on the patio, wrestling with covers for the garden furniture, covering it up for the winter. She cannot articulate what she is feeling, does not know if it is pain or anger, resentment or regret, or whether it is simply a yearning to be able to turn back the clock, to the time before Isla's death, before Andrew's treachery. Before her life veered out of control.

Pulling some Dijon mustard from the fridge, she begins to make a dressing which she'll keep to one side until she's ready to serve. Upstairs, the boys are in their bedrooms. All she wants is for them to have some semblance of a normal family dinner despite the fact that all four of them know there is nothing approaching normality about their family right now.

It was at Nicole's insistence that they'd made a collective trip to the police station on Thursday evening for fingerprinting. Andrew hadn't been keen, had thought it would look odd, the whole family turning up en masse. But Nicole had pointed out that the boys couldn't very well go alone, and that it might be sensible for them to put on a united front.

Mixing the dressing, she recalls her conversations with Nathaniel and Jack on Wednesday evening, breaking the news to them about the discovery of her car and the implication that it had been involved in a collision. It was Nathaniel she'd told first, watched the horror spread across his face: *Do the police think your car was involved in Isla's death?* Nicole had reassured him that there'd been no such suggestion, even as the same question plagued her too. Knowing how Nathaniel felt about Isla – knowing the unrequited crush he'd tried unsuccessfully to conceal over the past couple of years – she could not begin to imagine how he might be feeling at this latest turn of events.

Jack's reaction had been different: quiet, withdrawn, as though he were retreating into his own private thoughts to which Nicole had no access. She'd wrapped her arms around him, reassured him it would be okay, wished she could know what he was thinking, but he'd remained silent, remote.

Nicole makes a mental note to schedule a call with Jack's psychologist, to take a temperature check on how he's doing, whether his feelings about his ADHD diagnosis have changed at all.

Andrew enters the kitchen, offers her a tentative smile. She turns away, does not know if she is incapable of reciprocating or just unwilling.

The doorbell rings, and Nicole wipes her hands on a tea towel, walks into the hallway, opens the door.

'Where is he?'

Abby glares at her, and panic floods Nicole's body. She knows, instinctively – in the split second between opening the door and seeing the fury on Abby's face – that the walls of her house are about to crumble, that there is a finite amount of time until the whole edifice comes crushing down, and that there is nothing she can do to stop it.

'What's wrong?' Her eyebrows rise with faux-innocence. Nicole knows she must not give anything away, not yet, not until Abby confirms the cause of her anger.

Abby does not reply as she barges past Nicole, into the hall, through to the kitchen. Nicole follows close on her heels, to where

Andrew is marinating steaks, wearing a 'World's Best Dad' apron that Jack bought him for Father's Day last year.

'You pervert.' Abby pushes Andrew hard in the chest, so hard that he stumbles. He glances briefly at Nicole, alarmed, as if in hope that perhaps she will come to his aid, perhaps she will rescue him from this calamitous mess he has created.

Nicole does not speak, is not sure she could muster any words even if she tried.

'She was seventeen. *Seventeen*. You've known her her entire life. How could you do that?'

Abby spits the words at Andrew, thrusts her palms into his body again, while Andrew holds up his hands in pre-emptive surrender.

'I'm sorry. I don't know how it happened, I know it was wrong—'

'*Wrong?* You seduced my seventeen-year-old daughter and you have the audacity to say it was *wrong*? How dare you even look me in the eye. You're an abomination.'

Andrew cows his head in shame, and it is the first time Nicole has seen him truly penitent. The first time she has seen him genuinely fearful of the consequences of his actions. All those conversations she and Andrew have had, all the times he has apologised, cried, pleaded for forgiveness. Now she understands – in a moment of such sharp enlightenment it is as though a spotlight has been shone on her previous naïvety – that those were nothing but crocodile tears, nothing more than tactical remorse. Nothing beyond a desire to appease her and restore the marital status quo. The realisation is so pronounced, so profound, it is as though her mind is fast-forwarding – Andrew moving out, Nicole instructing a solicitor, negotiations over money and the house and the split of pension pots – and she understands in that moment that whatever else happens, her marriage to Andrew will not survive his betrayal.

'Was it you?' Abby's voice is quiet, suddenly, as though someone has turned down the volume.

'What do you mean?'

Abby eyes Andrew: unblinking, unflinching. 'Did you kill my daughter?'

Nicole's blood chills in her veins. She has not yet told Abby about her car, could not find the courage to reveal that her missing 4x4 has been discovered on an industrial estate, that it bears signs of having been involved in a collision.

'Don't be ridiculous, of course I didn't.'

'Why's that ridiculous?'

Abby pushes Andrew again, and he flounders, takes a step back, tries to regain his balance.

'What happened? Did you get bored of her? Was she threatening to tell someone?'

Nicole watches as heat bleeds into Andrew's cheeks, and she knows, in an instant, that in her fury Abby has chanced upon a facet of the truth. It is a truth Andrew has kept meticulously concealed. He has given Nicole no indication – not even a hint – that perhaps there was animosity between him and Isla. He has told her only that it ended because he realised what a terrible mistake he had made, how egregiously he had wronged Nicole and the boys. Now she wonders if there is a single grain of truth in anything Andrew has said or whether his entire narrative has been a fabrication from start to finish.

'Tell me! It's the least you owe me. Tell me what happened!'

Abby is shouting, and Nicole thinks about her boys upstairs, about the secrets that are festering in her home like bacteria in a wound. She doesn't dare risk exposing a revelation that has the power to contaminate her entire family.

'Please, Abby, I know you're furious, and you've every right to be. But please don't do this now, not with the boys upstairs.'

Abby

Abby spins around to where Nicole is standing behind her. Seeing the dread on Nicole's face as to what this may do to her family, Abby's contempt for her is almost as engulfing as her hatred of Andrew.

'*Your kids?* So your kids should be protected from what your husband has done while my daughter is what – collateral damage?'

'Of course not—'

'Did you know?' Abby is aware she is shouting but she does not care if Nathaniel and Jack hear. They *should* hear. They have a right to know what kind of a monster their father is. What he is capable of.

There is a moment's hesitation in which Nicole's eyes dart furtively towards Andrew, then down at the ground, refusing to meet Abby's gaze. And in that fleeting moment, Abby knows.

'You knew? You *knew* and you didn't tell me? You didn't stop it? For god's sake, what is *wrong* with you? How could you just stand by and let it happen?'

'It's not like that. I only found out a few weeks ago—'

'*A few weeks ago?* You've known for *weeks* and you haven't said anything?' Rage boils in Abby's chest and she does not know how to withstand its ferocity.

'Abby, believe me, I'm as appalled by it as you are—'

'Are you? Are you really? You're so appalled that you've still got him living in the house with you? Still playing happy families? Pretending nothing's happened?'

'No, not at all—'

'All this time you've been *comforting* me, pretending to be my *friend*, pretending to *care*, and the whole time you knew that your husband had been sleeping with my daughter? How can you not have told me?' Abby clasps her head in her hands, fingertips digging into her scalp until it hurts, wishing she could claw all thoughts from her head.

'It's not Nicole's fault. I put her in an impossible situation. This is entirely on me.'

Abby does not acknowledge Andrew's plea for clemency. She wants nothing whatsoever to do with him. All she wants is for the police to investigate him – investigate him seriously – as a suspect in her daughter's death.

'I'm so sorry.'

Abby feels a hand on her arm, looks down as if at some foreign object, sees the familiar Asscher cut diamond on Nicole's fourth finger. Shrugging Nicole's hand from her sleeve, she stares at her, bewildered. 'How can you still have him in the house with you? How can you even bear to look at him?'

Abby watches as Nicole opens her mouth to speak, closes her lips, seems to decide against whatever she was going to say. She sees Nicole glance over at Andrew as though they are in this together, as though they are two musketeers in league against a common enemy, and she is aware of something rising up within her: a sense of indignation that she should be facing this alone, that Stuart is dead while Andrew is alive, that Nicole and Andrew have one another to help navigate this ordeal while she is by herself. She is overcome by a sense of injustice that Nicole has the option to rug-sweep this whole sickening episode; that she can carry on as though nothing has happened, can maintain the charade of their perfect, happy family until time immemorial if she so chooses. And the inequity of it – the violation that Andrew and Nicole have imposed on her – is too much, and she feels her voice harden, consonants solidifying in her mouth.

'Did you know Isla was pregnant? That Andrew paid for her to have an abortion six weeks before she was killed? Did he tell you that?'

Nicole

The words assault Nicole as though she has been hit with bullets.

She looks at Andrew, expecting to see disbelief on his face that Abby would concoct such an outrageous story. What she finds, instead, is an undeniable expression of guilt.

'Is it true?' Nicole knows it is a rhetorical question, but she needs to hear him say it, needs him to face up to what he has done.

For a few seconds, Andrew says nothing, eyes darting between Nicole and Abby like a rabbit caught in the headlights. 'It's not what you think—'

'Not what I think?' Nicole cannot believe he has the audacity to evade it, that even now he is incapable of accepting responsibility for his actions.

The kitchen door clicks open, and Nicole panics to see Nathaniel standing there, glancing between the trio of faces.

'What's going on?'

Maternal instinct kicks in where all other reason fails. She cannot have Nathaniel hearing this, not now; she cannot allow Andrew's mistakes to implode their lives any more than they already have. 'Nothing. We're just talking. Can you give us a minute?'

Nathaniel eyes her suspiciously, and she knows he will not be so easily fobbed off, knows that the atmosphere in the room is so thick it is like wading through a London smog.

The front doorbell rings, jolting Nicole like an electric shock. 'Sweetheart, would you mind answering that?'

Nathaniel hesitates before turning and leaving. It will, Nicole hopes, give her a few seconds to think, to strategise, to try to persuade Abby that Nathaniel does not deserve to be party to this scene, that there is nothing to be gained in punishing him for his father's sins.

But before she has a chance to say anything, the kitchen door opens again, and Nathaniel returns, trailing two police officers behind him. The officers scan the room, and Nicole wonders whether they can detect the tension immediately, whether years of experience have taught them to identify a house filled with incandescent rage.

'Mrs Forrester?'

Nicole nods. 'Yes, that's me.'

'And you are?' The male officer looks to Andrew and then to Abby.

'I'm Nicole's husband—'

'I'm a family friend—'

Their voices collide, and the officer pauses before turning to Nathaniel. 'And you must be Nathaniel?'

Nathaniel nods. Nicole notices how the colour in his face has drained even paler than usual, how he has folded his arms across his chest, taken a step back as if to separate himself from the scene.

'Mrs Forrester, we've got an update on your car. Perhaps we could discuss that with you in private?' He glances towards Abby, waits for her to take the hint, but she does not move.

'You didn't tell me your car had been found.' Nicole hears the note of challenge in Abby's voice, does not know what she can say to mitigate the fact of having withheld the information from her.

Nicole begins to gabble, explaining in short, breathless phrases that her car was unearthed three days ago on an industrial estate a mile and a half away. She feels her voice falter as she relays that it showed signs of having been involved in a collision, that the police are carrying out forensics.

Abby stares at her, dumbfounded, before turning to the officers.

'Is there any chance that Nicole's car was involved in the death of Isla Richardson?'

There is a steeliness to Abby's voice that Nicole has never heard before.

The officers exchange a confused look. 'I'm afraid that's not something we can discuss. I'd be grateful if you'd give us some time alone with Mrs Forrester.'

Nicole watches as Abby visibly bristles. 'Isla Richardson was my daughter. If this has got anything to do with her death, then I have a right to know.'

The female officer shoots a glance towards her colleague, takes a moment to compose herself. 'I'm so sorry, Mrs Richardson, we didn't realise.'

Abby ignores her, turns to Nicole. 'You don't mind me staying, do you, Nicole?'

Nicole feels herself squirm, knows there is no feasible way she can ask Abby to leave, not after the revelations Abby has brought into her home. Not given the damage Abby could wreak on her family, given all she knows.

Nicole nods her consent. 'It's fine. Abby can stay. She's practically family.' The words claw in her throat; six weeks ago, they were unfailingly true. Now they are an insult to everyone present.

The officers turn to each other: one shrugging, the other raising a resigned eyebrow, and seem to decide this is not a point that requires pedantry.

'As you wish, Mrs Forrester. Forensics have dusted your car for fingerprints, and they haven't been able to find any that don't belong to a member of your family.'

The words flail in Nicole's head, and she cannot straighten out her thoughts. It is Andrew who finds an appropriate response.

'What does that mean? That whoever stole my wife's car wore gloves?'

One officer looks at the other, raises an eyebrow, and then the female officer turns to Nathaniel.

'How would you describe your relationship to Isla Richardson?'

Every nerve ending across Nicole's skin goes on high alert. She looks at her son, sees his fear, and understands, with a knowledge that goes beyond language, that he has something to hide.

Abby

'What's Nathaniel got to do with Isla? Or with Nicole's stolen car?' The words fire from Abby's lips as thoughts collide in her brain.

The male officer adjusts the key chain clipped to his belt loop. 'We're just making enquiries at this stage, Mrs Richardson.'

Abby shakes her head, flabbergasted that the officers can be so obstructive, infuriated that Nicole and Andrew can just stand there, flagrantly ignoring the enormous, trumpeting elephant in the room. But Abby will not let them get away with it.

'Did you know that Andrew' – she nods towards him – 'seduced my daughter? That he was sleeping with her? A seventeen-year-old girl he's known his entire life. Did you know that he got her pregnant? That he paid for her to have an abortion just weeks before she died? If anyone needs investigating in connection with my daughter's death, it's him.' She points a finger at Andrew, watches him shake his head, hears him protest, proclaim his innocence. Her blood seethes at the spectacle of Andrew trying to deny what he has done. She sees Nicole dart an anxious glance at Nathaniel, sees Nathaniel's face contort with horror or disgust, she is not sure which. She watches Nicole place a hand on Nathaniel's arm, trying to shield her son from truths that can no longer be hidden.

The female officer holds a hand in the air to silence Andrew. 'Thank you for that information, Mrs Richardson. I'm sure

Detective Webb will look into that as part of his investigation. I'll get him to call you as soon as we're done here.'

Confusion spirals in Abby's mind. She has just told two police officers the identity of the forty-eight-year-old man who predated on her seventeen-year-old daughter in the months leading up to her death, and they are treating the information as though it is of no consequence.

The female officer turns back to Nathaniel. 'As I was saying, I wonder if you could tell me a bit about your relationship with Isla Richardson?'

Nathaniel shrugs. 'We were friends.' His voice is unsteady, and something pricks in Abby's ears; there is a false note in it, something she needs to be attuned to.

'They've known each other since they were born. They were practically siblings.' Nicole's tone is urgent, defensive, as though the sand in an hourglass is draining at speed and she needs to be heard before it runs out.

Abby can stand the charade no longer. 'Siblings? Are you mad? Everyone knew Nathaniel had a crush on Isla, that he'd been pining after her for years. Have you any idea how uncomfortable it made her feel?'

'Abby, please—'

'What?' Abby experiences a stab of fury at Nicole's attempts to maintain the illusion of her perfect family. She does not care, in this moment, about the scarlet rash blooming on Nathaniel's neck, spreading into his cheeks. 'Are you saying it's not true?'

'Can we all calm down, please.' The female officer's voice is firm, decisive, and she turns to Abby. 'It really would be best if you went home now. We'll make sure Detective Webb calls you as soon as possible with an update.'

Abby stands resolute. 'I'm not going anywhere. Nobody ever returns my calls, and I want to know what's going on.'

The male officer shakes his head. 'I'm sorry, Mrs Richardson, but it's really not helping things, you being here. I'm going to have to insist that you leave.'

The officer's voice is firm, and Abby cannot believe she is being ousted from the scene, that they are behaving as though she does not have the right to be there. She is about to respond, to insist she be allowed to stay, before she thinks better of it, decides there are other ways around the situation.

She does not look anyone in the eye as she exits the kitchen and closes the door behind her.

Nicole

The front door slams with a loud, furious thud. The two officers look at each other before turning back to Nathaniel.

'Did you know already about your father's affair with Isla Richardson, before it was mentioned today?'

Nicole's breath halts in her chest. Never in her life has she more desperately wanted her son to be ignorant of something.

Nathaniel shakes his head, and Nicole experiences a rush of relief.

The male officer raises his eyebrows. 'Do you know anything about a series of anonymous emails that were sent to Isla Richardson in the months before she died?'

Fear tiptoes along Nicole's spine as she watches Nathaniel's eyes flit around the room, before landing on the floor.

'No.'

'You sure about that?'

Nathaniel nods, but Nicole can see it clearly on his face, as if it were written in indelible ink: the barely concealed lie.

'So you don't know anything about an account with the name FSW23BS that was sending Isla abusive emails over the summer?'

Nathaniel shakes his head. 'No.'

Part of Nicole wants to scream, to urge him to tell the truth, whatever that may be. To pause time so that she can grab both her boys, bundle them into Andrew's car, transport them as far away from here as possible. To save them both from this unholy mess.

'That's interesting. Because we've obtained the IP address of those emails and it's registered to your parents' account. Might you know anything about that?'

There is a deafening silence. Nicole stares at Nathaniel, wills it not to be true even as she witnesses the guilt on his face. She sees Andrew shaking his head, experiences a moment of unmitigated hatred towards him.

'Are you suggesting it was Nathaniel who sent all those emails to Isla?' Nicole hears the fear in her voice, can do nothing to contain it.

'It wasn't me. I didn't do anything.' Nathaniel's voice is thin, unconvincing, and there is no mistaking – at least not to Nicole – the culpability in it.

Nicole thinks back to the emails Abby showed her – the venom, the abuse, the vulgar misogynistic language – and she does not want to believe that her son – her gentle, kind, thoughtful boy – is capable of such bile. But when she looks at Nathaniel, it is not possible to deny the guilt in his expression. She experiences a surge of regret that she did not force a conversation with him sooner about his feelings for Isla, that she never noticed his crush had taken on a different dimension.

The thought strikes her that if Nathaniel sent all those emails, then he has known for months about his father's affair with Isla. He has lived alone with that terrible knowledge, has borne by himself that dreadful burden. She cannot imagine what it must have done to him, learning that the first girl he ever loved was sleeping with his father. All she knows is that she will never, ever forgive Andrew for putting their son in that hideous position.

'Nathaniel?' Nicole places a hand on his arm but he shakes her off.

The female officer continues. 'We know how you felt about Isla. Your feelings were well known among your school friends.'

'It wasn't me—'

'Do you know it's an offence to send abusive emails?' The male officer's voice is stern, challenging, goading Nathaniel into a response.

'Oh, come on – he's clearly upset. If he did do it – which there's no tangible evidence I can see that he did – it's not a big deal. Kids are always doing stuff like this online.'

Nicole winces at Andrew's belittling tone. She assumes he has not seen the emails Isla was sent, does not understand their level of malice.

The male officer eyes Andrew with something bordering contempt. 'I'm afraid it's a bit more serious than that. Malicious communications carry a maximum sentence of two years' imprisonment.'

'Two years?' Nicole experiences a flash of alarm. She looks at Nathaniel, registers his panic.

'Can you tell us where you were the night Isla Richardson was killed?'

Nathaniel swallows hard, his Adam's apple rising and falling. Nicole silently implores him not to lie, not to make things even harder on himself.

'I was at a party.'

'The party at Meera Rani's house? The party Isla attended?'

Nathaniel nods. Despair lodges in Nicole's throat. She knows he was not at the party. Sita Rani told her so. A voice screams in her head for Nathaniel not to be so foolish. But she knows she cannot intervene, that she may make things even worse for him if she does.

'See, we've spoken to a lot of people who were at that party, and nobody can recall you being there. Nobody recalls you even being invited.'

The officer leaves the point hanging, does not ask a question, the ellipsis at the end of his sentence lingering in the air, waiting for Nathaniel to incriminate himself.

'I wasn't there for long.'

'So where were you for the rest of the evening?'

Nathaniel hesitates, and it's as if Nicole can pre-empt what falsehood he is going to deliver before he even speaks.

'I was at a friend's.'

'Which friend?'

'Elliot. Elliot Mercer.'

Apprehension coils in Nicole's stomach. The officers exchange a knowing look, as though, unbeknown to Nathaniel, they have been involved in a game of chess, and her son has just been outmanoeuvred.

'But Elliot Mercer was at the party.'

'Not all night. We left early—'

'Nathaniel.' Nicole's voice is more febrile than she intended; she does not want to betray the extent of her anxiety, does not want the officers to think she has reason to be scared.

Her son turns to her, and her heart seems to shatter as tears pool at the corners of his eyes.

'Nathaniel, we know Elliot Mercer was at the party right to the end because he gave a statement to officers when they arrived at the scene. So, I'm going to ask you again: where were you the night Isla Richardson was killed?'

Nathaniel shakes his head, blinking away his tears. 'I wasn't anywhere, I was just hanging out, I didn't have anything to do with Isla's death, I swear.'

'Come on, you can see he's distressed.' Andrew steps forward, tries to take control of the situation. 'There's no way he'd have anything to do with what happened to Isla.'

Nicole remains rooted to the spot, paralysed with fear.

It is the female officer who speaks next, who says the words Nicole has been dreading, words she hoped so fervently never to hear.

'Nathaniel Forrester, I'm arresting you on suspicion of causing death by dangerous driving and for offences under the Malicious Communications Act. You do not have to say anything . . .'

The rest of the officer's caution bleeds into Nicole's ears as she witnesses the bewilderment on Andrew's face as though he has never, for one moment, contemplated the possible repercussions of his actions. She sees the terror in Nathaniel's eyes, and is acutely aware that the house of cards is tumbling down around her.

FOUR WEEKS BEFORE ISLA'S DEATH

Isla

Isla sat at the desk in her bedroom, eyes glazing over the chapter of a chemistry textbook she was supposed to read before the start of term in eleven days' time. It seemed surreal that in less than a fortnight she would return to Collingswood, take up her post as Head of School, begin the final two terms before sitting her A-level exams. It was only six weeks since the start of the summer holidays but it felt like a lifetime ago: a time before her pregnancy, before the abortion, before Andrew unceremoniously dumped her. Before her life began to unravel.

Picking up her phone, she opened WhatsApp, entered her archived messages. Not a single communication from Andrew for two weeks: nothing since the evening of their last meeting, after she'd stormed away from him when he had ended their relationship.

> *I know you're hurt and angry, but I really think it's better for both of us if we can part on good terms. I'm truly sorry it's had to end like this, but I do honestly believe that, in time, you'll see it's for the best. For now, I'll do my utmost to stay out of your way for as long as possible to make this easier on you. But it's not going to do either of us any good to lash out. I know you're upset, but telling anyone what's happened really isn't the answer. I know right now*

you think it would make you feel better, but do you really
want your mum to find out? Or your school friends? Or
your teachers? How do you think it'll impact your uni
reference if everyone knows what's gone on between us? It
won't only be Nicole, Nathaniel and Jack that you'll hurt.
You'll be hurting yourself too, and your mum. I don't
think you want that, not really. Let's try to be grown-up
about this. I promise you, in a year's time, this will all
seem like a distant memory.

Isla re-read the message, throat tightening with a compound
of emotions: hurt, anger, resentment, impotence. Humiliation at
her gullibility, self-loathing for her naïvety. Memories taunted her
of how, during their relationship, she had, on occasion, indulged
the fantasy that perhaps Andrew would leave Nicole, perhaps they
would set up home once she'd finished university. Perhaps they had
a future together.

Instead, she now realised, their relationship had been nothing
more than the indulgence of Andrew's clichéd midlife crisis. She
felt used, exploited, discarded. The foolish participant in a tawdry
fling. And yet, however much she hated Andrew for the way he
had treated her, it was nothing compared to the abhorrence she
felt about herself.

She thought about those times he had driven by and given her a
lift, and she had known, deep down, it was an unlikely coincidence
that he just happened to be passing. She thought about the first time
he had kissed her, a voice shouting in her head that it was wrong,
dishonest, immoral. She thought about those afternoons lying in
a hotel bed, suppressing her feelings of guilt about what she was
doing, about the carousel of loved ones she was hurting. How she
had consciously quashed her fears as to what would happen – how

perceptions of her would change, how her reputation would be destroyed – if anyone found out.

Isla laid her head on the desk, closed her eyes, tried to squeeze the memories from her mind. Tried not to think about all the lies, the duplicity, the untruths she had told.

Her phone buzzed, and she swiped open the screen, found a message from her swimming coach.

> *Hi Isla. Just checking in to see how you're doing? Do you think you might be okay for training this week? With the nationals so close, every day really is crucial. Hope you're keeping up the exercises. Let me know how you're getting on.*

Guilt hounded her at the thought of the excuses she had given as to why she'd skipped training for the past fortnight: first, a phantom tummy bug, then a sham shoulder injury. The same lies replicated for her coach, her swim mates, her mum. She knew there was no medical reason why, two weeks after the abortion, she shouldn't be swimming. She just didn't want to. The thought of it made her squeamish, sloshing around in water so soon after what had happened. It was irrational, she knew, but she couldn't escape the feeling that it would be wrong for her body. She'd go back when school started; she just needed a bit more time.

There was a gentle knock on her bedroom door.

'Can I come in?'

Isla swallowed, lifted her head from the desk, instructed herself to behave normally.

'Course.'

Her mum opened the door, stepped inside. 'How's the studying going?'

Isla forced herself to smile. 'Okay.'

'Well done for getting on with it. Perhaps you could have a word with your sister, see if some of your conscientiousness might rub off on her. She's done none of the holiday reading she was set.'

'That's because there's nearly two weeks before school actually begins.' Clio appeared in the doorway, face contorted with irritation.

'Clio, you've had six weeks to read two books for English and you haven't even opened them yet. How are you going to read two entire novels in eleven days?'

Clio raised a disdainful eyebrow. 'I'm nearly sixteen. You don't need to nag me about my homework.'

'I'm not nagging you. I'm just saying that you could take a leaf out of Isla's book and get on with your holiday work. You don't have much time left.'

For a few seconds, Clio said nothing, simply eyed their mum with a withering expression. 'I'm sure you'd have been much happier if you could have cloned Isla and got two perfect daughters, but I'm afraid you'll just have to make do with me being such a colossal disappointment to you.'

Clio turned around and slammed Isla's bedroom door behind her.

Isla's mum sighed. 'Why is it that in every interaction with Clio, I always manage to say the wrong thing?'

'You don't. She's fifteen. She's just figuring out her place in the world.'

'You were never like that at fifteen. I never had to remind you to do your homework, and you've never looked at me with contempt like she does. I just don't know how to get through to her when she's so angry all the time.'

Isla swallowed against a familiar pressure constricting her throat: the perception of her as a perfect teenager, who never felt angry or frustrated, anxious or exhausted. Who never felt beleaguered with homework and training and the expectation of achievement at every turn. The assumption that she spun effortlessly all the competing plates in her life, that she never wished the world would pause, just for a day or two, and let her step off the relentless treadmill.

She shrugged. 'We're all different. Clio's fine. She just needs to find her own way.'

Her mum placed a hand on Isla's back. 'I hope you're right. Anyway, how's the shoulder feeling? Any better?'

For a brief moment, Isla was overcome by a desire to tell her mum everything. The truth, the whole truth, and nothing but the truth. To confess there was nothing wrong with her shoulder, that there had never been a tummy bug. To confide in her everything that had happened over the past five months: Andrew's manipulations, her own stupidity, the betrayals, the deceptions, the profusion of lies. The pregnancy and the abortion and the emotional turmoil since. The certainty that a termination had been the right thing to do and yet the waves of profound, overwhelming loss ever since. Moments of grieving for something that had never truly come into being.

But then she looked at her mum's face – at the trust, the love, the unshakeable belief that Isla would never do anything to disappoint her – and she felt the truth close in on itself like the petals of a waterlily. It was as though she could see, frame by frame, what would happen were she to tell her everything; her mum's perception of her swinging one hundred and eighty degrees from good to bad, trustworthy to deceitful. From kind to callous, thoughtful to selfish. And even though a part of her was desperate not to be alone with her secrets any longer, the thought of her mum's reaction – the unalterable, permanent change in her mum's opinion of her – forced her to close the door on the truth.

'It's a bit better.'

'That's a relief. It's such bad timing for you, straight after that tummy bug. I know Paul's keen to get you back to training as soon as you're ready, but just don't rush, okay? I know you're desperate to be ready for the nationals, but if you push yourself too early, you'll only do more damage.' Her mum leaned forward, hugged her, and Isla tried to suppress the sense of her own unworthiness.

'Dinner will be at about half seven, okay? I'm doing a Sri Lankan curry – it's a recipe Nicole recommended.'

Isla tried to conceal her discomfort at the mention of Nicole's name. She imagined them all – Andrew, Nicole, Nathaniel, Jack – sitting around the kitchen table, eating homemade Sri Lankan curry, the picture of the perfect happy family: laughing, joking, exchanging stories of their day, while Isla had been holed up in her bedroom, wondering how her life had spiralled out of control within the space of a few foolish months.

'I'll leave you to it.' Her mum kissed the top of her head before leaving the room, closing the door gently behind her.

Tears pooled in Isla's eyes. An image of her dad suddenly slipped into her mind: at the helm of their boat, steering them out of Chichester Harbour, across to the Isle of Wight.

Almost every night for the past few weeks, she had dreamed of her dad, and almost every morning she awoke to the painful remembrance that he was gone. Some days, it felt as though her grief was as intense as the first few weeks after he died; an unquenchable yearning to see him, speak with him, be held by him.

Her phone buzzed with a message, her heart sinking as she saw Nathaniel's name on the screen.

Are you free to meet up?

Isla instructed herself to act normally; not to act like a person who had recently been dumped by Nathaniel's dad.

Why? What's up?

234

She watched, waited, as her phone indicated that Nathaniel was typing.

There's something I need to talk to you about.

What is it? I'm in the middle of chemistry prep.

I can't say. It's about Callum. Meet me outside the café in the park in 15 mins?

Isla felt a wave of dismay at the prospect of having to hear Nathaniel rail against Callum yet again.

In the fortnight since the abortion, she'd been plagued by regrets about her break-up with Callum. There were moments when she could not believe she had been so rash, so foolish as to end their relationship for the sake of a man who had proved himself so unworthy of anyone's love. There had been times – fleeting, at best – when she'd imagined her and Callum getting back together, of them picking up where they'd left off, of her pretending that the past few months never happened, like tearing out the unwelcome chapters of a book. But she knew it was nothing more than a fantasy. She would never forget the way Callum had looked at her the day he saw her emerge from Andrew's car, or the expression on his face whenever he had seen her since: disappointment, disillusionment, disbelief.

The last thing she wanted today was to hear yet more of Nathaniel's animosity towards Callum. But she'd manufactured so many excuses to avoid Nathaniel lately, and it least it would give her a reason to postpone her chemistry reading.

Taking a deep breath, she tapped out a response.

Sure. See you in a bit.

◆ ◆ ◆

'What's up?'

Isla approached Nathaniel, leaning against a tree outside the café, his bike propped up next to him.

'How's the work going?'

Isla feigned a smile, felt it strain in her cheeks. 'Not great, to be honest. Can't quite find the motivation.'

Nathaniel raised a sceptical eyebrow. 'Isla Richardson not feeling motivated? That's got to be a first.'

Isla felt herself blanch at the arch tone in Nathaniel's voice. She forced a shrug. 'I guess there's a first time for everything. Anyway, what did you want to talk to me about?'

Nathaniel eyed her for a few seconds, and Isla could hear her friends' voices echoing in her ears.

Doesn't it creep you out, the way he's always watching you?

It's weird, the way he waits for you in the common room like a faithful puppy.

You know he's borderline obsessed with you?

'Remember I told you about seeing Callum and Yasmin together?' Nathaniel paused, chewed at his thumbnail. 'I saw them again. There's definitely something going on.'

Isla allowed herself a beat. After everything that had happened over the past couple of weeks, the possibility of a relationship between Callum and Yasmin was the last thing she wanted to think about.

'Aren't you upset?' There was a note of challenge in Nathaniel's voice, as though he wanted – needed – to provoke a reaction.

'Why would I be? What Callum does is up to him.' Even as she said it, she was aware of a twist of jealousy; not just about Yasmin – she still didn't quite believe that to be true – but for the knowledge that, one day, Callum would hook up with someone else, and Isla would have to live with the fact that she had ended their relationship – a relationship with someone good and kind, who had loved her, respected her – to pursue a fling with a man who never really cared about her at all.

And then it suddenly struck her that if Callum and Yasmin were getting close – platonically or otherwise – perhaps Callum would break his promise: perhaps he would tell Yasmin about her affair with Andrew. Even the thought of it made her feel nauseous.

'Yasmin's not Callum's type. If they're hanging out, it's because they're friends.' Isla could hear the defensiveness in her voice, wished she could have restrained it.

A small, satisfied smirk curled the corners of Nathaniel's mouth. Isla was struck by a stab of dislike of him, a perplexity as to why she had defended him all these years.

'They weren't just hanging out. They were having lunch – just the two of them – in the garden of The Hope and Anchor. He was all over her.'

Impatience burrowed under Isla's skin. 'What were you doing in The Hope and Anchor?'

Colour flushed his cheeks. 'I wasn't in there. I was just cycling past.'

'If you were just cycling past, how did you see them long enough to decide there was something going on?'

Nathaniel's eyes shifted, left and then right. 'My chain had come loose. I was fixing it.'

The lie hung heavy in the air between them. An imagined scene slid into Isla's head, so clear it was as if she were watching a film: Nathaniel on the cycle path that ran alongside the pub garden, spotting Callum and Yasmin; a frisson of excitement that he had discovered them together again; concealing himself behind a tree and watching, spying, to see what might transpire.

'What Callum does is his business. It's nothing to do with you, and it's certainly nothing to do with me. Why are you so obsessed with whether Callum's seeing Yasmin? What's it to you anyway?'

There was a moment's silence, Nathaniel's eyes narrowing at the edges. 'I suppose you don't think it's anyone else's business if two people are fucking each other? I suppose you think it should just be their dirty little secret?'

Shock blindsided Isla for a moment. 'Why are you being so aggressive? All I'm saying is that I don't think it's anyone else's business if Callum and Yasmin are seeing each other.'

Nathaniel fixed his eyes on her face, unblinking. 'What about if someone's sleeping with someone else's husband? Or someone else's dad? Is that anyone else's business?'

Three short questions, but in their chiselled consonants and sharp venom, Isla understood that Nathaniel knew everything.

'I'm going—' She turned to leave but a hand gripped her bare arm, fingers digging into her flesh. 'Let me go.' She glared at Nathaniel.

'Are you denying it?' His grip tightened on her arm.

'Denying what?'

Nathaniel shook his head with contempt. 'Are you denying that you've been screwing my dad for months?'

The words hit Isla as though she had been knocked to the ground. 'What are you talking about?' She sounded weak, desperate.

'You know exactly what I'm talking about.'

'No, I don't—'

'For fuck's sake, don't lie. I *know*. I've got *photographic evidence*. And if you keep lying about it, I'll post that evidence all over my socials and we can see if your precious reputation survives. Is that what you want?'

Thoughts scrabbled to find a foothold in Isla's brain. She tried to imagine what photographic evidence he might be referring to – photos of her and Andrew kissing or holding hands or being out together somewhere they shouldn't – but she knew she couldn't dwell on that, that she had to concentrate on what to do, right now, to defuse the situation. 'It's over.'

Nathaniel eyed her with disdain. 'You expect me to believe that?'

'It's true, I swear.'

He stared at her, unflinching. Isla felt his eyes boring into her as though he were intent on tearing her apart, one piece at a time.

'How long have you known?' She had to find out what she was dealing with, what damage limitation she could feasibly employ.

'Long enough. Enough time to know that you shouldn't be allowed to get away with it.'

A memory snagged in Isla's mind, and she tugged it until she'd managed to wrest it free. 'But all that stuff you said . . . a few weeks ago . . . about being worried about your dad . . .' Isla felt like a rabbit trapped in a snare.

Nathaniel smirked. 'Just thought I'd test the water. See if you had any conscience at all. I told you I was worried my dad was seriously ill and even then you didn't see fit to tell me the truth.'

'So all those things about your mum and dad, about him being all over her . . .'

Nathaniel leered at her, eyebrows raised, as if challenging her to articulate any grievance about the fact that he had lied to her.

'How did you find out?'

He laughed – a bitter, acrid laugh. 'What, because you've been *so* discreet.' He shook his head. 'Whose idea was it for my dad to pick you up half a mile from school? Thought nobody would see because it was *so* far away? Was that your great mastermind or his?'

The derision in Nathaniel's voice grated on Isla like nails down a blackboard. She thought about those first few weeks of her relationship with Andrew: him collecting her after school before driving them to a pub in the countryside. Their meeting place a small, residential cul-de-sac, no chance of bumping into anyone she knew on their way somewhere else.

The reality dawned on Isla like a lightbulb switching on above her head. 'You were following me?'

Heat flooded his cheeks, and all at once it became clear to her. Nathaniel's crush tipping into an obsession. Nathaniel following her – for how long before her relationship with Andrew, she had no way of knowing. Nathaniel watching her get into his dad's car. Nathaniel knowing everything, right from the very beginning. 'You have, haven't you? You've been following me for months?'

He wiped the embarrassment from his face, replaced it with self-righteousness. 'Is that all you've got to say? You've been screwing my dad, and all you care about is whether I've been following you?' He shook his head. 'I've seen you. I've seen you coming out of that fucking hotel every Thursday night. You and him. Did you really think nobody knew?'

He spoke with such hatred that, for a few moments, Isla couldn't speak, couldn't think. And then she remembered that day, on the train, on her way back from seeing Andrew: Nathaniel stepping out onto the platform beside her. His excuse about getting his bike fixed; how, when she had asked him about it a few weeks later, he seemed to have forgotten. Now, she realised, he must have been following her every Thursday for weeks: stepping into a different carriage on the same train to Waterloo, following her from a distance to the hotel where she met Andrew, waiting outside for two or three hours, following her home again afterwards. The thought of it made her feel queasy, sullied, violated.

'You literally have no shame, do you? You waltz around pretending to be so perfect, like butter wouldn't melt in your fucking mouth, when all the time you're nothing more than a . . . a whore. Do you get off on fucking men old enough to be your dad? Needed

240

to find a father figure because your own dad's dead, so you thought you'd fuck mine?'

There was something familiar in the cadence of Nathaniel's malice, something Isla knew she had heard before: a similar level of misogyny, hatred, bile. And then it hit her. 'It was you, wasn't it?'

'What?'

'It was you who sent me all those anonymous emails.' The thought of it – the thought of Nathaniel, whom she'd known her entire life, with whom she'd been friends for as long as she could remember, writing such horrible, hateful things to her – made her flesh crawl.

'So? It wasn't as if any of it wasn't true.' He glared at her defiantly, challenging her to contradict him. And she could see, in that moment, the depth of his anger: the painful sense of inadequacy, his fury that she had chosen Andrew over him. His unmitigated resentment that she had never found him remotely attractive, that she would not have dated him in a million years.

She felt her voice strengthening. 'It's over between me and your dad. It would be pointless telling anyone. It would just hurt people for no reason.'

'Hurt *you*, you mean. Hurt your precious reputation. Don't want people thinking you're a slut? You should have thought about that before you fucked my dad.'

'It wasn't like that. He pursued *me*, for god's sake. It wasn't like I went *looking* for a relationship with him.'

Nathaniel's mouth curled into a contemptuous snarl. 'Yeah, right. You're pathetic, you know that? People have a right to know what you're really like.'

Fear tightened around Isla's throat. 'Please, Nathaniel. I know you're upset. But there's nothing to be achieved by telling anyone now.'

'Isn't there? I think there's a lot to be achieved.' He hissed the words at her, small particles of spit erupting from his lips. 'Did you ever stop to think *for one second* about my mum? Or my brother? Or me? Did it bother you *at all*, the shit you were causing my family?' He glared at her. 'You shouldn't be allowed to get away with it.'

The venom in Nathaniel's outburst – the knowledge of how much damage he could do – floored Isla for a moment. But then a self-preservation instinct kicked in and she knew she could not allow herself to be near him any longer.

'I'm asking you, for everyone's sake, not to tell anyone. I know how much you want to punish me, but believe me, I've been punished enough already. It's over and there's nothing to be gained from anyone finding out. All that'll happen is a lot of people will get hurt, most of all your mum. She's the one whose life you'll destroy if you say anything. So just think about that, please.' She turned around, began walking away, instructing herself to put one foot in front of the other.

'You won't get away with it. I won't let you.'

Nathaniel's anger trailed after her. But Isla did not look back, would not face any more of his vitriol. She kept walking, through the park, towards the exit, trying not to imagine the litany of repercussions should Nathaniel follow through on his threat.

THE PRESENT

Nicole

Nicole hears the police officer's words, cautioning her seventeen-year-old son, feels as though she has stepped into someone else's life.

The kitchen door flings open, and there are Abby and Jack, standing in the doorway, and it takes a moment for Nicole to absorb what she is seeing; she thought Abby left the house fifteen minutes ago, that Jack was safely upstairs, ignorant of all that was taking place. Abby's hand grips Jack's arm as though to restrain him from making their presence known, and Nicole can see immediately from their expressions – Abby's horror, Jack's fear – that they have heard too much already.

She pulls Jack towards her, wraps an arm around his shoulders, leaves Abby standing alone by the door.

For a few seconds, nobody speaks.

It is the male officer who breaks the silence. 'Mrs Richardson, we asked you to leave. It's not appropriate you being here. Nathaniel, we'll need you to come down to the station to be interviewed under caution.'

Nicole watches Nathaniel's eyes widen, sees his terrified glance towards Andrew, then to her. She registers the alarm in Jack's expression, watches him open his mouth to speak but no words emerge. She perceives the fury in Abby's furrowed brow, the pain these revelations are causing her. And even though all this happens in a matter of seconds, it is as though everything around her has slowed down, as though she is watching it in decelerated time. As though the moment is being protracted beyond all comprehensible bounds to punish her for what her family has done.

'Mum . . .'

The desperation in Nathaniel's voice jolts her back to reality: back to the frame of time in which sixty seconds fill a minute, in which two police officers are arresting her son for a crime she knows – beyond any reasonable doubt – he did not commit. The words blurt from her lips as if they have a life of their own.

'It wasn't Nathaniel. It was me. I was driving. I killed Isla.'

Abby

The words puncture Abby's ears. She feels them reverberating inside her, defying any coherent meaning.

'Mrs Forrester – are you admitting to driving the car that killed Isla Richardson?'

Abby listens to the officer's question, watches Nicole's eyes dart around the room – to Andrew, to Nathaniel, to Jack – before she responds.

'Yes.'

Abby feels as though she has stepped into a parallel universe where everything has been debased, corrupted, contorted beyond recognition. She cannot get her bearings, like a sailor lost at sea, no compass to show her the way.

'Nicole, what the hell—'

'Mum, please—'

'Mum, don't—'

Abby hears the trio of voices – Andrew, Nathaniel, Jack – and watches as Nicole exhales deeply, squeezes Nathaniel's arm, pulls Jack tight into an embrace, whispers something into his ear that Abby cannot hear.

'I don't understand.' Abby looks around the room, stunned that they are all standing there, immobile, as though Nicole has not just placed a bomb in the centre of the kitchen and detonated their lives.

Nicole turns to her, tears in her eyes. 'I'm sorry, Abby. I don't know what to say.'

The words are like treacle in Abby's ears, and she cannot make sense of what is happening. Nicole is her best friend, has been her best friend for almost two decades. It is not possible that what she is saying is true.

But then Nicole begins to talk, her confession an unrelenting torrent, and they are words Abby does not want to hear, words so vivid and graphic that she wishes she could close her ears to them, knows they will haunt every dream and plague every grief-stricken moment.

Nicole describes how she had been driving to the late-night pharmacy to get some medicine for Jack – Jack, who'd had a terrible upset stomach, who'd not been able to stop vomiting, more ill than Nicole had seen him for years – and she was texting Andrew, asking when he was going to be home, angry with him for being so late yet again, annoyed that she'd had to leave Jack by himself because Andrew was still at the office. She only glanced at her phone for a few seconds – sporadically at that, keeping half an eye on the street – but it was late, dark, her visibility impaired, and then a figure ran across the road – just bolted into the path of Nicole's car, like a deer startled by the headlights – and there was no time for Nicole to stop, no time for her to slam on her brakes. She wasn't even speeding, there just wasn't time. It all happened so quickly, the impact and the sound and the terrible realisation of what had happened. She didn't know it was Isla – she turns to Abby and swears she didn't know it was Isla – but she panicked, and she doesn't know what came over her, doesn't know what happened in those few brief, heinous seconds, doesn't know what she was thinking, only that she understood something awful had happened, something truly terrible. She felt as though she was in a nightmare from which she could not awaken: no clear thoughts in her head, just blood roaring in her ears, hands shaking so much she could not keep them still. She does not remember making a decision, does not remember the moment in which she put the car into reverse, turned it around, averted her eyes from the scene she was leaving behind. She does not remember the thought process that led her to drive away, in the opposite direction, does not know what sent her to the industrial estate, a place she had driven past countless times but never visited, does not know what it was beyond desperation that made her park on a derelict piece of land and leave her car there. She only knows that this is what she did. She ran the one and a half miles home as fast as she could, her whole body convulsing with shock, knowing she needed to get back to look after Jack before Andrew and Nathaniel arrived home and saw she was on foot, clocked that her car was missing, began asking questions for which she had no answers that would not destroy all their lives. Nicole talks and talks, about how everything spiralled out of control, about how it was only later – she promises Abby it was only later – that she heard about Isla, made the connection, realised the true horror of what she had done. How she knew, at that point, it was too late to confess, that time and circumstances had overtaken her. She could not bear to contemplate what it would do to Nathaniel and Jack if she admitted her crime. She knew she would go to prison for having driven away from the scene, could not bear the thought of what that would do to her boys.

And all the time Nicole is talking, she is crying, and Jack is crying, and Nathaniel looks stunned, and Andrew looks bewildered, and one of the police officers listens while the other makes notes in a small pocketbook.

And then the female officer is placing a hand on Nicole's shoulder, telling her she is under arrest on suspicion of causing death by dangerous driving, and Jack is pleading with Nicole not to go, and Nathaniel is clinging to Nicole as though he may be able to prevent her from leaving, and Nicole's expression is that of a woman whose heart is being ripped from her chest. Abby watches, unable to move, as Nicole wrests herself from her boys, allows herself to be led away by the officers, out of the kitchen, trailed by Andrew asking which station she is being taken to, when they can see her, what will happen next, Nathaniel and Jack following closely behind.

And then Abby is left alone, unable to believe that this is real, this is happening, that this is not some sort of terrible, cruel, sick joke.

Nicole

The walls of the interview room are dark blue, comprising large panels of cushioned hessian, much like Nicole imagines a padded cell in a psychiatric institution might look. There is no window, and Nicole cannot escape the thought that this is what it might be like in prison; this tiny, airless room might be a foretaste of what is to come.

Attached to the ceiling in one corner of the room is a small camera, and she wonders if she is being filmed, whether somebody is watching the interview live in a different room, analysing the tone of her voice, her body language, the guilt on her face. The thought fills her with unparalleled dread, and she tries to concentrate, to focus on the questions she is being asked.

'Let me get this straight, Mrs Forrester. You were texting your husband, while driving, and Isla Richardson ran into the road in front of your vehicle. You weren't able to apply the brakes in time, and you collided with Ms Richardson. You were aware that you had knocked somebody down – though at the time you didn't realise the identity of the victim – and then rather than stay at the scene and call the emergency services, you drove away, hid your car on an industrial estate, and later that evening reported the vehicle stolen?'

Nicole listens to the story relayed back to her, words congealing in her mouth. She nods her head.

'Can you give me a verbal answer please, Mrs Forrester, for the tape.'

Nicole looks down at the recording machine on the table, cannot escape the sense that this is surreal. 'Yes, that's correct.'

'And you told nobody what had happened?'

The interviewing detective – a different officer to the ones who brought her here – cannot restrain the scepticism in his voice.

In the chair next to Nicole, her solicitor – someone Andrew must have found at breakneck speed, Andrew not foolish enough to leave her to the mercies of a duty solicitor – leans forward, advises her to answer the question.

'No, I didn't.'

'And you maintain that you didn't discover your husband's affair with Isla Richardson until after the accident? Until the day of Isla's funeral, in fact, fifteen days later?' It is there again, the cynicism in the detective's voice, and Nicole shakes her head before remembering the tape and giving a verbal answer.

The clock on the wall tells her it is a quarter past nine. She is not sure what time she arrived, knows it must have been after six-thirty, but beyond that, it is as though time has taken on a different dimension, as though it is being stretched and then contracted from one minute to the next until it is warped beyond all recognition. All she knows is that she has told the detective the same facts again and again, has confirmed the details over and over, a seemingly endless array of clarifications. It is as though the four of them – Nicole, her solicitor, the interviewing detective and the taciturn officer – are trapped in a Groundhog Day of questioning.

The door opens, and a policewoman – the female officer who was at Nicole's house earlier today – enters the room, whispers something into the interviewing detective's ear. The detective frowns before speaking.

'Interview paused at . . .' He studies the clock on the wall. 'Twenty-one eighteen.' Pressing a finger down on the tape machine, he pushes his chair back from the table and stands up.

Without further explanation, he leaves the room, closing the door behind him. Nicole turns to her solicitor who tells her not to worry, it is all quite normal. The remaining officer studies whatever notes she has made in her book, does not make eye contact.

The minutes tick by – 21.19, 21.20, 21.21 – and Nicole is aware of sweat pooling in the small of her back. Her mind is awash with speculations as to what is taking the detective so long, and she tries to reassure herself that interruptions like this must happen all the time. But doubts escalate in her mind, and she picks up the cup of water in front of her, sips from it, tries to wet her parched lips.

Recollections rush to fill the empty time. She recalls the collective shock that greeted her confession earlier this evening and wishes that so many things in the past had been different, that the future she has been dreading were not now a reality.

The thought runs through her head that she does not know when she will see her boys again. She does not know if – when the questioning is over – she will be released on bail or held on remand. Whether it will be hours or days or even weeks before she can hug them again. The prospect of being separated from Nathaniel and Jack is like a vice tightening around her throat, a possibility she dare not dwell on for too long.

The door opens, and the detective returns, carrying an iPad. There is a silent, visual exchange between the detective and the officer seated at the table, a tacit communication Nicole cannot decipher.

The detective retakes his seat opposite her, presses a finger on the tape machine to restart it, announces the continuation of the interview at nine twenty-eight p.m. He looks at Nicole for a moment as though trying to solve an impenetrable puzzle, the iPad still in his hand, its screen concealed from Nicole.

'Is there anything else you'd like to tell us, Mrs Forrester? Anything you think might be relevant about the night of Isla Richardson's death?'

The palms of Nicole's hands are clammy, and she wipes them on her trousers. She feels as though she has stepped onto the wrong path and now cannot find her way back. 'I don't think so, no.'

The detective pauses. 'That's interesting.' He takes in a deep breath, lets it out again slowly. 'Just humour me for a moment, will you, while I tell you a little story.'

Nicole

There is something in the detective's tone that causes the hairs on Nicole's arms to bristle. She glances across at her solicitor, but his face is impassive.

The detective does not wait for a response before continuing.

'We've just received some information from a local cab driver. This cab driver has been in Australia for the past five weeks, visiting his daughter. He left, in fact, the day after Isla Richardson was killed, hadn't heard anything about the incident until he got back yesterday and happened to look through a local newspaper.'

The detective pauses, places his elbows on the armrests of his chair, clasps his hands together as if in prayer.

'Reading the story reminded him of an incident of his own the night before he'd gone to Australia – a near-collision with a speeding car. Not unusual in his line of trade, but the news story brought it to mind. This cab driver has a dashcam fitted to his car, and he's very diligent about downloading all the footage every night; he likes keeping a record of every journey. Sounds like he's had too many altercations not to be vigilant. Today, he had a look at this footage and was quite surprised by what he found. He brought it into the station this evening, and the officers agreed it made for interesting viewing. I've just had a look at it myself, and I thought you might like to see it too.'

There is faux-chumminess in the detective's voice, and Nicole reminds herself to remain on guard.

'Before I show it to you, I just want to check there's nothing else you'd like to tell us about the night of Isla's death. Nothing at all you can think of that might be relevant?'

Nicole's thoughts sprint through a thousand things she could say but she dares not articulate any of them. She shakes her head, tells him no.

The detective pauses, his gaze unflinching. 'Okay. In that case, I wonder if you could explain this to us.'

He does not take his eyes from her face as he activates the iPad, places it on the table in front of her, presses the play button.

A video begins, and Nicole looks at it, watches the knitting together of one frame to the next: a road in the evening, tipping into darkness, lit by streetlamps and city light pollution. An oncoming vehicle with no headlights on. A sudden swerve, a near-miss. A freeze-frame at the moment the cars almost collide. Clarity of images telling an indisputable story.

Nicole watches, paralysed, wishes she could tear her eyes away, that she did not have to see it: the scene she had hoped never to come to light. A truth she had hoped never to be exposed.

THE NIGHT OF ISLA'S DEATH

Isla

'It's none of your business. Just stay out of it, okay?'

Isla glared at Callum, furious with him for shining a light on the mess her life had become.

'I'm worried about you. You're just . . . you don't seem very happy. You've been like it ever since we went back to school. What's going on?'

Callum's voice was kind, gentle, and somehow that made it worse. She didn't deserve his concern. She didn't deserve anything from him, given the way she'd treated him. She wouldn't blame him if he never spoke to her again.

'I'm fine.'

'But you're not. You know you're not.' Callum paused. 'What's wrong?'

Isla shivered despite the warm September night. She looked at Callum, leaning against a garden wall, part of her wishing she could tell him everything, another part of her knowing, unequivocally, that she couldn't.

For the past month, she had barely slept. Every waking moment she had felt on high alert, waiting for all the ugly truths in her life to emerge. Waiting for Nathaniel to tell everyone she'd been sleeping with his dad, anticipating the moment her life imploded. Every time she walked into the sixth-form common room, she was convinced people were whispering about her. Every time she returned home at the end of the day, she expected to see her mum at the kitchen table, face contorted with disappointment, her friendship with Nicole destroyed because of what Isla had done. Four weeks since Nathaniel told her what he knew, and now a part of Isla wondered if she wouldn't rather he just publicise it, get the horror show over and done with, like the swift removal of a plaster, instead of this horrible, nauseating suspense as to what he might say, to whom, and when.

From Meera's house across the road came the gentle thud of music. Isla wished she hadn't come to the party, wished she'd stayed at home, got an early night. She needed to be at the pool at the crack of dawn, knew how important her training was given her absences over the summer, but she'd wanted to do something normal, wanted to *feel* normal. She'd thought coming to the party would reconnect her to whatever it was she had lost. It was over six weeks since the abortion; she should, she was sure, be feeling okay by now. Instead, she was plagued by a persistent sense of being removed – distant – from everyone around her: family, friends, teachers, swim mates.

'Isla?'

Turning back to Callum, she shook her head. 'I'm okay.'

'You're clearly not.' He hesitated. 'I'm guessing it's to do with *him*. I'm assuming it's over?'

Heat blazed in Isla's cheeks. 'It's got nothing to do with you.'

'Jesus, what a scumbag.'

'Just leave it, okay?'

'You know you're better off shot of him, right? He's a total fucking shit, taking advantage of you like that.'

Isla's hand swung through the air without her having any conscious awareness of it. It wasn't until she heard the crack of her hand against Callum's cheek, felt the sting in her palm, that she realised what she'd done.

He recoiled, took a step back, brought a hand to his face.

'I'm sorry. I didn't mean to do that. Are you okay?'

He stared at her in silence.

'Here, let me look.' Isla reached out to check his cheek, but he took another step back, shook his head.

'Just leave it.'

'I'm sorry. I don't know what happened. I just . . .' She searched for words to explain what was going on in her head; how, just a few months ago, she felt as though her life was like a well-organised cabinet in which everything had its place and she could find whatever she needed right away. But then a chain of events had shaken it up so badly that it was now in utter disarray: thoughts and feelings jumbled in a clutter of emotional chaos. But she couldn't find the words to articulate any of that without divulging more than she dared.

Callum was silent for a few moments before turning and walking away.

'Don't go, please.'

He raised a hand in the air, called over his shoulder. 'Take care of yourself, Isla.'

Isla watched as he left, rounded the corner, and disappeared out of sight.

A shriek of laughter came from Meera's house, and Isla looked across the road, checked she was alone. She didn't want to see anyone, didn't want to speak to anyone. She couldn't face going back to the party. Couldn't face going home, either. Leaning against a wall, she pulled out her phone, opened WhatsApp, went into her archived conversations even as a voice in her head screamed at her not to. But the part of her bent on punishing herself scrolled down to the thread with Andrew, opened it, began to read: back through time, back to the beginning, to the message that had started it all.

> *Hey. Great to chat earlier. Any time you need a lift, you know where I am. I want to do everything I can to support a future Olympian. ☺ x*

She scrolled up, one message at a time, the missives getting more personal, more intimate, as the days went by. And then, there it was, the message that had taken things to the next level. The message she knew she should have deleted immediately, put an end to it before it could begin.

> *Isla, I'm about to go out on a limb here, and I sincerely hope I don't live to regret it. I can't stop thinking about you . . .*

She read it in full, the message that had led to their first planned meeting, their first kiss, the beginning of something that should never have started. Scrolling further, she read message after message, outpourings of infatuation and desire that she had mistaken for love. Hungrily, she ingested them all as though they would fill her up, nourish her, instead of leaving her empty, bereft and achingly lonely.

And then she reached the final message, the nail in the coffin of their relationship: a relationship she had thought was solid, real, only to discover it was made of nothing more than teenage fantasy.

> *I know you're hurt and angry, but I really think it's better for both of us if we can part on good terms . . .*

She read it again, so engrossed in her own misery that she did not, at first, notice the SUV pull up beside her. It was only as she clocked the abrupt cutting of the engine that she became aware of it. Looking up, she saw darkened windows preventing her from seeing inside.

Fear scuttled across her skin. Her hand slipped into her bag, found her keys, clutched her fist around them. She turned, began walking swiftly away, back towards the party. Behind her, a car door opened, and she quickened her step.

'Isla.'

She looked round, took a moment to compute who had spoken, so unexpected was their presence.

'Jack?' Relief washed over her. 'What are you doing here?' She registered the car, the open driver's door, Jack standing beside it. 'Did you *drive* that? Whose car is it?'

He inhaled a deep breath before answering. 'My mum's.'

'And you *drove* it?' Isla's fist relaxed around the keys. 'Why did you do that? Your mum'll kill you if she finds out.'

Jack stared at her: impassive, unspeaking.

'Are you okay?' Walking towards him, Isla saw that his hands were shaking. 'What's wrong?' Reaching out, she placed a hand on his arm. Jack recoiled as though she had lunged at him with a sharp object.

'Get off me! Don't touch me!'

'What is it? What's the matter?'

Jack said nothing.

'Let me call Nathaniel, ask him to come and get you—'

'Don't!' His voice sounded urgent, panicked.

Isla paused, tried to stymie the dread rising into her throat. 'What's going on? Whatever it is, I just want to help.'

'I don't want anything from you. I know what you've been doing . . . with my dad.'

The shock hit her like a tidal wave. 'What do you mean?' Her voice sounded thin, taut, like a piece of elastic stretched almost to breaking point.

Jack gripped the edge of the car door, knuckles white. 'I know you've been . . . shagging him. I've seen photos on his phone. I know he's planning to leave my mum for you.'

Isla felt herself flinch. 'Where did you get that from?' Thoughts tore through her mind, wondering if Nathaniel had finally enacted his threat to tell people what he knew.

'I heard him, on the phone, talking to an estate agent about houses. I know he's leaving us.'

Confusion swirled in Isla's head. For a moment, she thought that perhaps Andrew had experienced a change of heart, that he was going to tell her he'd made a mistake, he was sorry, that of course he didn't want to end their relationship. That he was planning to leave Nicole, buy a new house, that they would no longer have to meet in hotel rooms by Waterloo station. For a brief moment, she imagined him asking her if she could ever forgive him for his terrible behaviour. But then she recalled the patronising way he had spoken to her when he'd dumped her, the icy tone of his final message, the radio silence since. The clear indication that he wanted nothing more to do with her. And suddenly, all her fury with Andrew – for his manipulations, his lies, his subtle emotional coercion – came flooding back, and she reminded herself that she would never forgive him, even if he begged. 'I don't know what you're talking about—'

'Stop lying! I've *seen* the photos on his phone. All those . . . pictures of you with him. I've *seen* them.'

Isla recoiled at the thought of what Jack may have seen: semi-naked photos of her in bed with Andrew, pictures that were only ever supposed to be viewed by the two people involved in them. She was incensed that Andrew had been so careless, so negligent, that he had not better protected his phone. Furious he had been so arrogant, so nonchalant as to let Jack anywhere near his mobile given the bombshell it contained.

She tried to steady her racing thoughts, but they were speeding faster than she could keep pace with. She had no way of knowing if Jack had discussed it with Nathaniel, if Nathaniel had admitted he already knew, whether they were already hatching a plan to expose her. All she knew was that she must try to salvage the situation, calm Jack down, limit the potential damage he could do.

'Jack, your dad's not leaving your mum—'

'You're lying—'

'I'm not.' Isla took a deep breath. 'Whatever you heard, it's not what you think.'

'I don't believe you. You're just saying that—'

'Stop! Will you just listen to me, please. I'm telling the truth. There's nothing going on between me and your dad now. I promise.'

Jack shook his head, murmuring quietly to himself, and Isla took another step forward, knowing she had to reduce the risk of Jack rushing home, blurting out everything to Nicole. She couldn't have this whole sorry mess getting out just at the point she knew it was time to move on.

'Listen to me. Your dad isn't leaving your mum. He loves your mum.' She swallowed against the humiliation scratching at her throat. 'The best thing you can do is let me take you home and forget all about it. It doesn't matter any more.'

'It matters to me! It will matter to my mum. I hate you for what you've done.' Without allowing time for Isla to respond, Jack got back into the driver's seat, buried his head in his hands.

Isla's body throbbed with panic. Reaching out, she grabbed hold of the car door, held it open.

'You can't drive. You're not old enough. Just think about what'll happen if you get caught.'

'Let me go!' He yanked the handle of the door, pulling it against the full force of Isla's grip.

'Please, Jack, let me take you home.'

'Leave me alone. I don't want anything from you.'

With one decisive pull, he wrestled the door from her grasp, slammed it shut, locked it and started the engine.

Isla banged on the window. 'Open the door. You don't know how to drive. Just get out and calm down, please.'

The engine continued to rev, but the car didn't move, the tinted windows too dark for Isla to see what he was doing inside. She clasped her phone, wondering if she should call Nathaniel, get him to come, or whether that would only make things worse. She cursed herself for having told Meera not to invite Nathaniel tonight, for not wanting him anywhere near her since he'd confronted her a month ago.

The gentle thump of a bass line emerged from Meera's house across the street, less than half a dozen houses away, diagonally from where she stood now. She could be there in twenty seconds, could get Jules or Kit – someone she could trust – to talk some sense into Jack, persuade him not to drive his mum's car.

Behind her, the engine revved even louder, but still the car didn't move, and Isla wondered what Jack was doing in there, what he was thinking, how he was feeling. She knew she had to stop him driving, had to look out for him. This was all her fault, her and Andrew's: Jack being upset, Jack driving his mum's car, Jack being in such a state. It was all their responsibility.

Turning around, without looking back, she ran at full speed across the road.

THE PRESENT

Nicole

Nicole stares at the dashcam footage that the detective has played twice now, panic clouding her thoughts.

The evidence is irrefutable. The identity of the driver who almost crashes into the cab is unmistakable in the frozen image.

Her little boy, behind the wheel of her car, the date and time stamped in the top left-hand corner of the clip telling a story she has tried so hard to conceal.

Something inside her seems to splinter, as though pieces of her are fragmenting, never to be restored in any semblance of order. As though she will never – can never – be the same again.

She thinks about Jack, at home, just a few hours ago; how she had been able to feel his panic, his despair when the officers were arresting Nathaniel. How she had known he was only moments away from a confession. How determined she had been to prevent him from speaking, to do everything in her power to shield him from a fate she has been dreading for the past five weeks.

Nicole looks up at the detective, feels the walls of her throat narrowing.

So many times she has imagined this scene, but now it is here she cannot believe it is actually happening. Cannot believe it has come to this. Cannot comprehend that, in the end, she was not able to protect him. Her one job – her main priority as a parent – and she has failed.

'Mrs Forrester. This footage clearly places your son – Jack – behind the wheel of your car very close to the location of the incident, just moments after it took place. So, I'm going to ask you again. What do you know about the death of Isla Richardson?'

THE NIGHT OF ISLA'S DEATH

Nicole

The front door slams and then the door to the sitting room flings open.

Nicole looks up, sees Jack's tear-stained face, leaps up from the sofa. 'What is it? What's wrong?'

Jack stares at her, his whole body shaking. Fear thuds in Nicole's chest and she places her hands either side of her son's face, tries to make eye contact. 'What's wrong? What's happened?'

He shakes his head, tears coursing down his cheeks. 'I only wanted to talk to her, I just wanted to know what she'd say—'

'Who? What do you mean?'

'I just wanted to talk to Isla . . .'

For a moment, Nicole is confused. '*Isla?* What did you need to speak to Isla about?'

He looks at her, then averts his eyes.

'Jack? What's happened? Please, just tell me.'

He sniffs, tears blotching his cheeks. 'I just wanted to ask her about it. About Dad.'

He hesitates, and the neurons in Nicole's brain fire in every direction. 'What about Dad?'

Jack swallows hard, and she can see his distress.

'Dad . . . he . . . he's sleeping with her. With Isla.'

It takes a few seconds for Nicole to understand what Jack is saying. 'Isla? *Our* Isla? Don't be ridiculous, of course he's not.'

Jack shakes his head. 'I'm not being ridiculous. I saw photos of her. On Dad's phone—' He stops abruptly as though a guillotine has sliced through his words.

Thoughts sprint through Nicole's mind as if in pursuit of a finishing line she cannot see. 'That doesn't mean anything, sweetheart. Of course Dad's got photos of Isla on his phone. I've got dozens of Isla – and Clio – on mine.' She rubs a finger along Jack's wet cheek, studies his troubled face, wonders if – in spite of her vigilance – she has nonetheless underestimated how upset he has been by his ADHD diagnosis.

Jack wrests himself free from Nicole's hands, quick breaths juddering in and out of his lungs. 'You don't understand. The photos . . . They weren't normal. They were . . .' He stops, buries his face in his hands, shaking his head as though trying to rid it of whatever thoughts are rampaging through his mind. 'They were in bed.'

The words buzz in Nicole's ears like a fly she cannot swat away. It does not make sense. 'You must be mistaken. Dad wouldn't . . . Not with Isla.'

'I'm not mistaken! I looked up the dates on the photos. It's been going on for *ages*.'

It takes a few seconds for the information to sink into Nicole's head, like water dissolving into caked earth. She feels dizzy, vertiginous, her brain refusing to believe it is true. She cannot comprehend that Andrew would do that, that he would betray her so abominably. That he would betray Abby, or abuse his position with Isla in that way. That he would do something so repugnant, so selfish, so reckless. So completely and egregiously immoral. But then she looks at Jack's face, sees his angst, knows he would not say something so unutterably awful unless he wholeheartedly believed it to be true.

She thinks about how erratic Andrew's behaviour has been over the past few months: furtive and tense one moment, animated and exuberant the next. She thinks about how, a few months ago, he began obsessing about his weight, his health, the greying of hair at his temples, and suddenly what Jack is saying does not seem as outlandish as she wishes it to be. Suddenly it seems painfully, horrifically plausible.

'I only went to talk to her . . . I wasn't going to do anything . . . I didn't mean it . . . You've got to believe me.'

Jack's words are garbled, no clear ending of one sentence, no distinct beginning of the next, but the panic in his voice causes a knot to tighten in Nicole's throat. 'What are you talking about? What happened?'

'I didn't see her . . . It was an accident . . . She just ran out into the road . . . My foot . . . the accelerator . . . I don't know what happened.'

Fears chills Nicole's blood. 'Where were you, Jack? What were you doing?' Suspicions needle their way into her mind but they are too dreadful to contemplate.

And then a story is tumbling from Jack's lips, amidst the tears and the breathlessness, and he is telling her how he couldn't stand what his dad had done with Isla, how angry he was, so angry he thought he was going to explode with it – with the secret and the hurt and the certainty that his dad was going to leave them – and he just wasn't thinking straight, he just couldn't think clearly. He just had to get out of the house, be somewhere different. He took Nicole's car, hadn't even known where he was going, he just needed to do something.

As Nicole tries to compute all this information, she restrains herself from reprimanding him, from asking what on earth he was thinking, driving her car illegally when he doesn't know how beyond his Saturday go-karting, but she knows this is not the time, knows he is too distraught, that he would not hear her anyway. What she needs to do now is calm him down, elicit from him the story he is struggling to tell.

And then Jack is explaining how he drove to the party – the party that Nathaniel was going to, the party at Meera's house where he knew Isla would be too – and that he only wanted to talk to her, only wanted to ask her why she had done it, why she had ripped his family apart. He hadn't meant for it to happen, he thought she was just going to walk along the pavement, he didn't know she was going to run into the road, that she would run so fast, without any warning. He hadn't meant to push his foot down on the accelerator, it just slipped, too far, too quickly – the pedal was so different to a go-kart, it felt completely different – and the car went off so fast, he couldn't control it, it all happened so quickly. And then he panicked, and he didn't know what to do, he just sat there, shaking, and he couldn't bear to look, couldn't bear to get out of the car to see what he'd done, so he put it in reverse, backed away and drove home. And maybe she was okay, maybe Isla was fine, maybe it was just a knock and she got up and went back to the party, he doesn't know, he just had to get out of there, and now he doesn't know if he hurt her or not. And Jack is asking Nicole what he's going to do, what will happen to him, will he go to prison, imploring her to tell him it will be okay, that she believes him, that she believes it was just an accident.

Jack's teeth are chattering, and Nicole pulls him into her arms, tries to calm him down, struggles to grasp what he has told her.

'You didn't see anything? Before you drove away? You didn't see if Isla was alright?'

Jack shakes his head. 'She'll be okay, won't she?'

Nicole tries to think, to collect her thoughts, but they are like spheres in a pinball machine, ricocheting from one side of her brain to the other.

276

Glancing down at her watch, she sees it is almost nine-thirty. Nathaniel must still be at Meera's. The realisation hits her that someone at the party might have seen something, recognised her car. Somebody, right now, might be calling the police to report a hit-and-run.

Something clicks into place inside Nicole's head: a sense of urgency, of maternal imperative. An ancient, febrile instinct to protect her son.

'Where's the car now?'

Jack's breaths jolt in and out. 'In the driveway.'

Nicole forces herself to think. 'Just stay here a moment, okay? Don't move.'

She waits until Jack has acknowledged her, and then she grabs her phone, heads out into the hallway, through the front door in her bare feet, into the wide sweep of their driveway. Activating the torch on her phone, she bends down, examines the front of the car.

On the right-hand side of the bumper is a deep dent, the metal disfigured, the plastic casing of the light cracked and broken. The damage is too great, surely, to be nothing more than an innocuous tap. And yet, Nicole remembers one time, years ago, when she hit a rabbit late at night on a country road – she hadn't even been going that fast – and even that had caused a sizeable dent in her bumper.

A dozen possible scenarios play out in her mind.

She imagines calling Nathaniel, asking if he is still at the party, asking if Isla is there, whether she is okay.

She imagines calling Abby, ascertaining whether Isla has come home yet, checking whether she is back safe and sound.

She imagines calling Meera's house, hoping someone will answer the phone, asking them to go out into the street to see if Isla is there.

But as each option hurtles through her mind, she knows she cannot pursue any of them. Because they all lead to the same inevitable outcome.

They all lead to suspicion. To questions she does not want to answer. To Jack being prosecuted, found guilty, being sent to prison. He has driven illegally, underage. He has hit a pedestrian and left the scene of the incident. It is a catalogue of crimes, and he will surely be punished.

Terror grips her throat, and she knows she cannot allow it to happen. He is only fifteen. He is just a child. He has made a terrible, foolish mistake, a mistake precipitated by his father's disgusting behaviour. She cannot – will not – allow him to pay for it for the rest of his life.

There is not time, right now, for her to speculate about what may have happened to Isla; all she can do is hope – pray – that she is okay. For now, she must focus on destroying the evidence so that, whatever Isla might say, Nicole can refute it, convince people it is not just untrue but impossible.

Racing back inside the house, she thrusts her feet into a pair of trainers, dashes into the sitting room where Jack is still standing, immobile. 'The keys, where are the keys?'

Jack stares at her, as if in a daze, and she grabs his arm, tries to keep her voice calm even as hysteria billows in her chest.

'Where are the keys, Jack? The car keys?'

Something seems to snap awake in him, and he reaches into the pocket of his jeans, pulls out the keys that Nicole had not known, until a few minutes ago, were missing.

'Come on.'

Clutching hold of Jack's arm, she leads him through the hallway, collects her house keys from the entrance table, shuffles him out of the front door, closing it behind her. Unlocking the car, she opens the passenger door, bundles Jack inside – Jack, like a little boy, dazed, compliant – fastens his belt around him. She cannot leave him at home alone, not when he is in such a terrible state. She cannot risk Andrew or Nathaniel arriving back and seeing him like that, cannot risk Jack telling anyone else what he has done. She has to protect him, even if that means taking him with her for the task she now faces.

As she passes around the front of the car, she cannot help glancing down again at the bumper, sees the deep indentation, imagines the impact. Forces herself to look away.

Sitting in the driver's seat, she tells Jack it is going to be okay, that she is going to take care of everything. Jack is silent, unresponsive, and Nicole tells herself that she will manage his shock later, when she can think how best to handle it, but for now she must deal with the immediate urgency in front of them.

Opening Google Maps on her phone, she zooms into her home address, moves out little by little, eyes scanning the streets, an area she knows so well – she has lived in this neighbourhood for almost twenty years – and yet now she cannot think, cannot get her bearings, cannot figure out where to go.

Her eyes dart from one side of the map to the other – north, south, east, west – and she can feel her desperation escalating, can feel the seconds ticking by, knows that time is closing in on her; Nathaniel might soon be home, Andrew might have left the office already, Isla may already be telling people what Jack has done.

And then her eyes land on it – the perfect place – and she jabs a finger at the screen, sees that it is only five minutes' drive away. She studies the reverse journey on foot, is quoted eighteen minutes but knows they will be able to do it in twelve if they run, which they must, if they stand a chance of getting back before anyone else is home.

Setting the location, she reverses out of the drive, speeds down the road, Jack silent beside her. Thoughts outstrip each other in her mind as she tries to figure out what to do, what to say, how to get Jack out of this.

She does not know how fast she drives, but in what seems like no time at all they are pulling off the main road, towards the industrial estate. Silently, she prays there will be somewhere she can leave the car, somewhere inconspicuous so it will not be discovered immediately. Somewhere that will buy her time, buy Jack an alibi, enable her to strategise their way out of this disaster.

The entrance to the industrial estate appears out of the darkness and she experiences a wave of relief. It is bigger than she'd imagined, enormous in fact; there is a road through the middle with warehouses on either side, each with their own parking lot. But she knows she cannot leave the car in one of those, knows she must find somewhere better to conceal it, somewhere it will not easily be detected.

Next to her, Jack emits a loud sob, and Nicole puts a hand on his thigh, tells him it is going to be okay, drives on through the industrial estate. A clock ticks loudly in her ear, and she knows that time is running out, that she must abandon the vehicle soon, that they must make their way home if they are to stand any chance of arriving before Andrew or Nathaniel.

And then they are at the end of the road, and Nicole fears she has got it all wrong, she has made a bad decision; they should never have come here. She should have spent longer studying the map, finding a better place, but now it is too late, there is no time to search for an alternative, no possibility of travelling somewhere new and still having a chance of reaching home in time.

And then, as her eyes scan the perimeter of the dimly lit industrial estate, she spies a narrow path to her right: an overgrown track adjacent to the final warehouse, trees on one side, a high wall on the other. Without a second thought, she turns into it, edges the car into the confined space beneath the overhanging branches, inches forward until she has reached the end. Quickly, urgently, she instructs Jack to get out of the car, watches as he pushes open the door as far as it will go, stumbles out, closes it behind him. Nicole gets out of her side, squeezes through the narrow gap, looks left and then right, can see nobody around, looks up at the buildings, does not catch sight of any CCTV cameras.

Reaching overhead, she pulls at a branch, tugs it until it breaks free, yanks off another and then another, leans them up against the back of the car, throws them onto its roof, her hands sore, her forehead drenched with sweat. And then she looks at her watch, sees the time – almost a quarter to ten – a fresh injection of adrenaline spiking her blood, and she tells Jack they have to go right away. She grabs his hand, hauls him out of the alleyway, over the uneven ground and the long grass, looks over her shoulder, sees that the car is pitifully camouflaged, that if somebody happens to venture down that track for any reason, they will see it immediately, but it is the best she can do in the time available.

Jack is still shaking, and she tells him that he has to run home with her – that's all he has to do, just run a mile and a half home – and she will take care of everything. And even though Jack's eyes are glassy, his expression vacant, he nods, and she tells him she loves him, that it is all going to be okay. And then she holds his hand tightly and together they run through the industrial estate, out onto the street, along the main road towards home.

And all the way, a plan formulates in Nicole's head, the details slipping and sliding until there is something solid, something that has a chance of being believed, something that may yet save Jack from the fate that otherwise awaits him.

If the house is empty when they get home, she will give Jack temazepam, send him to sleep, render him unconscious from this catastrophe in which they find themselves.

She will wait until somebody notices her car is missing, will feign ignorance, stoke the fire of belief that it has been stolen. She will report it to the police, say that the last time she saw it was when she collected Jack from football practice earlier that evening, that they'd arrived home at seven o'clock – a small dose of the truth to pepper the lies – that it could have been stolen any time since; she wouldn't have noticed, she had not been out of the house all evening.

When Isla tells people what happened – because Isla will be okay, surely – Nicole will say it's impossible, that Jack was at home with her all evening, that Isla must be mistaken; perhaps it was Nicole's car that hit her, but it must have been a stranger driving it. The thought of it, the thought of casting doubt on Isla's story – Isla, whom she has known since she was born, whom she has loved like a member of her own family – makes her flinch with pre-emptive remorse, but she cannot indulge it. Right now, she can think only about protecting Jack. Because if Jack is discovered to have been driving underage, if he is proven to have hit someone – to have hit the young woman with whom his father has been in a sexual relationship – it may be alleged that he did it on purpose, that he meant to run her over. And Nicole dares not contemplate what the ramifications of such an accusation might be.

Alongside her fear for Jack is her fury with Andrew. Rage for his infidelity, rage that of all the people in the world he chose to seduce, he selected the daughter of their best friend; a teenager who should have been able to trust that a man she'd known since she was born would never exploit her in that way.

Andrew has put their entire family in jeopardy; it is his behaviour, his choices, that have precipitated Jack's actions tonight. Had Andrew not betrayed them all – had he not been so unscrupulous, so corrupt, so egotistical – none of this would be happening.

But for now, she will feign ignorance, will pretend to know nothing. Because if she does not know about Andrew's relationship with Isla – if Jack has no knowledge of it either – then there can be no viable link to the accident. There can be no meaningful motive. In concealing her knowledge of Andrew's betrayal, she will shield Jack from any suspicion of involvement.

Holding on tight to Jack's hand, her feet pound along the pavement, one in front of the other. That is all she can do for now, put one foot in front of the other. Get Jack home, get him to bed, find them a route out of this labyrinthine nightmare.

The plan goes round and round in her head, and she knows, beyond all reasonable doubt, that she will do everything in her power to protect her son.

THE PRESENT

Nicole

'Mrs Forrester. We have dashcam footage showing your son driving your car recklessly and illegally, very close to where Isla Richardson was killed, just minutes after her estimated time of death. That vehicle has subsequently been discovered abandoned on an industrial estate, showing clear signs of having been involved in a collision. Forensics experts are carrying out further tests on the car, and officers will be on their way shortly to arrest Jack and bring him in for questioning—'

'No, please, don't.' Nicole hears the desperation in her voice. She cannot bear the thought of Jack being arrested; Jack being taken away in a police car, being brought here – to a soulless room like this, to be questioned – without her to support him. 'Please, let me go with you. He's only fifteen.'

The detective shakes his head. 'I'm afraid that won't be possible. We'll ensure he has an appropriate adult with him. But the best thing you can do for Jack now is tell the truth. You want to help him, don't you?'

Nicole is aware that the detective is goading her, trying to trap her into betraying her son, but she is paralysed with fear, does not know what to do for the best.

Her thoughts rewind to the night it happened. Arriving home to an empty house, relieved for once that Andrew was working late, that Nathaniel was still out. Bundling Jack up the stairs, medicating him with temazepam, putting him straight to bed. Sitting beside him, stroking his hair – telling him over and over that it was going to be okay, that she knew it was just an accident, that she would look after him – until his breaths deepened and he fell into a drug-induced sleep.

She recalls Nathaniel's return not long after, his eagle-eyed observation that her car was missing, the guilt she felt as she performed her planned charade, pretending not to know where it was. Her relief when it was Nathaniel – not her – who suggested it had been stolen, who proposed calling the police.

She remembers Andrew arriving home not long after, how it took every last vestige of her self-control not to pound him with her fists, not to shout, to swear, to scream at him for his unforgivable duplicity. Not to throttle him for the damage he had caused, or ask him if he realised what his depraved behaviour had cost them. How she let him kiss her, even as her stomach roiled with disgust for what he had done to her, to Isla, to all of them. How she knew that the best way to protect Jack was to pretend to be oblivious to Andrew's transgressions.

She remembers – as though the scene were frozen in time – the moment Nathaniel looked up from his phone, announced that Isla was dead, that she had been killed in a hit-and-run. How Nicole's entire body hummed with grief and panic in equal measure. How she contemplated shaking Jack awake, grabbing their passports, going to the airport, getting on the first available plane – anywhere, it didn't matter where – to remove him from danger. How the minutes ticked by all night long as she lay awake, replaying the events of the evening in her mind, too horrified to think clearly about what to do next.

And then the following day. Waiting until Jack awoke – late, the temazepam had done its job – sitting on the side of his bed, delivering the news she knew would throw his life into perpetual turmoil. Witnessing his terror, trying to reassure him that she would make it okay, schooling him in what to say, rehearsing the narrative about a fictitious vomiting bug that may yet save him. Watching Jack's confusion as he tried to absorb her instructions, her apprehension that he was still too much in shock, still too groggy from the temazepam to reliably remember the story. How she promised him over and over that she would look after him, that she would not let him come to any harm.

She remembers the following days and weeks as though they have been seared onto her memory. Jack retreating into himself: becoming quiet, withdrawn, pale, monosyllabic. How she oscillated between the desire to talk to him and the awareness that she did not want to pick at the scab of his anxiety. How the realisation dawned on her that perhaps she could save Jack from prosecution but she could not purge him of the crushing sense of his own culpability.

She remembers all the nights she lay awake thinking about the events of that evening, worrying whether she had done the right thing, whether she would do anything differently if time were rewound and she could live those moments again. Worrying about her car on the industrial estate, fearing she had not taken it far enough from home, had not hidden it sufficiently well, had not thought through the likelihood of it being found. And yet, at the same time, knowing it was out of her control, that she could not revisit the location, that it would be catastrophically foolish to do so.

And then there was Abby. All those hours she had sat with Abby, consoling her, comforting her, knowing what she knew. Listening to Abby rail against the monster who had killed her daughter, knowing that Abby's monster was in his bedroom, listening to music at top volume through his headphones to drown out the torture of his own thoughts. Those repeated moments of dread every time Abby relayed how she had harangued the police in search of answers. The remorse, the shame, the guilt about her own complicity in Abby's torment. And yet, her deep, profound belief that Isla's death had been an accident; Jack had been reckless, impetuous, distraught but he had never meant to harm her.

And then, Abby's discovery of the anonymous emails, her awareness of Isla's relationship, and Nicole's desperation that Abby would not uncover the identity of the man who had exploited her daughter. Not for Andrew's sake; Nicole stopped caring about him the day she found out. But for Jack's sake. Because the closer the net was trawled to their family, the greater the likelihood that Jack would be caught.

Nicole thinks now about the expression on Abby's face earlier this evening when she admitted responsibility for Isla's death: the unmitigated shock, horror, hatred. Nicole cannot blame her. It may not be true that she was driving the car that killed Isla, but her accountability for Abby's suffering is almost as great.

Her memory aches as she thinks about the past eighteen years, about all that she and Abby have been through together. The pregnancies, the tribulations of early parenthood, the endless self-doubt of motherhood. The commemoration of their children's milestones: first words, first steps, first days of school. The celebration of birthdays, Christmases, Easters, bank holidays. The sharing of countless bottles of wine, long weekends away, conversations deep into the night.

She thinks about the many times over the past five weeks she has come close to telling Abby the truth. But every time she has been on the verge of a confession, thoughts of Nathaniel and Jack have stopped her: thoughts about what would happen to them if the truth emerged, how it would destroy their lives as well as hers. She has lied not to protect herself, but out of love for her boys.

She raises her head, looks up at the detective, tears pooling in her eyes.

'Please let me see him. He's only fifteen.'

Abby

Abby sits on the sofa in her living room, opposite the family liaison officer, unable to digest what she's just been told.

Jack killed Isla.

Jack took Nicole's car, drove it illegally, and killed Isla.

And Nicole covered it up.

The news seems unreal, as though she has found herself in the narrative of someone else's life.

'Do you think it was an accident, or . . . ?' Abby cannot bring herself to say it explicitly.

The family liaison officer shakes her head. 'It's too early to say. But it does seem possible that what happened was a terrible accident. That's what both Jack and Nicole maintain.'

Abby nods, still unable to take it in.

She thinks about how she has watched Jack grow up over the years. How he has always been such an uncomplicated boy – personable, friendly, well behaved – how she and Nicole have often joked that at least they both have one teenager who never gives them any trouble.

Except now one of those children is dead and the other is in police custody.

She is overcome by such a complex mesh of emotions that she does not know where one ends and another begins. Anger with Jack for being so reckless. Fury with Andrew for seducing her daughter.

Resentment at Nicole for her multitude of lies. Frustration with Clio for having made Abby suspect – even for a moment – that she may somehow be involved.

'Can I get you anything?'

Abby shakes her head. There is nothing, she knows, that will ever completely dispel these feelings. Anger is only the tip of the iceberg. There is also her grief. Huge, unwieldy swathes of grief: for Isla, for Stuart, for her friendship with Nicole.

She thinks about the past five weeks, about Nicole sitting beside her on the sofa, wrapping her arms around her, grieving with her. She thinks about Isla's funeral, how Nicole had taken care of everything – the flowers and the catering, the transport and the wake – and how Abby was in such a daze she did not even think to thank her at the time, had felt so guilty about that later. She thinks about Nicole's daily check-ins – the visits, phone calls, messages – the care she has bestowed on Abby and Clio. She thinks about the unfailing interest Nicole has taken in the progress of the police investigation: interest that made Abby believe Nicole was almost as invested as she was in Isla's killer being brought to justice. Now, she realises, Nicole's enquiries were nothing more than calculated self-interest.

There can be no recovery, she knows unequivocally, for her relationship with Nicole.

The door to the sitting room opens, and Clio stands beneath the architrave. Her eyes clock the family liaison officer and she hovers, uncertain, like the inquisitive child she used to be in the not-so-distant past.

Abby does not know how to tell Clio what has happened, does not know how to convey that her sister was killed by a boy she has known since she was born, or that the crime was covered up by one of the most trusted adults in her life. She does not know if there are words to explain all that. For now, she opens her arms, invites Clio inside, and wraps her in all the love she has to give.

Nicole

'You've got five minutes.'

The officer opens the door to the interview room and Nicole steps inside.

Jack looks up from where he is sitting between Andrew and a man Nicole assumes is Jack's solicitor, in an otherwise empty room, his face pale, dark rings hammocking his eyes.

'Mum . . .' He stands up, falls into her arms.

Nicole holds him, Jack's breath hot against her neck. 'It's okay, sweetheart. It's going to be okay.' The words strain at her throat, and she does not know if she can do this, does not know how, in a few minutes' time, she will leave him. It seems impossible that she will say goodbye to him not knowing when she will see him again.

'What's going to happen to me?'

Panic laces Jack's words, and it slips into Nicole's bloodstream, infects her like a virus for which she knows there is no cure.

She hunts for phrases to reassure him, understands how woefully inadequate they will be. She does not possess the power to perform the magic trick she needs to enact: cannot turn back time, cannot undo what has been done. She cannot halt the future that is rushing to meet them.

Stepping back, she holds his face in her hands, studies his tear-stained cheeks. She does not know how her heart is still beating when she is sure it is broken.

'We're going to get you through this. I promise, we'll get through it.'

He nods but she can see he doesn't believe her. His face is awash with confusion, and she can sense his body is flooded with adrenaline and uncertainty for what the next few hours hold.

Pulling Jack back into her arms, the muscles in her throat constrict. There is no knowing when she will be able to do this again. If a judge on Monday decides not to grant Jack bail, if she herself is remanded in custody, she does not know when she might see him again. And the thought of it – the thought of her little boy in a juvenile detention centre, surrounded by strangers, surrounded by people who may choose to do him harm – is too unwieldy, and she has to expel it from her mind.

Holding on to Jack, she remembers the day he was born, two weeks early, such a tiny scrap of a thing. How she had cradled him in her arms – so small, so vulnerable – and had understood immediately, viscerally, that she would do anything to look after him. How she had known, without a shadow of a doubt, that she would die for him, if need be. That she would die for both her boys if, one day, it was required of her.

And yet, now here she is, powerless to stop whatever fate awaits him. Her sense of impotence is profound, and she does not know how she will survive the coming hours, days, weeks.

Behind her, a voice calls her name.

Nicole clings on to Jack, will not let him go, will not let them part her from her son. He is only fifteen. He is just a child. She cannot allow them to take him where he might be going.

The officer repeats her name, and she feels a hand on her shoulder, feels herself being prised away, but Jack is clasping hold of her, his arms around her shoulders, and she whispers in his ear, tells him she loves him, she will never stop loving him. He is crying – huge, uncontainable sobs – and he is telling her he's scared, he doesn't know what's going to happen to him, he doesn't want to be sent to prison. She kisses his cheeks, tears wet against her skin. And then the officer tells her she needs to come now, her time is up, but it seems impossible that anyone is going to make her leave Jack, that anybody has the power to force her to leave her son when every maternal fibre in her body is telling her she must stay, she must be with him, she must look after him.

But then the officer's hand grips more firmly on her arm, leading her away, and it is as though she can feel an invisible cord between her and Jack lengthen and stretch, pull taut on her heart. She looks at Jack's face, feels his desperation, tells him she is sorry, she is so sorry that she could not do more to protect him, tells him again that she loves him. She watches as Andrew gets out of his chair, puts his arm around Jack's shoulders, watches the two of them stand in the midst of that oppressive room as she is led out of the door, away from her son, with no knowing when or where she might see him again.

Abby

Abby says goodbye to the family liaison officer, closes the door behind her. Walking back into the sitting room, Clio is seated on the sofa still reeling from the story Abby has told her about Jack killing Isla, and Nicole covering it up.

'I just can't believe it. Jack's so . . . nice. I don't get why he'd do that?'

Abby inhales deeply, knows that the time for secrets is over. Her voice is steadier than she anticipated as she narrates to Clio a story that still sounds incredible to her own ears: Isla's relationship with Andrew, the pregnancy, the abortion. The lies, the duplicity, the betrayals of trust. Their two families – intertwined for so long – now irrevocably ruptured.

Clio is silent for what seems an inordinately long time. Abby is not sure whether to interrupt – to ask what she is thinking – or let the revelations sink in. She bides her time, does not want to pressurise Clio into a response, knows how much there is to absorb. 'Are you okay?'

Clio nods. 'I just can't get my head around it. It's so . . . *un-Isla*. I can't imagine her doing something like that.'

Abby does not know what to say, wishes she had a response to explain what she, also, is unable to understand. 'I can't either. But we just have to keep hold of the Isla we knew and loved. None of this changes that. She's still the same person, even if she did have secrets from us.'

Clio says nothing for a few seconds, picks at the skin around the edge of her nails. 'I just can't picture it. Isla with Andrew? It's so . . . weird. He's like . . . an uncle, or something. I don't understand how it even happened.'

Abby allows herself a beat. It is a question to which she does not have an answer. A question to which she will never have an answer because she cannot ask Isla directly. 'I honestly don't know. I'm not sure we ever will. All I know is that what Andrew did is sickening in every way imaginable.' She tries to keep her voice steady but her disgust at what he has done cannot be swallowed, cannot be silenced.

For a few moments, neither of them says anything. Clio pulls the sleeves of her hoodie over her hands as if wanting to hide herself from view. 'Can I say something without you getting angry with me?'

Abby nods, wonders whether Clio is going to tell her about the doctored photos or about spying on her sister, or about what she has really been doing all those Friday nights she says she is sleeping at Freya's.

Clio breathes in slowly, self-consciously. 'Sometimes I think you'd be happier if I'd been killed instead of Isla.'

The shock momentarily destabilises Abby. 'Don't say that, of course I wouldn't. What makes you think that?'

'Because she was the perfect one. She was the one everyone loved. She was amazing at everything—'

'And so are you. You can't compare yourself to Isla. You're completely different people. You're both special in your own way.'

Clio shakes her head. 'I'm not. I know I'm not.' She tugs at her sleeves. 'I know Isla was your favourite.'

Abby wrestles Clio's hands from inside her jumper, squeezes them tightly. 'That's just not true—'

'It is. Isla was everyone's favourite.'

Guilt tightens around Abby's throat. 'Parents don't have favourites. That's not how it works.' She pauses, wonders how honest to be with Clio, decides that secrets have brought nothing but trouble to their family so far. 'When I got pregnant with you, I remember worrying whether I'd be able to love another child as much as I loved Isla. I told your dad, and he said I was being silly, that millions of people have more than one child and find enough love for them. But I did worry about it. And then you were born, and there was such a rush of love for you. I hadn't understood it before, but every child opens up a new reservoir of affection inside you that you hadn't known existed.' She brings Clio's hand to her lips, kisses it. Clio – unusually – does not resist. 'I absolutely promise you that I've always loved you and Isla equally. My relationship with each of you is different, but I've always loved you the same.'

She is overcome by a profound wish that she could turn back time to the months after Stuart's death, to see them again through Clio's eyes. Wishes she had not been so mired in her own grief, that she had been able to put herself in the shoes of a ten-year-old girl and understood just how bewildering the world had become. 'I'm sorry I've made you question how much I love you. I'm sorry you've ever doubted that for a second. And I'm sorry you've not been able to tell me you feel like this until now.'

Holding Clio tight, Abby rocks her back and forth, lets her daughter cry.

'I miss her, Mum. I miss her so much.'

'I know you do, sweetheart. I miss her too.'

'But I was horrible to her. I was jealous of her and I was horrible—'

'You weren't—'

'I was. And now I wish I could have her back, just for one day, and tell her I was sorry. She thought I hated her and now I can never tell her . . .' Clio's voice tapers off.

'She knew. She understood how difficult things had been for you since Dad died. You've had so much to contend with over the past few years.'

Clio blows her nose, takes a deep breath. 'I think I could have stopped it happening.'

'What?'

'The accident. I could have stopped it.' Clio hesitates for a moment, wipes her nose. 'I saw her, the night she died.' She pauses again. 'Literally, just before she died.'

Abby thinks of the grainy photographs on Clio's phone, understands this is not the time to confess what she already knows. She appreciates the importance of Clio telling this story for herself. 'Where?'

Clio's eyes flit towards Abby and then down at the floor. 'I sometimes, sort of, just . . . kind of spied on her a bit.' She stops abruptly, and Abby strokes the back of her hand, encourages her to continue. 'I used to watch her sometimes, when she didn't know. At school, mostly. I know it's weird. I honestly don't know why I did it—'

'It's not weird—'

'It is.' Clio sucks in a deep breath. 'I saw her having a row with Callum, the night she died. I even took photos of them.'

Abby forces herself to pause. 'It's okay. Just tell me what happened.'

Clio bites her bottom lip. 'Isla and Callum were arguing – I don't know what about, I couldn't hear. And then Isla slapped Callum, and he stormed off.'

'And then what happened?'

She shakes her head. 'Nothing.'

'What do you mean?'

'I left. Isla was just standing around looking at her phone. The drama was over. I thought there was nothing more to see. So I went to Freya's and then I came home.' A furrow of grief lines Clio's forehead. 'I can't stop thinking about it. What if I'd stayed? What if I'd hung around for a bit longer? Maybe I could have done something. Maybe I could have stopped Isla being killed.' She sniffs, wipes her sleeve across her eyes.

Abby places the palm of her hand against her daughter's cheek. 'There was nothing you could have done. You couldn't have stopped Jack stealing Nicole's car. You couldn't have stopped him going to find Isla. You certainly couldn't have stopped him running her over—'

'But if I was there then maybe I could, and Isla would still be here.'

'Clio, look at me.' Abby thinks carefully about each word she is about to say, knows the importance of getting this right. 'Isla's death was not your fault. There is absolutely nothing you could have done to prevent it. You are in no way responsible.'

'But what about—'

'There are no buts. What happened to Isla was a tragedy. Perhaps it was a terrible accident or perhaps it was deliberate. We may never know. But there's a whole slew of factors that led to it. And you not being there is not even close to being one of them.' The litany of circumstances leading up to Isla's death hurtle through Abby's mind. It is Andrew she blames the most, even more so than Jack. If Andrew had not taken advantage of her daughter, if he had not abused his position in every conceivable way, Isla would still be here. It is Andrew who bears the brunt of Abby's fury.

Wrapping her arms around Clio, Abby tries to confront the fact that it is just the two of them now. That their family quartet has been reduced to a duo in the space of five years. It seems inconceivable that she will not get to watch Isla become an adult, will never discover what the future held for her. All those experiences they will now never share. Collecting her A-level results. Driving her to her first day at university. Watching her graduate. Witnessing her falling in love and being there to console her when she fell out of it again. Encouraging her in whatever career she chose. Perhaps watching her get married, have children. Whatever made her happy. All the hopes and dreams she has had for her children from the moment they were born. And yet she has been robbed of them all.

She breathes into Clio's hair, rocking her daughter gently back and forth. There is such a tumult of emotions, she cannot separate one from another: the rage from the disbelief, the grief from the despair. It had taken so much to carry on after Stuart's death, and just as she had begun to learn to live without him, just as she had begun to accept that it was the three of them from hereon in, she must reconfigure their lives yet again.

Jenna

Jenna slots her key in the front door, supermarket shopping bags bunched around her ankles like anxious children.

The smell of toast greets her, and she realises Callum must finally have surfaced. He was still asleep when she left just after eleven, and she'd decided not to disturb him on a Sunday morning.

'Do you want a hand?' Callum appears in the small, square hallway, wearing a pair of shorts, chest bare.

'Thanks, love. Can you grab the other bags?'

She carts the shopping through the living room, into the compact kitchen, uses every available space – floor, work surface, draining board – to stow the bags before she unpacks. Behind her, Callum brings the last of it through, places it under the fold-out table.

'What time did you wake up?'

'About half eleven.'

Jenna pulls out frozen salmon, a bag of peas, a tub of Callum's favourite ice-cream, and manages to cram them into the freezer compartment at the top of the fridge. 'You obviously needed a lie-in. Hopefully it'll have done you good.' She hears the formality in her voice, knows that at some point she has to confront Callum about what's been going on. Ever since the call from Mr Marlowe on Friday evening, Jenna has been burying her head in the sand, hoping that all the uncertainties will somehow magically disappear. She has been deluding herself that she doesn't need to ask Callum the truth about what's been happening at school, about his rekindled friendship with Liam Walsh, about what happened the night Isla was killed. Every time she thinks she is on the verge of broaching it, her courage abandons her, too fearful of what the answers may be.

Placing two cartons of milk in the door of the fridge, she knows she cannot leave it much longer. The doubts are burning a hole in her chest, keeping her awake at night.

'Do you want a cup of tea?'

Callum nods, mouth full of toast. Jenna fills the kettle, pulls two mismatched mugs from the cupboard above the microwave, places a teabag in each.

'There's something I need to ask you.' The words are there, released into the ether, before her brain has time to stop them.

Callum eyes her with mild caution. 'Okay.'

Jenna pulls a teaspoon from the drawer, twiddles it between her fingers like a majorette with a baton. 'Have you seen Liam Walsh lately?'

She trains her eyes on Callum's face, witnesses the hesitation: the weighing up of the scales, contemplating truth versus fiction.

'Why are you asking?'

'He came here, a couple of weeks ago—'

'Liam came here? How did he even know where we live?'

Jenna scrutinises her son's expression, searches for any trace of deception, but finds nothing. Either her son has become a skilful liar or he's telling the truth. 'I don't know. I was hoping you could tell me.'

'I honestly don't know. I've never told him. Maybe he . . . I dunno . . . followed me or something.'

Jenna allows herself a pause. She has no idea how he will respond when she tells him what she knows. 'He said you'd seen him lately. Been hanging out with him—'

'That's a lie—'

'So you haven't seen Liam? You haven't seen him since that day in court?'

There is a momentary silence, such a narrow sliver of time, and yet enough for Jenna to discern the answer to a question that has plagued her ever since Liam's visit.

'Why, Callum? Why would you start hanging around with him again?'

'I haven't—'

'I thought we were beyond all that. I really thought that when you got your place at Collingswood it was going to be a fresh start—'

'It is—'

'But now you're hanging around with people who are only ever going to get you into trouble—'

'Mum, will you just stop and listen, *please*.'

Behind Jenna, the kettle boils, but she does not turn around, keeps her eyes locked on Callum's face.

'It's not what you think. I haven't been hanging out with him.' Callum picks up a t-shirt from the back of the kitchen chair, slips it over his head and through his arms. 'The night Isla died, she and I had a row, at the party. I left. I was going to come straight home but I was angry and I just needed to walk it off.'

Jenna waits, listens, dreading whatever he is about to tell her.

'I was on the high street, near the bridge, and I saw Liam, outside the off-licence.' Callum swallows. 'He was with a couple of mates – I don't know who, I'd never seen them before.'

He pauses, and Jenna has to restrain herself from urging him to continue.

'Liam was being really friendly, asking how I was getting on at my posh school—'

'How did he even know where you go to school?'

'I dunno. Someone must have told him.' He runs a hand across the back of his neck. 'And then three other blokes turned up and started cussing Liam—'

'What blokes?' Jenna can hear the alarm in her voice, a thousand different permutations hurtling through her mind, each worse than the last.

'I don't know. But I think Liam might be dealing.'

The kitchen feels claustrophobic suddenly, as though the walls are closing in on them, trapping them both.

'I promise I won't be angry, love. Whatever's going on, we'll sort it out. I just need you to be honest.'

He takes in a deep breath. 'These blokes were talking all kinds of shit, and then one of them pulled a knife—'

'Jesus, Callum—'

'It's okay. I just turned and ran. One of them tried to chase me but I lost him within a couple of minutes.'

Jenna tries to steady her racing thoughts, imagining what might have happened – how that night might have turned out – if Callum hadn't got away.

'That's how I got that mark on my face. I was climbing over a wall and I banged it against the brick.'

Jenna's memory rewinds to the night of Isla's death, to Callum's return, to the red streak across his cheek. 'I thought Isla had hit you.'

A rueful smile upends one corner of Callum's mouth. 'Actually, she did. But not hard enough to leave a mark like that.'

Assumptions recalibrate in Jenna's mind, like squares in a game of Tetris. 'And you haven't seen Liam since? He hasn't been in touch?'

Callum shakes his head. 'I haven't, I swear. I blocked his number ages ago. I haven't seen him since that night.'

There is an earnestness to his voice, and Jenna is sure he is telling the truth.

'So the CCTV footage the police found of you running away, near where Isla was killed – you were running away from this gang?'

Callum nods.

'Why didn't you say so at the time? Why didn't you tell the police?'

He sighs with an air of resignation. 'Because it would have got me into more trouble. The police wouldn't have believed I'd just bumped into Liam. They'd have assumed I'd been with him intentionally, that I was dealing too. They'd probably have thought I was carrying a knife as well. You know they would, with my track record.'

Jenna wants to dispute it, but she knows Callum is right. She has seen it too many times, in her line of work. Innocent kids tarred with a criminal brush because of one prior mistake. Fingers pointing towards a child who comes from a broken home, an undesirable neighbourhood, a working-class family. Knee-jerk assumptions of guilt when a kid fits a profile the police are seeking.

She recalls the accusatory eyes of other parents at the sixth-form play when Callum was taken in for questioning, the certainty that the right person was being apprehended, as though it was only ever a matter of time before the police came for him.

Guilt needles her thoughts. For days – weeks – she had allowed other people's prejudices to make her doubt her son, to entertain suspicions that now fill her with remorse. To imagine that perhaps he'd fallen back in with the wrong crowd. That perhaps – god forbid – he was in some way implicated in Isla's death.

Looking at Callum now, something solidifies in her: a determination that she will never again allow anyone to make her question her son's integrity.

'What were you arguing about that night? You and Isla?'

Colour pinks Callum's cheeks. 'Promise you won't say anything if I tell you?'

Jenna nods.

Callum pauses before speaking. 'Isla was having a . . . a thing . . . a relationship with Andrew Forrester. As in, Nathaniel's dad. It's why she dumped me.'

For a few seconds, it seems too preposterous to be true. But then Jenna allows herself a moment for the revelation to slot into the narrative, like the missing piece of a jigsaw puzzle.

It never really made sense to her, Isla's abrupt ending of her relationship with Callum. One day they were so in love, and then suddenly she announced it was over.

But Isla and Andrew?

She thinks about Abby and Nicole, about how envious of their gilded lives she has been since Callum started at Collingswood: their affluence, their wealth, their confidence. But now she thinks of Abby and what she must be going through: the double loss of her husband and daughter in the space of five years; the rage she must be feeling towards her best friend's husband; the impotent fury that she wasn't able to prevent it. And then she thinks of Nicole, her seemingly perfect life shattered by a middle-aged man taking advantage of an emotionally vulnerable seventeen-year-old girl. Jenna has seen this predatory narrative play out many times during the course of her career but never so close to home.

She looks at Callum and knows that for all their imperfections, for all the frustrations of their daily lives – the bills, the inconsiderate neighbours, the inequality – she would not swap places with Abby or Nicole for all the money in the world.

'I don't know what to say. I'm just so sorry you've been going through all that on your own. I'm sorry it's been such a hard time. And I'm sorry for Isla, sorry that she got . . . coerced by that man. God, what a mess.'

Callum chews the edge of his lip. 'Can I tell you something without you going apeshit at me?'

Jenna forces her voice to be calm, neutral. 'Course.'

He pauses, breathes. 'I'm not sure I want to stay at Collingswood.' His voice is tentative, as if testing his weight on the edge of a frozen pond.

'But it's only a few months until your A levels.'

'Can't I just study for them at home or something? I've got all the textbooks. We'll have covered all the syllabus by Christmas anyway.'

Jenna studies his face, sees his unease. 'What's wrong?'

He shrugs. 'Nothing. I just don't feel it's the right place for me.'

Indignation rises into Jenna's cheeks. 'Of course it is. You can't let them make you think that—'

'I'm not, it's just how I feel—'

'It's not how you felt this time last year. You loved it then.' She pauses, tries to gather her thoughts, steady her voice. 'You *earned* your place there, Callum. You can't let people make you doubt yourself just because they live in bigger houses, or their parents have more money, or they go on fifteen flipping holidays a year. That does *not* make them better than you. And it certainly doesn't give them the right to make you feel unwelcome in a school you've every right to be at—'

'They're not. And I know all that. I just don't feel like I fit in. I never will—'

'Listen to me, Callum. Loads of kids would have fallen apart after what you went through with Liam and Ryan. They'd have gone completely off the rails. I've seen it a hundred times before.

But you picked yourself up, got on with your revision, passed your GCSEs with flying colours. Got a place at Collingswood. Do you realise how much courage that took? How much resilience? It's an incredible achievement. And you must never – for a second – think of giving up on an opportunity like that because of some misplaced belief that you're not worthy of it. You deserve that education and all the opportunities it brings just as much as a kid who happens to have rich parents. You deserve it more, in fact, because you've had to work harder for it. Do not let other people's attitudes get the better of you. If you do, you'll regret it for the rest of your life.'

Callum is silent for a few seconds before he nods – hesitantly at first, and then more definitively – and Jenna knows, deep down, that he will not quit. Her son is a fighter. He is too smart to relinquish an opportunity like this. He will, she feels hopeful, manage to navigate his way through this turbulent patch, and when he emerges, he will be all the stronger for it.

ELEVEN MONTHS LATER

Jenna

Jenna follows Callum along the narrow, pedestrianised streets, through the honeyed archway. The wheels of Callum's suitcase rattle behind her, and she quashes the feeling of self-consciousness, tells herself that nobody is paying her any attention, they are all too preoccupied with their own children.

Heading into the Porter's Lodge, they wait in a queue to collect Callum's key, to be directed to the room he has been allocated. Stealing a glance at her son, he turns his head, catches her eye. His smile is filled with excitement, and she is relieved that it is only she who is nervous about this new chapter in his life.

When it is Callum's turn, she watches as he chats with the porter, shares a joke about his terrible sense of direction, swells with pride at how he is taking it all in his stride. He has been here only three times before – once for an open day, once for his interview, and a third time over the summer, to familiarise himself with the city – and yet he seems so comfortable already, as though a part of him knows this is where he belongs. As though he understands intrinsically that he has found his academic home.

The porter gives Callum the key to his bedroom and a map of the college, patiently explains where they need to go even though he must have given directions countless times already today. Callum listens, nods, while Jenna thinks about the fact that, in a few hours' time, she will leave Callum here, in this Oxford college founded over five hundred years ago, to begin his university career and his life as an adult.

As she follows Callum across the quad with its immaculately mown lawn – Callum carrying two enormous rucksacks, Jenna pulling the wheelie suitcase behind her – a passing student asks if they need a hand with anything, and Callum thanks him, says he's all good. Jenna allows herself a flicker of reassurance that it will be okay, the other students are nice, Callum will find friends here and be happy.

'You alright, Mum? You sure you're okay with that suitcase?'

Jenna pulls her face into an optimistic smile. 'Honestly, love, I'm fine. It's not as if you've got any free hands anyway.'

Callum grins and looks back down at the map.

So many times over the past year, Jenna has worried whether Callum will ever get here; whether he will achieve the grades he needs, overcome the difficulties he's experienced, realise his potential.

In the days after the revelations about Isla's death became public – Jack killing Isla, Nicole having covered it up, Andrew and Isla's relationship – the school community seemed to exist in a state of shock. But gradually, as the weeks passed, life reverted to normal. Mr Marlowe had shown unwavering care for Callum's wellbeing, and the school had gone to exceptional lengths to support him; in time, Jenna had accepted that Collingswood were not looking for a reason to castigate her son but in fact wanted nothing but the best for him. By the new year, Callum had reintegrated socially, got his head down, studied hard. He had put his energies and focus where they needed to be. When she and Callum stood in the quad at Collingswood on A-level results day, A4 envelope in Callum's hand, and he read them out – four A-stars – she had wept with both pride and relief.

'I think this must be it.'

Callum checks the numbers on the wall against the key in his hand before leading them up a narrow, spiral staircase. At the top, he finds the right room number, slots the key in the lock, opens the door.

'Wow.'

Following him inside, Jenna's eyes widen. The room is beautiful: leaded windows overlooking the courtyard, ivy curling around the frames, a desk beneath the view. A single bed, an armchair, a sink against the wall. To the right of the desk is a line of shelves that await Callum's textbooks. A slim wardrobe is tucked into an alcove by the door with a mahogany chest of drawers next to it. It is everything Jenna imagined an Oxford college room to be.

'Not too shabby, is it?' Callum smiles at her, and it is as though she can see the next three years playing out in her mind. Callum settling into university life. Him making friends, friends he will have, hopefully, for a very long time. Callum joining the athletics club, the cross-country team, the film club. Him taking notes in lectures, offering ideas and opinions in seminars, writing essays at his desk under the window. Finding a girlfriend, perhaps, and falling in love. Finally – hopefully – relinquishing the ghosts of the past.

Callum hauls the oversized rucksacks from his back, uses them to prop open the door, pulls the duvet cover from one and throws it onto the bed.

'Hey.'

Both Jenna and Callum turn to find a teenage boy – tall, wiry, wearing a Radiohead t-shirt – standing in the doorway.

'Hey.'

'You a fresher too?'

'Yep. I'm Callum.' He holds out his arm and they shake hands.

'Tom. My room's two doors down. I was going to have a look around, check things out if you want to come, or do you want to get sorted?'

Jenna watches Callum hesitate, can almost hear his thoughts whirring; he will feel guilty leaving her here alone when they've only just arrived.

'It's fine, love – you go. I'll get things unpacked and see you when you get back.' She keeps her voice light, breezy, as though this is the most normal thing she has ever done: bringing her son to one of the most famous universities in the world, watching him make his first friend, seeing him metamorphose before her eyes.

'You sure?'

'Course. See you in a bit.'

'Okay. I won't be long. Don't leave before I get back.' He grins at her before heading out of the door with Tom. As they walk down the corridor, towards the stairs, Jenna hears the beginning of their conversation – Tom is studying history, he comes from Manchester – and she waits until their voices fade before unzipping the suitcase, pulling out a pile of Callum's hoodies.

Lowering herself onto the edge of the unmade bed, she looks around the room, does not know how to reconcile her feelings: the pride with the loss, the excitement with the trepidation, the hopes with the fears. The concern that perhaps, in coming here, Callum is not just starting university, but is embarking on a journey that will take him away from her forever: educationally, culturally, geographically. It is both a fear and, paradoxically, a desire; she wants Callum to have better opportunities than she had, has fought so hard to help him succeed, knows how much he has to offer. And yet, sometimes, she cannot help worrying that the young man who graduates from Oxford in three years' time will be unrecognisable from the teenager she has brought here today.

She instructs herself to stop being maudlin. This is a wonderful opportunity for Callum, everything she has ever hoped for him. And she feels cautiously optimistic that however far his education may take him, he won't lose a sense of who he is, where he comes from, the values she has taught him: integrity, kindness, a sense of social responsibility.

As she puts his jumpers away in a drawer, she thinks of Abby and Nicole, of how they might be occupying their time this week. She wonders how Abby is feeling, whether she dares acknowledge what she would be doing in a different, parallel world – taking Isla to university, just as thousands of other, luckier parents all over the country are doing – or if the thought is too painful, an alternative reality Abby cannot allow herself to imagine. She thinks of Nicole, how she might be coping, and what Nathaniel may have decided to do with his future. The irony does not escape her that two years ago it would have been unthinkable that it is Jenna, of the three of them, who is the lucky one.

Glancing at her watch, she wonders when Callum will get back, what time she will leave him here today. The prospect of returning alone to their empty flat – returning from work every day to Callum's absence – is not something she can bear to imagine. It is going to take time to adjust, and she is choosing not to contemplate it until she needs to.

Tucked between Callum's pants and socks, she finds a framed photograph. It is a picture of the two of them in Spain this summer, outside the Guggenheim Museum in Bilbao, from the long weekend they spent there to celebrate Callum's A-level results. He looks happy, relaxed, grown-up. He will thrive here in Oxford, she is in no doubt.

Placing the photo back where she found it – it is for Callum to decide if he wants it on display – she begins to make his bed, the last time she will do so until he is home for the Christmas holidays. Waiting for Callum to return, she knows it is almost time for her to leave him, and she feels as sure as she can be that, when she does, he will be just fine.

Nicole

Nicole sits in the waiting room on a grey plastic chair, eyes trained on the door. Glancing up at the clock on the wall, she sees it is almost two-thirty, feels the now familiar tangle of nerves she encounters every fortnight when these visits take place.

On the chair to her right, a woman sits impatiently, knee jerking up and down, and Nicole looks quickly away, knows better than to stare at people in a place like this. It is knowledge she wishes she did not have, but this is where circumstances have brought her, and she now has experience of things she had never even contemplated before.

The door at the far end of the room opens, and Nicole scans the faces of those entering, searching for familiarity. Anonymous bodies swarm in, each one knowing how precious every moment is, and Nicole cranes her neck, strains her eyes, wills him to come into view.

And then there he is, his face filled with uncertainty, despite the regularity of these visits. Nathaniel's eyes skim across the room, in search of Nicole, and she raises a hand, waves, the clock ticking loudly in her ears as the first of their allotted sixty minutes slips by.

As he catches her eye, she sees that Nathaniel is not alone. Her throat tightens with gratitude as she spies Jack behind him. Her chest contracts to see him here – no place a sixteen-year-old should ever have to come – and yet she is so happy he has made the effort. He did not accompany Nathaniel on the previous visit, and Nicole had been torn between disappointment and understanding.

'Hey Mum.' Nathaniel smiles awkwardly, hugs her stiffly. It takes all her self-restraint not to hold on to him – it is such a rare dose of physical contact, such a small ration of affection – but she releases him quickly, knows she will be reprimanded by one of the guards if she doesn't.

'Are you okay?'

Nathaniel nods, sits down at the small low table in the prison visiting room, well-drilled now in the protocol.

Jack hovers tentatively to one side, as if awaiting instructions as to what he should do next.

Reaching out and pulling him towards her, Nicole breathes in the smell of him, whispers into his ear. 'Thank you for coming. I've missed you.' There is an almost infinitesimal nod of Jack's head before Nicole gestures for him to sit down next to his brother, watches him take a seat, sees him glance nervously around the room.

Sometimes, when Jack comes, she wonders whether it is the experience of visiting his mother in prison that unsettles him so much. Other times, she speculates that perhaps a part of his mind is elsewhere, thinking about what might have been: about how narrow his escape was from a similar fate, had his own sentencing turned out differently.

As Nicole sits down, there is the humiliating rustle of the neon orange tabard she must wear to distinguish herself as a prisoner. 'How are you both? How've you been?' She tries to keep her voice light, colloquial, but there is an inescapable formality to prison visit conversations, and in the five months Nicole has been here, she has not yet found a way to overcome it.

Nathaniel begins to talk. He is so good, so diligent, at keeping the conversation flowing, as though he feels that, in Andrew's absence, it is incumbent upon him to be a responsible adult. Nicole listens, grateful for this temporary diversion from the monotony of prison life, for this brief insight into normality.

In a different world, Nathaniel would be starting university this week. Instead, he is telling her about his new school, the school to which he has transferred to repeat the second year of his A-level courses. It was the February half-term break when Nathaniel confessed to Nicole that he'd done no revision, that he couldn't concentrate, couldn't focus on maths and physics when he was so preoccupied with Nicole's upcoming trial. Her guilt had been overwhelming, but she'd known that apologies were not what he needed. Instead, she had listened, strategised, removed the pressure, put a plan in place. It had been such a traumatic time for them all – Nathaniel being issued with a police caution for sending anonymous emails to Isla, on top of everything else they were all going through – and Nicole did not want to jeopardise his wellbeing further by forcing him to sit exams for which he was unprepared.

She and Nathaniel have talked at length and in depth about those emails to Isla. It seemed to Nicole so out of character for Nathaniel to do something like that – she had never heard him utter a sexist word before, let alone that kind of misogynistic bile – and she was worried that perhaps he'd been indoctrinated by an online forum or incel culture. What transpired was, in some ways, both better and worse. His unrequited feelings for Isla, together with Isla's relationship with Andrew, had left him feeling angry, resentful, humiliated. Full of misdirected rage, and with a warped sense of love, relationships, trust. In the months between Nicole's arrest and her sentencing, she had worked hard with Nathaniel, helping to reset the barometer through which he engaged with the world. Helping him understand that Isla was a victim not a perpetrator, that she deserved their compassion, not their antipathy. That no seventeen-year-old girl should ever end up in a sexual relationship with a forty-eight-year-old man, least of all one she has known – like a second father – her whole life.

Now, Nicole's priority is for Nathaniel to be happy and settled at his new school, a school she chose in part for its unparalleled pastoral care. To find his tribe, make new friends. She thinks back to a year ago, how oblivious she was to Nathaniel's social isolation. She recalls the night of Isla's death, her belief that Nathaniel was at Meera's party, having fun with his friends. It was only later – after so many other, more difficult truths had emerged – that he told Nicole where he'd really been that night; sitting in the park by himself, scrolling through his phone in the dark, too embarrassed to come home and confess that, for the fourth weekend in a row, he had not been invited to whatever social gathering was taking place.

It was Nicole who had insisted – even before her trial began, long before her custodial sentence was handed down – that they sell the house, move out of London, settle the boys somewhere they could begin afresh, free of the stigma that now surrounded their lives. Andrew had been resistant – he'd wanted the boys to stay in London – but it wasn't, in the end, his decision. After the divorce, the boys chose to live with Nicole, and she took the decision to move to Surrey, find a smaller house, apply to a boarding school for Nathaniel and Jack, so that if she was sent to prison, the practicalities of their daily lives would already be taken care of.

It is difficult, now, for Nicole to think about Andrew without deep-seated hatred. That night in the police interview room, when she was asked whether she'd confided in anyone about what had happened, it struck her that the reason she hadn't told Andrew about Jack killing Isla was because she knew he wasn't to be trusted. She knew by then the extent of his betrayals; treacheries that proved to be the catalyst for the devastation that followed.

Now Andrew lives alone in a flat in Shoreditch, and the boys refuse to see him. She cannot blame them. The irony – the bitter irony – that Andrew was the cause of this succession of tragedies and yet he is the only one who has escaped scot-free – in judicial terms, at least – provokes a sense of fury she suspects will never fully abate.

Nathaniel finishes talking, and Nicole tells him how happy she is that he is settling into boarding school life, that he is making friends and is focused on his studies. For the first time since Nathaniel left Collingswood last February, she feels a glimmer of hope that he might be okay; that the upheaval of the past year may not ruin his chances at this critical juncture in his life.

Turning to Jack, she asks how he's finding the new school, watches him hesitate before he tells her it's good, he likes it. She can see his desire to reassure her, wishes there was some way to impart to him the truth about motherhood; that, having witnessed your child's every facial response since the day they were born, their expressions are like words in a book – as legible and clear as sentences on a page. Nicole can sense, immediately, that Jack has not embraced his new school as easily as Nathaniel, that he may still need additional support, and she resolves to call his Head of Year the next time she is allowed access to a phone.

Changing the subject, she asks Jack about his football training, sees him begin to relax, though his shoulders are still tight, his hands clasped one inside the other as though it is the only way to keep his emotions in check.

Listening as Jack tells her about his football fixture last weekend, it strikes her that he is – in the circumstances – coping remarkably well. Whenever she begins to think about what might have happened, she has to forcibly stop herself going down that particular rabbit hole. It is a form of self-harm, she knows. She is only too aware how lucky Jack is, how his life could have diverted onto so different a path had the judge not decided against a custodial sentence; had they not concluded that there would be no benefit in sending him to a young offenders' institute, had they not taken into account the extenuating family circumstances leading to the accident. The judge had accepted Jack's version of events – that he never meant to harm Isla, that he merely wanted to talk to her, that he was upset, flustered, that he never meant to slam his foot down on the accelerator. The judge took on board Jack's guilty plea and his obvious, profound remorse. Instead of sending him to prison, she issued him with a twelve-month youth referral order and instructed him to write a letter of apology to Abby. She also recommended he undergo counselling, which has, Nicole thinks, been good for him in so many ways. But she knows Jack's guilt is, at times, crippling. It manifests itself in nightmares, anxiety, in periods of all-consuming self-loathing. Nicole will forever be grateful that Jack is not serving a sentence in a young offenders' institute – she dares not imagine what that might have done to him – but she knows he will serve a different sort of life sentence nonetheless. He will forever have to live with the fact that he took another person's life, and there is nothing that anyone – not Nicole, not Nathaniel, not Jack's therapist – can say or do to change the debilitating truth of it.

She thinks about Callum, as she so often does, about the second chance he was given, just like Jack. She blanches at the thought of her lack of generosity towards Callum when he first started at Collingswood. She regrets the fact that she never stood up for him when other parents were jumping to conclusions, even though she knew categorically he wasn't involved in Isla's death. Now, she can only hope that Jack will not face similar whispers of judgement if peers at his new school discover his own troubled past.

Glancing up at the clock, she sees that their time is already half spent, feels the familiar stab of panic that, in thirty minutes, it will all be over for another two weeks; she will hug her boys, say goodbye, knowing that she will not be allowed to see them again for another fourteen days. It is, for her, the harshest reality of prison life; being separated from her children is the gravest punishment she can imagine, the experience she finds most difficult to bear.

And yet she understands that she, like Jack, has got off relatively lightly. Only half her fourteen-month sentence for perverting the course of justice will be spent in prison. In two months, she will be released – in time for Christmas, she hopes – and reunited with her boys. They will be able to come home from school every weekend, or transfer to being day pupils if they so choose, as she expects they will. She can have both her children in her life. It is a luxury, she knows all too well, that Abby will never be afforded.

So many times every day, Nicole's thoughts turn to Abby; she thinks about those five weeks between Isla's death and the truth emerging. Lying to Abby was one of the hardest things she has ever done. For those thirty-five days, she felt as though she were living two parallel lives: the life in which nothing had altered, in which she was Abby's best friend, in which she was supporting her through the worst trauma any parent could face; and a separate, simultaneous existence in which she knew that everything had changed – changed beyond all recognition – and that the future would be altered irrevocably by what had happened.

She thinks about Isla, her promising future cut so tragically short, about the exploitation Isla suffered at the hands of Andrew. Often, she dreams of Isla; memories of the times they spent together merging with imagined scenes until she wakes, unable for a few seconds to separate truth from fiction. She grieves the death of Isla with a profound sense of loss even as a part of her feels she does not have the right to mourn her.

Over the past eleven months, Nicole has written countless letters to Abby: so many apologies, so many attempts at explanation.

She does not expect forgiveness, knows she does not deserve it. She carries her guilt like a heavy backpack slung over her shoulders. All she would like is for Abby not to be eaten up with hatred for her: Abby, who has already suffered so much. Nicole hopes that Abby's animosity towards her does not compound her already unimaginable grief.

Nathaniel begins telling a story about his new physics teacher, and Jack laughs – the first time Nicole has seen him laugh unselfconsciously for months – and she listens attentively, wants to ingest every morsel of family life with her boys despite these surroundings, despite the surreal situation in which they find themselves.

Her main aspiration now is that, at some point in the future, the past will be behind them. It is, she knows, not something they will ever get over. There is no forgetting, no time when the three of them won't think about what has happened. It is woven into the fabric of their family now, just as Abby's losses are braided into her and Clio's lives. All she dares wish is that there is hope for all five of them beyond the experiences of the past year: hope that each of them can rebuild their lives, find some form of happiness, some means of fulfilment. Some kind of peace.

Abby

Abby holds Clio's hand as the boat skims across the water. Behind them, the skipper looks steadily forward, eyes trained on the horizon. The wind bites Abby's cheeks, but both she and Clio have wrapped up warm – hats, gloves, scarves; they have both been here before, know how unforgiving the weather can be. But despite the harsh temperatures, the sun shines overhead, and Abby could not be more grateful. She knows how rare such a day is on the Snæfellsnes peninsula, knows from their previous trip, just over six years ago, that the weather in Iceland is nothing if not unpredictable.

Glancing behind her, the rugged land juts out of the water – craggy, unapologetic, as if the hills might, at any moment, transform into living beings – and Abby is reminded of the stories from Norse mythology that Isla loved reading as a child.

Grief tightens around her throat, and she breathes in the crisp, brisk air.

It was Clio's idea to come here on the first anniversary of Isla's death; back to the location of their final family holiday just two months before Stuart died. Isla was twelve, Clio ten, and they had all fallen in love with Iceland's dramatic landscapes: its snow-capped mountains, erupting volcanoes, theatrical geysers. Both Abby and Stuart had been amazed how far the girls were willing to hike – fifteen kilometres a day – to waterfalls and volcanic craters, past hot springs and glaciers. But it was here, on Breiðafjörður fjord, that they had experienced the highlight of their trip: a pod of orcas gliding through the water, six adults and a calf, a once-in-a-lifetime sighting. Isla had been mesmerised, talked about it for months afterwards. In the year before she was killed, she had researched volunteering opportunities in Iceland, said she was thinking of spending her summer before university helping out on an environmental project.

Clio squeezes Abby's hand, and Abby turns, smiles at her. It is remarkable how much Clio has changed over the past year. How much she has matured. All the chaos Abby found on Clio's phone – the smoking, drinking, socialising with older boys, messing about in cars which, Clio has insisted, she never actually drove – has been acknowledged, though Clio has said she doesn't want to discuss it. She has promised it was just a phase she was going through, assured Abby it is now behind her. They are aspects of Clio's past that Abby assumes – hopes – Clio talks about with the therapist she has been seeing twice a week for the past ten months. It has been transformative, Clio being in counselling, and Abby now regrets not finding therapists for both her girls when Stuart died.

Clio is no longer friends with Freya. She has a new best friend, Sophie, with whom her life seems calmer, less frenetic. In many ways, Clio is more reserved now – more introspective, more thoughtful – but in other ways she is undoubtedly more confident. A quiet confidence, a sense of self-belief she never had in the past. Sometimes Abby wonders – guiltily – whether Clio simply never had the space to flourish before, whether living in Isla's shadow was like being a sapling on the forest floor, unable to access the necessary light in order to grow. At other times, she wonders if Clio feels pressure now to be grown-up, to achieve things, to try to fill the enormous gap Isla left behind. Abby keeps a close eye on her, but for now, at least, Clio seems okay. She did surprisingly well in her

GCSEs given the year she'd had, seems to be settling into sixth-form life at Collingswood with relative ease. But Abby is well aware how skilfully teenagers can mask their problems and hide their secrets. She will not allow herself to miss any signs a second time around. She is careful not to repeat the same mistakes she made with Isla; not to rely emotionally on Clio, not to lean on her for comfort, support, for the kind of conversations she might be having with Stuart if he were still alive. She knows how important it is for Clio to be a regular sixteen-year-old, wants Clio to understand that she is not responsible for Abby's emotional wellbeing.

The skipper calls out to them, points to a trio of puffins sitting on a small, rocky island in the bay. Clio slips a glove from her hand, pulls out her phone, takes some photos. Abby watches, drinking in the scenery as the land recedes behind them.

A year after Isla's death, still not an hour goes by when Abby is not arrested by grief so strong it physically winds her. A sense of loss so profound it is as though an ancient god has scooped out her heart and is feeding it to birds of prey. Mourning so acute she does not know how she will survive it, does not want to survive it, cannot bear to be conscious through the intensity of it. A year on and it is still incomprehensible to her that Isla is gone. It makes no sense, and she still cannot absorb the fact of it. The cavity in her chest – that gaping wound – still has the power to shock her and yet, simultaneously, it is accompanied by an awareness that this is how it is now; this feeling of being permanently ripped apart is what her life has become.

It is wrong to talk of her heart being broken. Something that is broken has the possibility of being fixed. But Abby's grief for Isla can never be fixed. Her pain is not something that will ever be mended. It is a part of her, a permanent scar, a load that she carries. Isla's death is an indisputable facet of Abby's life. There is no restoration from grief like this.

She pauses her thoughts, recalls what her therapist often tells her. *Remembering those we've lost is key to our ability to live without them. One cannot exist without the other. We cannot learn to bear their absence if we do not allow ourselves to remember the significance of their presence.*

Abby thinks about Tuesday night, about the third instalment of her counselling course. She is enjoying it more than she'd envisaged. It had been Clio's suggestion that Abby train as a therapist. *You're a brilliant listener, Mum, and you always know the right things to say when people are upset. You'd be an amazing therapist.* Initially, Abby had been sceptical, had brushed the idea aside; it seemed such a huge leap of faith from stay-at-home mum to trainee therapist. But the idea kept niggling at her, like a finger jabbed gently in the top of an arm. Eventually she'd done some research, found a course, plucked up the courage to email the admissions office. A few months later she was accepted. It is still early days, but she would like to specialise in child and adolescent counselling, would like to help young people negotiate the increasingly complex world in which they live.

She thinks about Jack, as she often does, more often than she would like sometimes. She wonders how he is, how the events of the past year might anchor themselves to his future. The last she heard, the boys were at a boarding school in Surrey, and Nicole had bought a house nearby for when she is released from prison.

Still, to this day, Abby does not know how she feels about Nicole, about Jack, about the whole Forrester family. Except Andrew. Andrew she loathes with a deep, visceral hatred. There were days, at the beginning, when it took all her self-restraint not to do something stupid, something she would come to regret. Something that would land her in the same place as Nicole. The only thing that stopped her was Clio: knowing that she could not – must not – do anything to jeopardise Clio's future. It is only for Clio's sake that she has kept thoughts of inflicting harm on Andrew – slow, torturous harm – to nothing more than a fantasy.

But Nicole is different. Nicole has tried to explain herself – again and again – in long, contrite letters. Each time one arrives, Abby promises herself that she will not read it; Nicole has nothing to say that Abby could possibly want to hear. Each time, the letter is tucked behind a photograph on the kitchen mantelpiece for a day or two, Abby resisting the urge to open it. And every time, after a few days have passed, there is a moment when Abby's curiosity gets the better of her, when she picks it up, slides a finger under the flap, removes the handwritten pages inside. Reads what is written. She can sense Nicole's desperate need for forgiveness as if it is a living, breathing being, drifting up from the words on the page, like a genie released from a bottle.

The truth is that, in spite of everything, Abby misses Nicole. Nicole was a central figure in her life for almost two decades. After Stuart died, she was the adult to whom Abby was closest: in whom she confided the most, shared the most, laughed the most, cried the most. Life without Nicole would have been unthinkable a year ago. And yet, here they are.

There have been moments when her empathy has got the better of her, when she has found herself imagining what it must have been like for Nicole that night, to have been faced with such an invidious dilemma. She has wondered what she would have done in a similar situation – whether she would have lied, betrayed, perverted the course of justice to protect her child. She cannot, in all honesty, claim that she would not. A parent's love for their child is all-consuming; it goes beyond words, transgresses rational thought. Supersedes, sometimes, morality, conscience, the law. Abby knows she would do anything to shield Clio from harm, and she cannot definitively say that she would not do something illegal in order to defend her. And yet, in spite of this – in spite of understanding why,

331

perhaps, Nicole acted the way she did that night, in spite of the gnawing ache with which she sometimes misses her – Abby knows that their friendship is broken beyond repair.

A gull flies low overhead, and it reminds Abby of the last time they were here. She thinks about Isla that day: so young, so innocent, so full of hope and enthusiasm. It has not escaped her attention that Isla would be starting university this week. In a different world – one in which Andrew had never groomed Isla, in which Jack had never found out, in which he had never gone to confront Isla in a stolen vehicle he was not equipped to drive – Abby would be accompanying Isla to university, watching her take her first, tentative steps towards independence. A rite of passage towards adulthood that every parent should have the privilege to experience with their child, however it manifests itself. An experience she will cherish all the more with Clio, when the time comes.

Sometimes, thinking about what has happened over the past six years – the death of her husband, the death of her child – Abby thinks it is a gift in life that we do not know what awaits us. If we did, we may not have the strength to bear witness.

Her thoughts pivot to Callum, to how he might be settling in at Oxford. Abby has had only scant contact with Jenna over the past eleven months. Soon after the truth emerged about Isla's death, Abby went to Jenna's flat, apologised profusely to her and Callum for her behaviour, for having suspected Callum's involvement. Both Jenna and Callum were unfailingly magnanimous, and Abby felt humbled by their lack of grievance. Since then, her path has crossed only fleetingly with Jenna's at school events. They have nodded courteously, said hello, nothing more. When Abby heard about Callum's A-level results and his confirmed place at Oxford, she bought a card, posted it to Callum, sent Jenna a short WhatsApp message to congratulate them both. One of her greatest regrets about the last two years is to have judged Callum so unfairly; to have brought her prejudices to bear on a teenager who, it transpired, had more integrity than the adults she considered to be her closest friends. She hopes for only good things for Callum, hopes he is happy.

The skipper of the boat slows the engine, stills to a halt. Abby looks around. They are exactly where she wanted to be: far enough from the land to have a sense of space yet within sight of the mountains, close enough to feel safe.

She looks at Clio, who responds with a small, definitive nod. Reaching down to the rucksack wedged between her feet, Abby pulls out two square wooden boxes, each with an engraving on top. She hands one to Clio, holds one herself, and together they stand side by side at the edge of the boat.

The wind settles into a gentle breeze, and Abby leans over the side of the boat, eases the lid from the box she is holding, watches Clio do the same next to her. Gently, in unison, they begin to scatter the ashes on the surface of the water; Stuart and Isla returned together to a place they both loved. Grief narrows the walls of Abby's throat, and she glances at Clio, sees tears slip down her daughter's cheek. Slowly, tenderly, they empty the ashes into the water, watch them disperse, diffuse, until the boxes are empty.

For ten minutes, or twenty – Abby has no sense of time – she and Clio stand next to each other in silence, Abby's arm around Clio's shoulders, watching their father, husband, sister, daughter become part of the landscape. The only sound is the gentle lapping of waves against the hull, the call of gulls overhead, the whistle of the wind. She knows there is no perfect ending, no flawless goodbye. But this, she thinks – with the fortuitous blue sky and the golden sun, with the distant rocky mountains that will be here millennia after all of them are gone – is as close to a perfect resting place as it is possible to imagine.

Putting the lid back on the box she is holding, she turns to Clio, enfolds her in her arms. Today is not something any sixteen-year-old should have to experience.

They both turn their heads, look back out to sea. Somewhere among the fish and the phytoplankton, the whales and the dolphins, Stuart and Isla drift, dissolve, become a part of the ocean.

She does not know how long they stand there, saying their silent goodbyes as the boat rocks gently from side to side. Eventually, Abby looks over her shoulder at the skipper, gestures their readiness to leave, and the stutter of the engine slices through the silence.

As they're steered back towards the shore, through the labyrinth of islands jutting out above the water, Abby keeps hold of Clio's hand. It is just the two of them now. Stuart and Isla will always be a part of their lives, will always be present in spite of their absence. But, from here on in, it is all about her and Clio. And Abby knows – as profoundly as she has ever known anything – that she will do whatever it takes to be there for Clio: to love her, support her, to help guide her towards whatever their future may hold.

ACKNOWLEDGEMENTS

Thank you to the incredible team at Lake Union who've brought my books to a whole new readership. To my editor, Sammia Hamer, whose candour and honesty is such a breath of fresh air in the publishing industry: thank you for your energy, support and strategic brilliance. Thanks to the super-efficiency of Nicole Wagner, to Bekah Graham in marketing, to Andreina Guenni in production and to Liron Gilenberg for overseeing the cover, designed beautifully by Emma Rogers.

To the wonderful Sophie Wilson, as ever, who edits with such care, insight, collaboration and good humour: infinite thanks, and please never let me do a book without you.

Heartfelt thanks to those writers who are so generous with their friendship, their time, their editorial input and their support: Ruth Jones, Rachel Joyce and Alex Michaelides.

My mum remains my biggest champion (as all good mums are); thank you for being my loudest cheerleader, and for your love, your pride and (as always) your excellent proofreading. Everlasting thanks to my stepdad Jerry, in memory of his kindness, his encouragement, his love and his fantastic woodwork (Aurelia was very lucky to have him in her life, as were we all).

My biggest thanks, as always, to Adam and Aurelia. It was quite the eighteen months for all of us while I was writing this book, and it's a feat of our family fortitude that we got through it, and with incredible adventures to boot. Auri: I could not be more proud of everything you did – and everything you achieved – in the time I was writing this. Your hard work and determination demonstrated maturity and resilience beyond your years, and you deserve every exciting prospect that I know awaits you. Adam: you are the steady (and very wonderful) hand at the tiller of our family's odyssey, and none of it – from the quotidian to the extraordinary – would happen without you. I love you both beyond measure.

ABOUT THE AUTHOR

Photo © 2018 Adam Jackson

Hannah is an author, journalist and broadcaster. She is a book critic and features writer for a range of publications including the *Observer*, the *Guardian* and the *FT Weekend Magazine*, and was the book pundit on the Sara Cox show on BBC Radio 2. A regular chair at festivals and events across the UK, she has interviewed a range of writers and celebrities from Graham Norton and Nigella Lawson to Maggie O'Farrell and Kate Atkinson. She has judged numerous book prizes including the Costa Books Awards. *Three Mothers* is her fifth novel.

Follow the Author on Amazon

If you enjoyed this book, follow Hannah Beckerman on Amazon to be notified when the author releases a new book!

To do this, please follow these instructions:

Desktop:

1) Search for the author's name on Amazon or in the Amazon App.

2) Click on the author's name to arrive on their Amazon page.

3) Click the 'Follow' button.

Mobile and Tablet:

1) Search for the author's name on Amazon or in the Amazon App.

2) Click on one of the author's books.

3) Click on the author's name to arrive on their Amazon page.

4) Click the 'Follow' button.

Kindle eReader and Kindle App:

If you enjoyed this book on a Kindle eReader or in the Kindle App, you will find the author 'Follow' button after the last page.